Oriental Flyer

By

Charles Patton

Saber Books
Published by Indigo Sea Press
Winston-Salem

Saber Books
Indigo Sea Press
302 Ricks Drive
Winston-Salem, NC 27103

First Saber Books edition published December, 2015
Saber Books, Moon Sailor, and all production design are trademarks of Indigo Sea Press, used under license.

For information regarding bulk purchases of this book, digital purchase and special discounts, please contact the publisher at indigoseapress.com

Cover design by Stacy Castanedo
Photo by Robert F. Burgess

Manufactured in the United States of America
ISBN 978-1-63066-423-7

Dedicated

to those who didn't make it back.

—Charles Patton

Chapter One

Reconnaissance at Quyet Tien

David Beking found himself drawn with anticipation toward the images on his screen. He became silent and pensive for a moment. The low hum of the electronic equipment packing his tiny cloister provided most of the room's light and helped him concentrate as he stared at the monitor.

He switched the settings on his computer to pick up a reconnaissance satellite in low orbit, about a hundred and twenty-five miles up in space. It had been tasked to stay stationary over this area of Southeast Asia. The monitor showed static and then the signal cleared up. *There they are! They're out today*, he thought. He had been given strict instructions to check on this site daily and to record and print out any unusual activity. In a secretive meeting the year before Beking had been ordered to take any sighting reports two floors up and hand them over to a Navy captain, and not to reveal what he had seen, even to his own supervisor.

He fine-tuned the settings on the monitor for better resolution and could easily make out about a dozen men gathered in a small clearing. They appeared to be gathered around a freshly dug grave. One stepped forward and gestured as if he was speaking to the rest of the men. All of the men were dressed in striped, pajama-type clothing. They listen reverently for a few minutes and then walked back to their huts.

Beking knew from previous experience to zoom in to the roof of one particular hut. As in the past, a small hand-painted sign, about the size of a wooden shingle, was drying in the sun. It bore an inscription:

1

Major John "Buck" Elliott
USAF
1946—2013

Most of Beking's time was spent spying on Chinese Naval and Submarine bases in an effort to track and report naval activity, especially submarine traffic. This was the information that had made him a target of Chinese espionage. He did not know how they found out what he did, but about four years ago he had been casually approached by agents of the People's Republic of China who wanted to learn what he knew about Chinese submarine operations. The financial rewards were substantial.

He did not report the contact as he should have and as required by his work contract, his morals and ethics contract-and general patriotic grounds. This, however, did not bother him. In the beginning all he wanted was a good government job that would satisfy his strong interests in electronics and satellite technology and if possible, to be able to work alone without someone always looking over his shoulder. Now the interest from a foreign government fed his narcissistic ego.

Somehow his entrance interviews and psych exams had missed that high degree of narcissism. His level of intelligence and the way his mind was bent followed down a narrow path where only a few people fit a profile and qualify for jobs at the NRO or the NSO. Sometimes their level of intellect and quirkiness camouflaged certain social defects, such as narcissism.

He ordered the National Reconnaissance Office's (NRO) satellite to take a digital photograph of the men and the shingle, and to download the encrypted files to the NRO's offices in Chantilly, Virginia.

Although he was betraying his country he could not help but admire the resources and the way the NRO operated. It was responsible for developing and operating space reconnaissance satellites and gathering intelligence data for the Department of Defense and the CIA. It served as the eyes of the CIA, while its sister agency, the National Security Agency (NSA) worked as its ears, listening to overseas telephone calls and email messages with all of its eavesdropping satellites and listening stations around the world.

A few minutes before five o'clock he started the process of signing off his system. Another operator would soon take over his position for the next shift. He gathered his papers, nodded to the person sliding into his desk and walked toward the elevator. The ride to the captain's floor and office was one of the few things that made him nervous.

He knocked and heard a stern, "Enter". He opened the door, walked to the captain's desk and held out the folder containing the photos.

"Here's a couple of photographs that will interest you," he said.

The captain opened the folder and examined the pictures. He never said much and today was no different-just that same stern look that meant, S*ecret, secret, secret. Say anything and you are history.*

Beking felt uneasy as he walked out of the office. The captain always unnerved him. Not to mention that, today, he had a flash drive hidden in a secret compartment of his shoe. It contained Chinese submarine traffic information. And on a whim he had thrown in the two satellite pictures of the men in North Vietnam.

The whim would produce a whirlwind of life-changing events for him. He was to meet Mr. Wu at 5:45 pm. This meeting was designed to be held during the rush hour which would make following him a bit harder in case someone was interested.

Beking was to meet Mr. Wu at a bar halfway between the NRO and downtown Washington. Sometimes it was difficult to reach the intended meeting place because of traffic, which today was moving along at a steady pace. When he pulled in the parking lot of the bar he took a moment and removed the flash drive out of his shoe and placed it in his side coat pocket. He walked into the bar, stopped for a moment to let his eyes adjust to the dim light, spotted Mr. Wu, and maneuvered his way to the bar and sat down next to him.

He wondered if Wu was his real name. He had asked him his first name once but Wu told him he did not need to know. It did not matter one way or the other; he did not want to or need to know if his name was real or fake.

3

Beking looked at Wu and said, "Good afternoon."

Wu said nothing.

Crap, Beking thought, *today he wants to play games and use the coded phrases.*

He took a deep breath and said, "Man, I hate this Washington traffic."

"Maybe it'll get better when they finish upgrading the beltway," Wu countered.

After the introductory code phrases were over with they sat in silence briefly to help carry out the charade of two polite strangers sitting next to each other.

"Been sailing lately?" Wu asked. This was his code for asking if Beking had any naval information for him. Beking sometimes wondered if all this phraseology was really necessary. Wu, who had a healthy respect for the FBI and insisted on it.

"Yes, I took an interesting trip last week."

"Really, I'm always looking for new places to sail. Where did you go?"

"It was nothing exotic, just cruised around the marinas at Annapolis."

As they continued their banter, Beking stood up from his stool and tried to attract the bartender's attention. At the same time he slipped the flash drive into Wu's hand. Wu calmly put the drive in his side coat pocket away from Beking. They talked for another five to seven minutes.

During their conversation a man sat on a stool one down from Wu. Both men stopped talking. Their suspicion lessened when the man ordered a drink and started a conversation with an attractive lady next to him.

The man had rested his briefcase on his knee nearest to Wu. He pushed a button on the expensive burgundy leather and a device within the case searched a three-foot radius for any type of portable memory devices. Wu felt his leg tingle, but he thought it was a chill brought on by his body getting used to the cold temperature in the bar. Within thirty seconds it had copied the contents of the flash drive in Wu's pocket. The device was capable of uploading or downloading files, including viruses, onto Wu's flash drive. The FBI agent, who had been shadowing Wu for weeks, paid for his drink, left the bar and walked to a waiting car parked outside. The agent opened the door, sat down, removed the flash drive from his briefcase and plugged it into his partner's laptop.

"Got anything?" the first agent said.

"Yeah, looks like someone is selling what we know about Chinese submarine activity, the bastard."

"You think this will be enough to take them down?"

"Don't know. It's not our decision. Wait a minute, what's this?"

"What? What have you got?"

"There are two satellite pictures of some people in a forest or jungle."

"Interesting. Let's take it back and see what the Digital Forensics Lab can do."

Wu drove to his house and after a few minutes walked out his back door to a car waiting on a side street nearby. An embassy driver was waiting to take him downtown to Chinese Embassy on Connecticut Avenue.

As the car returned Wu to his residence a Chinese analyst took Wu's information and began the process of analyzing the submarine traffic information. After forty-five minutes he began analyzing the two image files. They puzzled him at first, but then he got a queasy feeling. He thought he knew what this might be. Occasionally, he had heard occasional rumors about this ever since he had been in the intelligence agency. He debated whether or not the photos were worth sending to Beijing, finally deciding to transmit the image files along with the submarine information.

Deep in space an NSA satellite intercepts the encrypted photo images. Although the NSA had not broken the Chinese message traffic code, they were able to decode image photo files depending on the level of security encryption they encountered. The decryption expert passed the image files on to a security analyst further up the line. Two hours later the analyst opened the envelope with the two photos and studied them. The coordinates printed on the photos put them in North Vietnam and only a mile from the Chinese border. Like the Chinese analyst, he also thought he knew what these were. He forwarded them to the CIA in a priority folder.

The next morning a CIA analyst sipped his coffee as he went through his morning mail. He had meetings and appointments all day long and had to prioritize his mail quickly. Coming to the envelope the NSA had sent him, he opened the manila envelope and read the cover letter:

"The enclosed two photos were intercepted at 11:06 pm, Wednesday, via satellite. They were sent from the Chinese Embassy in Washington and were intended for Chinese Intelligence in Beijing."

He flipped over the cover letter and looked at the pictures. He burned his mouth on his coffee and about crapped in his pants. They were the same two photos that he had received yesterday afternoon from the NSA.

How in the hell did the Chinese Embassy get them?, he wondered.

In the next few hours the level of anxiety rose to near panic. There were some seriously worried people at the CIA, Pentagon, and the White House staff. There had to be a spy at the NRO, and worse, the Chinese, and probably the Vietnamese, knew that the Americans knew what they knew. There were American POW's still being held in North Vietnam, and the Americans knew exactly where.

The Secretary of Defense, the Chairman of the Joint Chiefs of Staff, the FBI Director and the head of the CIA had an emergency meeting in the afternoon to decide what and how to tell the White House.

"Does anyone have any suggestions on how to present this to the President?" The Secretary of Defense asked.

Eventually the CIA Director said, "As we all know, in the past this subject, like another, had the directive of, 'Don't Ask, Don't Tell'. But now this can of worms has blown wide open. This could leak, maybe not from us but from unfriendly foreign governments, just to embarrass and put us in an uncomfortable position."

The Chairman of the Joint Chiefs of Staff nodded his head in agreement.

After fifteen minutes of discussion the Secretary of Defense ended the meeting by issuing orders, "General, have your people come up with possible rescue scenarios." He turned his head to the directors of the CIA and the FBI and said, "And you two. You either catch or kill that traitor. And I really don't care if it is the latter. It'll be less dirty laundry to air out."

As the room emptied the Secretary had leaned back in his chair, closed his eyes and composed in his head the general outline of what he would say to the President. The President would soon know about the POWs and would be forced to deal with the situation. He would want answers and solutions. The past few Presidents had not known anything about the POWs in North Vietnam. They had either not bothered to ask or did not want to know and no one in the intelligence community was inclined to inform them. The subject was political dynamite.

It did not take long for Beking to become the suspected spy. A courier was sent to the FBI to brief them on the situation. Beking was to be picked up as soon as possible. They needed to get him before he found out that he had been made as a spy. If he knew that his cover was blown then it would not be easy to locate him. The Chinese would make sure of that.

It was mid-morning and Beking had just gotten to the outskirts of Washington on the way to a satellite tracking station west of the beltway when his cell phone beeped. The message was from Wu.

"Fishing trip canceled, the mackerel has fled south."

Of all the coded crap he had to learn this was the one that he had

7

hoped that he would never receive: he had been discovered as a spy and he should try to leave the country by the southern escape route. Chinese agents would be waiting for him, but, he knew, many more American agents, especially the FBI, would be looking for him. At least until he got out of the country, then the CIA would be the pursuers.

He got off the interstate, found a deserted side road, took out his cell phone, removed the battery and threw both in a water-filled ditch beside the road. He had been taught that even though a cell phone was turned off it could still be tracked. The only way to stop the authorities from tracking the GPS chip in a phone was to take out the battery.

> *...Wait till the tempest is done,*
> *Hope for the sunshine tomorrow,*
> *After the shower is gone.*
> *Whispering hope, oh, how welcome thy voice*
>
> *Whispering Hope, Septimus Winner, 1868*

Chapter Two

In the Quyet Tien prison camp Navy Lieutenant Jay Carter walked back from the grave site and sat down inside the men's dormitory and reflected on the day. The dorm was made with wood saplings and interwoven with reeds. It worked surprisingly well as it allowed some breeze through but kept out the rain if woven right. It could hold about twenty men, but they were down to only fifteen men now. They had started out with seventy men at the camp down the road about thirty years ago. After that they had been moved around from one jungle camp to another, forced to do hard labor, mostly in logging. Over the years they had died out due to logging accidents, hard labor, and malnutrition. Some just gave up and died.

The Chinese and the Vietnamese had an armed border squabble shortly after the Americans got out of Vietnam and the men had been moved south for many years, but they had spent the last ten years here at a secluded camp a couple of miles from the regular Quyet Tien prison camp. Quyet Tien (pronounced "Wet Tin") was a special political prison for the Vietnamese very near the Chinese border and sometimes referred to as Vietnam's Siberia. The American's POW camp was isolated on purpose. They wanted as few people as possible to come in contact with the Caucasian prisoners.

They were all old men now, most in their sixties, a couple in their seventies. Life had been hard until a few years ago. When Dr. Duc Ho and his wife, Han had arrived at the camp conditions began to improve. Dr. Duc, as the men called him, had insisted on better food, medical care, and a reduction in amount of hard labor required.

9

As they had gotten older the only work they had to do was tend their gardens. Even the guards were friendly now. Dr. Duc had managed to get the one that mistreated them transferred out. The guards still watched over them and carried rifles, but were more tolerant now.

Jay had learned from one of the guards that the doctor and his wife were both from influential Hanoi families and had requested the assignment to care for the prisoners. He had intended to stay for only a few months, but he and his wife Han had become so caught up in the prisoner's plight and their stories that he had postponed a promising medical career in Hanoi for this medical, almost missionary-like, posting. Their families were not pleased with the decision, but supported them and used their influence to get better treatment for the prisoners at this camp.

Of all of the two or three hundred prisoners that Jay had ever seen, everyone had fit a certain profile. They were either from rich influential families or had strong scientific backgrounds. Many were academy grads who held engineering degrees. Others were officers who had helped develop weapons systems. Others were specialists in electronic weapons or evasion systems. For their first few years of captivity torture was prevalent and they had been questioned almost daily about what they knew concerning weapons systems and electronics, but as the years passed and technology passed by their level of technical knowledge they were interrogated less and less. The best and the brightest in these fields were clandestinely loaded into a truck and never seen again. Most felt that they were probably taken to Russia for debriefing.

As always, when he took time to reflect, his mind turned to his wife, Ameline.

"What'cha thinking about, Jay?" his friend Howie asked, but he knew where Jay's mind was headed.

"Amy."

"Come on Jay, don't do it. You know how it gets you down. Buck's funeral plus thinking of your wife; you won't sleep tonight."

"I know, but today's her birthday. I wonder what her life is like."

"I don't know Jay, I just don't know." He did not want to

10

speculate and he did not want Jay to think about it too long. Depression was a constant fight and danger here.

"I hope she's remarried to a good man who loves her as much as I do, or did, and is taking good care of our little girl. She was less than a year old when I was shot down. I never even saw her, just had a picture of her."

Howie had heard the story a dozen times but decided to get Jay to talk and maybe change his mood. He asked Jay, "Tell me again how you met Amy." He knew that talking about Amy, although potentially depressing, might just cheer him up.

"We met while I was in flight training at Meridian, Mississippi. Her full French name is Ameline Broussard and she and her friend, Clotille Savoie, are from Louisiana's Cajun country. They decided to have some adventure one weekend and set their sights on visiting the Naval Air Station at Meridian, Mississippi to see if they could meet some Navy Pilots. I spotted Amy as soon as she walked into the bar of the Officer's Club.

She was beautiful, not Hollywood beautiful, but cute beautiful. Her face was perfectly symmetrical, had jet black hair, white alabaster skin, and dark eyes that sparkled. In a few minutes I noticed that she kept looking at me and it embarrassed her when I caught her looking."

"Didn't you say that even someone in the band was watching you two?" Howie said.

"That's right. The band had come off break and the female lead singer sitting in the band area was watching us. She had noticed me and my friends and she had also noticed Amy and Clo when they walked in. I guess the attraction between us was not hard to miss."

"What were they wearing?", Howie asked. He knew what Jay was going to say.

"Oh man, this is the good part. They were braless. In the late 60's and early 70's it was a sign of the times. It was a badge of women's freedom to go braless.

The singer told me later that she had watched me as I walked over and asked Amy to dance. She said Amy's nipples had gone hard

11

under her thin, tight-fitting shirt, then when she realized her condition she quickly cross her arms in front of her. She said she didn't know what Amy was going to say because there had been a long pause between the time I ask her to dance and when she finally stood up and said yes. I remember that the singer quickly got the band going and started belting out a Juice Newton tune, "Dirty Looks". I love that song."

"Did she play hard to get"

"No, not really. For the next four months we were together every weekend. One weekend she would come to the Naval Air Station in Meridian and the next weekend I would leave on Friday afternoon for Broussard, Louisiana, a little south of Lafayette. I would get back to the Naval Air Station on Sunday night just in time to prepare for the next day's flight. I would study for a couple of hours and then crash."

"What's Cajun country like? You got to see the area, didn't you"

"Oh yeah, I loved it around Broussard; the French culture, the mixture of languages, and the exotic bayou food. One of Amy's ancestors had actually founded the town. Amy's family were true Cajun descendants, the people that the British forced out of Acadia, Canada, and re-settled in Louisiana."

"What about her father? Didn't you say he was a little cold at first?"

"He sort of avoided me at first, but once he realized that I truly loved his daughter and wanted to marry her, then, even he was onboard with the relationship. It also helped when I saw him struggling to build a storage shed in the back yard one weekend. I had worked on a maintenance and construction crew at my father's factory in the summers during high school and when I jumped in to help and practically built the shed—well, from there on her father treated me like another son."

"What about her mother?"

"Oh, we became good friends. I would come down from the guest room while she was preparing breakfast and talk to her. For her, it was like talking to another sibling. I think her mother thought that my mother had done a good job with me. This was a relief for Amy because her mother seemed to have a special intuition and could read people quickly and often told her who she should be dating or not."

"What about her friends?" Howie said, leading him on into the conversation.

"Her friends liked me, or at least the girls did. The boys took a while. It took some effort on my part, which included some drinking bouts at local dives and helping them with some Cajun cookouts. I didn't really learn to cook Cajun but I helped the other guys with the process. After a while the "good ole boys" took me in. If Amy liked me, then they would accept me, too."

"So how did you talk her into going to Texas with you?"

"I'm getting to that. The visiting routine continued until I was nearing the end of Basic Jet Training. I was doing well and in the top three of my class, which meant I could have fighter jets if I wanted them, and you know that I did want them, ever since I was a little boy I had wanted fighter jets. But the problem with this meant that very soon I would be sent to south Texas to the Naval Air Station at Chase Field near Beeville, Texas, for advanced training. It would be difficult to see Amy on the weekends."

"Is that when you proposed?"

"Yeah, one evening we were sitting in the swing on Amy's front porch. They had a big porch. You know, I had thought to myself several times that their house was right out of Hollywood casting. It was a beautiful southern home with large porches surrounding the house. It had live oak trees with Spanish moss in the yard—anyway I had a question for Amy."

"Did she know it was coming? What did you say?"

"I think so. I said, Amy, I know we have talked about this several times and we're both in agreement about our relationship. In about six weeks I'm going to be transferred to Texas for advanced flight training. It's going to be really hard for us to see each other on the weekends. So, I have a question for you. Her eyes opened wide and her eyebrows arched upward a little bit and she whispered, What?"

"Will you marry me?"

"Yes, of course. I've told you that before", she said.

"I know. I just wanted to make it official."

"When do you want to have the wedding?"

"Soon, before I get transferred to Texas. Can you get a wedding together in four or five weeks?"

"Umm. That's tight, but I'll make it happen, even if I have to have a magistrate to do it in our front living room."

"Were they able to put it together before you left?", Howie asked.

"They sure did. As it turned out Amy and her mother had a church wedding ready and prepared in five weeks. My training worked out to where I was able to finish basic flight training in the next five weeks. I managed to get two weeks off before I had to report to NAS Chase Field at Beeville, Texas.

We had the wedding at a local Church. Ninety per cent of the people attending were from Amy's family and the local parish. The other ten per cent were my family from North Carolina and a few of my pilot buddies. The wedding was traditional. My sister, Tancy, sang a couple of songs during the ceremony.

Jay paused for a moment and reflected on his sister. At the time, Tancy had been a senior at the University of North Carolina at Chapel Hill. She was pursuing a double major in music and business. It was an unusual combination. She loved music, but their father had insisted on the business degree also. He knew why. Their father's plan was for Jay to get out of the Navy and enter politics. His father felt sure that he could become a congressman, possibly a senator from the state.

It would be Tancy's job to run the family's manufacturing business. She really did not mind. Very few music majors can make a living with their music, besides; she actually enjoyed the factory, especially the factory floor. The workmen were craftsmen who turned out beautiful pieces of furniture, especially rocking chairs. Much of it had become mechanized, but there was still that element of craftsmanship that made their furniture so desirable.

"OK, so you're married now. Tell me about the honeymoon."

"After the wedding and the reception we were off to New Orleans for a three day honeymoon. That was all the time we could afford there. I had to get us out to Beeville, Texas to find an apartment and get settled before resuming advanced flight training the next week.

My father paid for the honeymoon. We stayed in a boutique hotel near Jackson Square in the heart of the French District. We had Bananas Foster for dessert, beignets pastries and chicory coffee in the mornings, took the carriage rides around the French Quarter, took in Bourbon Street, watched the street performers from the steps across from Jackson Square, and had a great dinner at a French restaurant every night. Those three days, the best three days of my life, went all too quickly. Reluctantly we packed the car and left but we enjoyed traveling to South Texas. We were on an adventure together."

They settled into an apartment in Beeville after a couple of days in a motel and Jay was immediately immersed into the fast pace of advanced flight training. It was more difficult for Amy. She was away from home and knew no one. It took about a month but she soon became involved with a group of other Navy wives who husbands were going through the same training as Jay and things became more enjoyable. She had noticed that all of Jay's friends were from the best of colleges. They were very smart and personable. They seemed to be an elite group and their wives were also. The wives were generally speaking, very beautiful, educated, and classy. She would find out that this would cause problems later on with husbands away at sea for nine months of the year. These beautiful and sometimes exotic women from pampered backgrounds would not put up with such long separations and within the first three to five years of their marriages the divorce rate would exceed fifty per cent.

The only thing that really bothered her was that student pilots seem to die in crashes about one every month, sometimes more often. She would be glad when Jay's time in the Navy was over so they could go back to civilian life.

A few months later Amy pinned Jay's Navy *Wings of Gold* on him at his graduation ceremony. For Jay it was extremely gratifying. It was the hardest thing he had ever done in his life and he had made it. He had orders for a couple months of specialized squadron training near San Diego and then he would join his assigned squadron, already at sea off the coast of Vietnam on the *USS Kitty Hawk*. Amy would go back to Louisiana and live with her parents. She was three months pregnant and would need her mother with Jay overseas. Jay was able to see Amy only one time while stationed those two months at San Diego. He got a four-day pass and flew in to see Amy before he shipped out the next week.

A tear formed in one eye.

"Jay, come back. You don't need to go there. This is depressing you," Howie said.

"I'm already depressed over Buck's funeral. I might as well dwell on my beautiful Amy too….Don't worry, Howie, I'll be alright tomorrow."

For the rest of the day Jay reviewed almost every moment they had together from the time of their courtship and marriage until the day he left to join his squadron on the *USS Kitty Hawk*, off the coast of Vietnam.

Later Howie sought out Jay, "Jay, I talked to Dr. Duc and he said he would give you something to help you sleep and stop the dreams."

"Thanks, Howie, but I want to dream. It's the only time I can escape from here."

"Well, OK….if it gives you some sense of peace or even hope."

"Maybe some peace, but I don't believe there's hope anymore."

"Jay, there's always hope."

"Maybe, but if there's any hope, it's a whispering hope."

Jay walked over to his cot and picked up his camp-made guitar, walked outside, sat down on a bench, and in a soft voice started singing the old gospel hymn, "Whispering Hope."

He was dreaming again and he was happy and free. Jay and his family were at the Fiddler's Grove Festival at Union Grove, North Carolina. He was seven-years old and playing a guitar that was almost as big as he was. His six-year old sister, Tancy, was playing a fiddle. The whole family had musical talent, especially his sister. She could play the fiddle almost as well as an adult, which amazed the old-timers. Dad was singing lead with Mom singing harmony to the song, *Will the Circle Be Unbroken*. Their family was a popular favorite at any fiddler or gospel singing convention.

His Dad owned and ran a furniture company near Hickory, N.C. They were well-off, but you would never know it by their clothes or the car they drove. They did live in a nice large house, though. It had a library and downstairs there was a music room. His dad was also a state senator and was in the state capital, Raleigh, quite often.

In his dream he remembered being at the Fiddler's Festival one day when a low-flying military jet overflew the convention field. Jay knew right then and there that he was going to be a jet pilot someday. He wanted the adventure.

The dream seemed to last for a long time. There were family trips, musical outings, Boy Scout trips, birthdays, church, and high school football games. Suddenly his F-4J Phantom was falling apart around him with fire everywhere. He started the ejection sequence by pulling the face curtain down over his face. He awoke with a start, sweating and breathing hard.

Howie raised his head from the cot, "You ok, Jay?"

He couldn't speak. He could only nod his head that he was alright.

It was daybreak. *Maybe if I go to Medical, Han will give me some coffee*, Jay thought.

Han enjoyed getting into the clinic early. It gave her time to think and prepare the rooms for the day. Her husband, Dr. Duc Ho, would be in later. She started percolating some coffee over a wood stove. Coffee was a luxury that she and her husband allowed themselves and occasionally shared with the camp commander and, on rare occasions, some of the prisoners. She had grown up hating what the Americans had done to her country but she had put most of that behind her when she got to know the prisoners and realized that they were just men who were placed in a terrible situation. She had developed great empathy for them. She spent much of her time talking to them and listening to their stories of how they got there and of their families.

Most had accepted their fate and were adjusting as well as could be expected. Four of the men had actually set up house with local women who were employed to help out at the prison camp with cooking and cleaning. These men were allowed to build some huts on the edge of the camp clearing and live there with their wives and children.

She knew from stories that her influential and well-connected parents had told her that the Vietnamese had great hopes of receiving vast amounts of ransom money from the Americans in return for the prisoners. They believed this because Fidel Castro had visited Hanoi in 1973 and had bragged about the reparations and ransom received from the United States for the prisoners from the Bay of Pigs. His argument was so convincing that the Vietnamese government believed it for years after the war ended.

She had come to believe, that had they given up all the prisoners at the end of the war like they said they were going to do, then the Americans would have eventually been more generous in their aid to Vietnam. America did not pay ransom for prisoners. It only encouraged more kidnappings and ransom requests, so now she had to watch these poor men suffer and die. *Americans should spit every time they hear Fidel Castro's name,* she thought.

In the early morning fog Han saw Mr. Jay walking toward the clinic. He was one that would never take a local woman as a mate. He would never get over his wife. Mr. Jay was special. He was the unspoken leader of the men. In many ways he was strong and a natural leader. Mentally, however, because of his compassion he felt for his men and strong feelings of loss over his family, he was vulnerable. This was especially so if he were to be placed in isolation, but fortunately, that was not used anymore.

Jay walked into her room and sat down. His swollen eyes showed that he had been crying. Han turned away from him, put her hand to her mouth and almost cried herself. She composed herself, poured a cup of coffee, and handed it to him.

She knew the reason for the swollen eyes. She knew it was from vivid dreams or nightmares. All of the prisoners seemed to be troubled by them. It seemed to get worse as they got older. For the lucky few, the dreams were peaceful and took them back to their earlier years, but the dreams often brought on depression. Others had terrible bouts with nightmares resulting from years of torture. It was the premise of an academic paper that her husband was writing and hoped to submit to a medical journal soon. Its premise was that isolation and lack of cultural stimulation for prisoners brought on vivid dreams to compensate for the lack of interaction with their culture.

"Mr. Jay, you had a bad night. I want you to help me today. I want you to pull all of the men's files out of the file cabinet and write an evaluation of each man's medical and mental well-being. Would you do that for me today?"

"Yes, I will. I need to get my mind going in a different direction."

Han smiled and they talked while they had coffee. They both knew what was wrong with him.

The day did not go as easy as he thought it would. When he went to the file cabinet there were files of all the other pilots who had died and of the few who remained alive. There were Rear Intercept Officers (RIO's), navigators, and others that had gone through the prison camp system.

He thumbed through some of his old friends files. It took him back to his last semester in college at North Carolina State University where he was an electrical engineering major. He had signed on with the Naval ROTC Department as soon as he could get accepted. It was his route to become a Navy pilot. Nineteen days after college graduation he was going through pilot training in Pensacola, Florida. It was not easy. Navy Flight School was a pressure cooker. Every day, every week was like the pressure that you endured in college during mid-terms or finals. There was that much study and pressure. It was that way for a year and a half, until he got his wings. Even then the pressure did not let up. You simply got used to it, and learned what was expected from you so that you would be ready when you were eventually assigned to your squadron. It was all very detailed and demanding. It was not like in the movies. You had to know the plane's hydraulics, pneumatics, electronics, and weapons system so that they were second nature. You did not have time to think about them or what their limitations were during a high-g turn in a dogfight.

He wondered what had happened to David Ferris. He was his best friend during the year and a half of flight training. They were able to stay together for the entire time until they got their wings but were then assigned different squadrons, but as luck would have it, both squadrons were assigned to the aircraft carrier, *USS Kitty Hawk*.

He and Amy had included David in most of their parties and outings. Their small circle of close friends was inseparable in their activities outside of the day-to-day Navy routine. He remembered one evening in particular. They had invited David over for dinner. It had been a long, hot, summer day in Texas with two training hops. David had been exhausted and thirsty. Jay poured David some champagne before dinner and he had downed it in one or two gulps. Jay smiled, shook his head, and poured David another glass full. David took a little more time with this one but still, it went down quickly. Jay joined Amy and helped her set the table. Meanwhile, David became very sleepy and had the strongest urge to lay down on the floor and go to sleep. Jay saw him nodding.

"David. Wake up buddy. Time to eat."

"Man, I didn't know I was so tired and dehydrated. I almost passed out in the chair."

"Yeah, I noticed. Come on over here. Get some food in you.
"And no more champagne for you", Amy added.

On board the *Kitty Hawk* they were extremely busy but usually found time to visit each other every day in their small staterooms, which as junior officers they shared with three other officers.

One night, after Jay and David had returned from a night operations mission, they were talking, trying to wind down. They had successfully landed their jets onboard the carrier at night; the hardest thing they had to do. They were discussing their missions and about the two pilots and their accompanying RIO's that had been lost that day. They had seen many of their squadron mates get shot down who were either killed or captured. It was becoming apparent to them that it was a real possibility that one or even both of them might not make it back home alive.

"David, do you think we can survive this cruise?" Jay asked.

"Hope so. We've only got thirty days left before we return home". David paused for a moment and then asked, "What do you think Amy and the baby will do if you get shot down?"

Jay sighed, lay back on his pillow and said, "Probably return to Louisiana and live with her parents. They're well-off and I know her mother would love to help her keep the baby. Actually, that's where she spends most of her time anyway."

"Well, I guess that's as good a place as any for them to wait for you until you get released from a POW camp."

They thought about this for a few moments and then Jay spoke, "David, if I don't make it back, will you promise me that you'll look after Amy and the baby, and make sure that the Navy treats them right? I know the Navy will listen to you since you already have a MIG kill. You're a big shot now."

"It's a promise."

Three days later Jay was sitting in his F-4 Phantom on the deck of the *Kitty Hawk*. It was hot and the sweat was running down from under his helmet. His forehead and face was covered in sweat. The canopy was up and a breeze was coming across the deck, but his flight suit and helmet made him feel like he was in an oven. He had been assigned "Alert Five" duty today. "Alert Five" meant that at least one plane was ready to be launched, if needed, when in a combat situation. If, suddenly, an enemy aircraft were to appear on the radar screen and it looked like they were headed toward the carrier then there would be at least one plane available that could launch within five minute to defend the carrier. In addition, if the situation was hot, then there would be two more planes on "Alert Fifteen".

"Andy, you OK back there?", Jay shouted to his back-seater, commonly known as a RIO (Radar Intercept Officer).

"God no. I'm sopping wet. I almost wish one of those MIG-boys would make a run at us so we could get up into some cooler air."

"Yeah, me too. I would love to get my chance at a MIG kill. You'd think that they would try to tangle with us every day."

"Well, we know that's not the case. They only showed up if they have an advantage, set a trap for you, or your plane was crippled.", Andy said.

As strange as it seemed, it was actually hard to get a MIG to tangle with you one-on-one. Most American planes were shot down by Surface-To-Air Missiles (SAM) or radar-guided anti-aircraft guns.

"Aardvark Eleven, prepare for launch", the Air Boss said.

Jay and Andy were both startled, but started going through the "Alert Five" checklist. It was rare for anyone to be launched while assigned to "Alert Five" or "Alert Fifteen" duty. *I wonder what's going on*, Jay thought.

"Aardvark Eleven, there's a real furball going on just outside Hai Phong Harbor. Some of the MIG's are getting a little far out. Make sure one doesn't head this way and you may have to help out if we have a cripple heading for the boat and a MIG is after it."

"Roger, understood."

The Air Boss's voice crackled through the air again, "Alert

Fifteens, get out of your ready room and get your planes into the catapults, your Alert Five now."

"Roger", they responded from their squadron's ready room.

Three minutes later the launch officer saluted Jay and two seconds later he was airborne at 140 knots; thirty seconds later they were already feeling cooler air as they climbed to altitude. They were hurtling toward Hai Phong Harbor at a little under 400 miles per hour. It would have been faster but they were still climbing. He reported in to *Red Crown*, which was a radar ship in the Gulf of Tonkin that relayed vital enemy air activity to the pilots.

Jay climbed through 15,000 feet and switched the radio to their tactical channel. The frequency was filled with a half a dozen pilot conversations going on. *"Watch it, Gopher, there's one on your tail!"....."Spice, drag him starboard so I can get a shot at him"...."Damnit, get him off my tail!"....."Nice shot Snake, you got him!"* Every thirty seconds or so *Red Crown* would cut in and announced further enemy activity. Finally, one pilot told *Red Crown* to shut up for a while. They knew where the enemy was and they were cutting in on vital pilot conversations.

Jay felt sorry for that *Red Crown* operator. They did a great job of letting the pilots know where the MIGs were and the pilots really appreciated them, but Jay knew how the pilot felt. When, in a real furball fight like that, they did not need the extra chatter.

As Jay arrived on station, the furball started to untangle and jets were bugging out on both sides. It reminded him of a schoolyard fight when one side decided to quit and the other side was damn glad they did.

As radio chatter died down, *Red Crown* came on the air again and warned everyone that four Russian-built MIGs-17s were screaming down from the north. They were coming down the coast, south of the Chinese border. This was unusual; either some Vietnamese pilots had flown low and to the east toward the coast and then started south or these were Chinese pilots out for some combat experience.

All of the Navy planes were low on fuel and did not need to deal

23

with this new threat, so Jay turned his plane toward the four MIGs.

"Jay, you gonna' take on those four bandits?" Andy asked.

"Hope I don't have to. Maybe they'll turn and run." More than half the time they did turn and run, but sometimes they stood and fought.

"Andy, set me up two Sparrow missiles."

"You want Sparrow missiles?" Andy said incredulously.

"Yeah, yeah, I know, they're practically useless." He knew why Andy was so surprised. The Sparrow had less than a ten percent success ratio. They were radar guided and were easily confused and had performed poorly so far in the war. "I'm going to try to scatter them with the Sparrows, I know they won't hit. Maybe it'll scare'um and make'um turn back."

"Jay, we're going to merge in about forty-five seconds. I'll have'um ready."

"Tell me to fire when we're fifteen miles from them."

"Will do"

At twenty miles, Andy started a countdown to fifteen. Jay fired off two Sparrow missiles. He felted the missiles come off the rail and averted his eyes. Their bright exhaust would blind you if you were not careful to look away for a moment. He called into the mike a general warning to all on his frequency, "Fox one! Fox one!" This meant two sparrow missiles had been fired.

"Jay, both sparrows missed, but they had to maneuver hard to get out of the way… Hey, I think it worked. I believe they're running for home."

"OK, let's hang around for a minute to see what happens.", Jay said.

Thirty seconds later Andy pressed his intercom button to Jay. "Two of them are headed home but the other two are coming our way."

Jay could imagine it in his mind. Two instructor pilots were out with trainees. They had sent the trainees back and the two instructors were teaming together to come after them. *I hope they aren't Chinese or Russian,* he thought.

"They're climbing high for an advantage!" Andy shouted.

"I'm going to fire two more sparrows. That'll mess'um up."

"There're ready. Go ahead."

"Fox one! Fox one!", Jay shouted into the microphone.

While the missiles were on the way, Jay slammed the throttle forward and started getting some altitude of his own while still aiming at the two MIGs. In the distance he saw an explosion.

"My God, Andy. One of those sparrows hit a MIG."

"Nooooo! No way!"

Jay keyed his radio and said, "This is Aardvark Eleven, splash one MIG-17." This was for the benefit of *Red Crown* so they would know and could record that they had shot down a MIG.

The other MIG started after them but suddenly turned away.

"Hum, guess he's had enough", Jay said to Andy.

"I don't think so. I've got several SAM sites locking on to us and firing. There's two…three…, there's five SAMs coming our way."

Jay pushed the throttle into afterburner and went straight up for a few seconds. Then he turned the plane straight down. Jay was hoping that the SAMs could not compute his turn down fast enough. Maybe they would fly right by him before they could ignite the fuse to explode. Four of them did just that, but the last one made the calculation and exploded about fifty feet off his left wingtip. It sounded like someone had thrown a load of gravel against his plane. But it was not gravel, it was shrapnel. Most of it seemed to hit behind his cockpit.

"Andy, you alright back there…Andy, talk to me!" No answer.

He wanted to strain his neck around to see if he could see Andy, but the plane was beginning to become uncontrollable. There was a muffled explosion and the cockpit became engulfed in flames.

"Oh God! I'm going to have to eject, Jay thought. A dozen thoughts screamed through his mind. *Am I slow enough to eject? Will I survive the ejection? What will they tell Amy and his parents?* But the overriding thought was, *Why won't Andy talk to me?*

He tried to pull the plane level to lose some airspeed but then the plane started to roll. He pulled the face curtain down over his face which started the ejection sequence for both he and Andy.

The wind blast was tremendous. He only had a second or two to try to bleed off airspeed before the plane became too uncontrollable and he had to eject. A four-hundred mile an hour wind hitting your body knocks you senseless for a few moments. He did remember a sensation that his back was being driven down into his seat from the jet pack that was blasting him free of the airplane. He did not remember the blast that separated him from his seat, but he definitely felt his straps jerk when his chute opened. It took a few moments to gather his senses and start looking for Andy. He could not find Andy's chute but he did see his plane impact the ground.

At five hundred feet he could tell that there were North Vietnamese soldiers everywhere. *I'm going to be captured. Not even a chance of a helicopter rescue,* he thought.

They were on him as soon as he hit the ground. One soldier was particularly Saber. He had raised his rifle butt to hit him in the head when a voice shouted for him to stop. A North Vietnamese Army (NVA) officer had arrived on the scene and had taken charge and stopped the beating. The officer knew that pilots were a valuable commodity and orders had been issued to get all air crews back to Hanoi in reasonable health. They tied his hands together behind his back and marched him a few miles to a truck and sat him in the back. He tried to ask about Andy but every time he tried to talk someone hit him. The officer who stopped his beating moved in front of him in the truck and said, "Pilot...*mort*." He knew *mort* was French for dead, but did he mean Andy or another pilot?

The journey to Hanoi took a week. At night, if there was no danger of American jets attacking the trucks, they would sleep in the trucks; otherwise they slept on the jungle floor. They never untied his hands. By the time Jay reached a prison camp near Hanoi his wrists were raw and infected. As soon as he entered the camp they untied his hands, threw some disinfectant on his wrists, and threw him into isolation.

After two weeks of isolation he was anxious to talk to anyone. That is when they started the interrogations. At first there was no torture so he answered their questions that did not pertain to military intelligence or military things that anyone would know. They wanted to know about his family and his background. Here, he unknowingly told them something that changed his destiny. When they learned that his father owned a furniture company they decided to keep him away from the prisoners in the Hanoi Hilton. He must be from a rich family and they could ask for ransom at the end of the war.

The prisoners in Hanoi would be swapped after the war, but he, along with certain other prisoners, would be kept separate and used to make sure that the United States paid reparations for all the war damage done to their country, which was in line with Castro's advice. These prisoners from rich families would be used as leverage to pressure the Americans to pay the ransom. Prisoners with technical degrees, along with advanced knowledge about weapons and electronics, would be sent to Russia and China. No one ever saw those prisoners again.

Jay Carter looked up from the medical records he was working on and rubbed his eyes. Han's idea of updating the medical records for the men had turned into a long-term project. Not only did the camp have on file the records of the seventy men who were first interned at this camp, but files of a couple hundred more flight crew who had died or were possibly at other camps like this one; although he doubted it. The guards had indicated to him that this was the only camp left with American prisoners.

He enjoyed the work; having something constructive to do, but it had its drawbacks too. The dreams at night were more intense and were a mixture of the men's files and his own past. He woke every morning, exhausted. Some days Dr. Duc would tell him not to come in the next day and give him a pill to sleep that night. Most of the time the pills worked, but occasionally they caused dreams that were so vivid that he would bolt upright in his bed and shake until the next morning. Han would take pity on him and give him coffee to soothe his nerves.

Today he finished the last paragraph in the medical record of a pilot who had died twenty years ago. He remembered him, but he was becoming blurred with so many others. He put the file away and opened the next folder containing the record of Air Force Captain Nehemiah Cross.

Nehemiah, a black man, was an electronic warfare officer and was still alive but very sick over in the men's compound. Dr. Duc said it was cancer, but he was not allowed to give him any special treatment other than what little he had here in the camp. He was having dreams too.

Chapter Three

David Beking was riding on the back roads of Virginia, heading south. He knew he had to change cars soon. The FBI had to be looking for him. He knew enough to stay off I-95 and not to use his credit or debit card. Everything had to be cash and he was running short of that.

He was in a small town in Virginia looking for a pay phone, which was hard to find since cell phones had made them almost non-existent. He finally spotted one at a rundown convenience store without outside surveillance cameras. He had been given two phone numbers in case of such an emergency. One was to be used if he had headed north out of DC and the other if he headed south. He called the number for the southern escape route.

"Hello."

He answered with the code phrase, "Hello, is this the number for the Dragon Fish House?"

There was a long pause. "Where are you?"

Beking gave him the address and city of where he was and where the convenience store was located.

"Hide your car as best you can. I'll be there in about forty-five minutes. What color shirt do you have on?"

"I have on a royal blue shirt with khaki pants." I'm about five-foot-nine and……", but the other man cut him off.

"I know what you look like. I will have a yellow tee-shirt and cut-off jeans. Hang tight"

Beking parked in the back of the convenience store and waited in the car for about forty minutes. He got out of the car and walked around the building near the front door. Six minutes later two cars pulled up.

A man in a yellow tee shirt and cut-off jeans got out of one of the cars, walked to him, and held out a set of car keys.

29

"Here, you need a new car. There is clothing, toiletry items, $10,000 in cash in the car, and a few passports. Here's a credit card. Use it one time only. It should be used for your final trip out of the Caribbean. Hopefully you won't have to use it and you'll find another way out, preferably by boat. For now, head south until you meet your other contact and then hopefully on to Cuba or Venezuela. Stay off I-95. There're a lot of people looking for you. Don't go to any airport, public or private. Now listen carefully. There's an envelope with money in the luggage. It also has information on who and where your contact is. Read it, memorize it, and burn it. Now go."

"Is that my car?" nodding toward the car the man got out of.

"Yes, it's the grey Ford Taurus, over there", he said as he pointed his hand in the direction of it. "You're a hot item right now, so it's a low profile-type of car. Good Luck." He turned around and walked over to the second car, got in, and left. He looked at the other man driving the car and said, "I give him a fifty-fifty chance of making it to Venezuela."

"Why Venezuela?"

"That's where, what the American's call, the "Terror Flight" leaves from. It leaves Caracas on an intermittent basis for Tehran, Iran, carrying agents and spies out of harm's way. From Tehran they can make it to their home country without any problem"

"Huh, that would be an interesting ride."

"You can't buy a ticket for it. It poses as a normal scheduled flight, but only government-approved personnel can get on it."

"Maybe we'll get to ride it someday."

"Let's hope not."

In Washington Eric Dawkins had left a meeting with a dozen other FBI agents. All had been assigned a section along the East Coast. They had been briefed on the spy David Beking, given photos of him, and had a long discussion as to where he might be headed. The general consensus was Cuba or Venezuela. He had been told that a CIA agent would contact him soon and shadow his search. The reason for this was if they discovered that the spy had been able to leave the FBI's jurisdiction of the United States and had gotten out of the country, then the CIA would take over. Their agents had a lot more latitude overseas than the FBI.

Eric had been assigned to coastal North Carolina. It was early fall. *At least it won't be so cold, and there are some decent seafood restaurants there. If I start now I should be able to make it by midnight,* he thought. *I wonder who the CIA agent will be.* He knew a few of their field agents. Most were a little strange, but effective. They had a completely different employment profile for agents than the FBI had. In the past you could spot a CIA agent by his dark suit, thin tie, and dress hat, but not anymore. They could be anyone.

At CIA headquarters in Langley, Virginia, a top-level meeting was in the process of matching up CIA field agents to shadow the FBI agents who had been assigned different areas along the East Coast. More experienced field agents had already been sent to various spots in the Caribbean to see if they could spot Beking. They did not think Beking was there yet, but the agents could get settled in and start their watch for the spy. Although their gut feeling was that he was headed south toward Cuba or Venezuela, they also stationed other agents in northern coastal cities and a few along the West Coast. They had to shadow the FBI agents because the CIA was forbidden to operate in the United States, but as soon as they found out that Beking had left the United States, then he would become their responsibility.

"Who do you want to send to the North Carolina coast?" one senior agent asked.

"I don't know, we've just about run out of experienced agents", replied another.

"Could we send one of our newer field agents?"

"Got anyone in mind?"

"I was impressed with that new girl that's out at Yuma, going through HALO training.

"Yes, she's good. She got good evaluations all through her training, but why in God's name is she going through HALO training?"

"She requested it; begged for it actually."

HALO training was short for High-Altitude, Low Opening. It was parachute training to the extreme. Not only was she being taught HALO, but HAHO also, which was high-altitude, high-opening. HAHO was particularly useful for inserting personnel into sensitive spots without the opposing party knowing about it. Additional training could enable an agent to jump out of a plane at 30,000 feet with a wingsuit, looking a lot like a flying squirrel, and glide nearly ten miles to the insertion point before having to pop the chute.

"Alright, send her down there with the FBI agent covering that part of the Carolinas. It'll be good experience for her."

"Is she the really good-looking girl that went through training a few months ago?"

"Yep, that's her."

"I don't know, she's almost too good-looking to be a field agent…too noticeable."

"Pretty girls have their uses too", one of the senior female agents said, almost under her breath.

Sudie Sexton was sitting in the business section of a jet headed toward Washington, D.C. She had finished HALO school yesterday at the Yuma Proving Grounds and had planned on spending a few days sightseeing around the Southwest, but she had been ordered back to Langley to be briefed for her first assignment. Today she had dressed down to what she thought the boys would call a five or a six. She could look like a nine or ten if she so chose, but she didn't want the attention today.

She had come a long ways in the last five or six years; from a teenage Melungeon girl in East Tennessee to Yale, and finally to the CIA. She smiled to herself and thought, *I bet I'm the only Melungeon to ever go to an Ivy League school and then become a CIA agent.*

Oriental Flyer

The Melungeon people's history is a little murky to say the least. They are thought to be of Spanish or Portuguese descent and DNA evidence has been confirming it recently. Present day Melungeons tends to show a DNA ancestry of European and Native American, along with about a five per cent Mediterranean or Saharan mixture. The early pioneer Melungeons of East Tennessee claimed to be of "Porty-Ghee" or Portuguese descent. How they got to the mountains of East Tennessee in the 1500 to 1600's is a mystery. Some people have speculated that they may have been part of the Lost Colony, but DNA does not support that theory. The DNA supports the theory that these people came from Northern Africa or Southern Spain and the Melungeon people tend to have unusual diseases that are common for people of the Mediterranean.

The most prevalent and well-accepted theory is that they were men from DeSoto's expedition that went through western North Carolina and eastern Tennessee from 1556-1568. DeSoto had one of his men, a Captain Don Pardo, build camps and small fortresses in those areas. Some speculate that several of Pardo's men were captured by Indians and integrated into the tribe; others say that when Captain Pardo left the area some of his men deserted and joined the Indians and took brides from the Cherokee and Creek Indians. There is no recorded history of warfare or animosity between the Indians and the Melungeons and many take this as proof that the Indians looked upon them as a cousin-type tribe.

When the early English pioneers first entered East Tennessee they encountered olive or dusky-skinned people, with European features. They all had black, oily hair and claimed to be of Portuguese descent. They kept to themselves because the white settlers mistreated them as if they were black, fortunately the government would not let them be considered as part of the black race, and therefore they could not be slaves.

Sudie's mother, a Melungeon, was almost abandoned when she was a year and a half old. Her mother had died and she had come under the care of her grandmother who was old, fat, and could hardly provide for herself much less an eighteen-month old child.

Doctor Williams, a country doctor, happened to drive by the grandmother's patchwork wooden shack one day and noticed the grandmother sitting on the porch in her rocking chair with a little girl playing at her feet. Intrigued, he stopped and talked for a while and then examined the child. It was evident that she was malnourished, dirty, and unkempt.

"Mrs. Collins, do you mind if I take this child into town with me and look after her for a spell? She has bronchitis and will soon have pneumonia and needs some doctoring", he said.

Mrs. Collins thought about it for a moment and said, "No, I don't mind. She is sick. Nobody around here will take her. They already have too many mouths to feed." She thought for a minute and said, "Doctor, do you think you could find someone nice to take care of her?"

"Do you mind if my wife and I take her in and look after her?"

A tear rolled down her face as she thought about the little girl's dead mother, her own daughter. "Lord knows I'll miss her, but I just can't care for her like she should be looked after. Would you bring her by every now and then so's I could see her?"

"Why sure Mrs. Collins; I'll try to bring her by when I know I'm coming your way."

She held out her arms for the little girl to come to her. Doctor Williams lifted her up and placed her in her grandmother's arms and lap. The grandmother gave her a long hug and kissed her on the cheek. The little girl winced at the hug and squeeze but did return the kiss on her grandmother's cheek. Her grandmother then held her out to the doctor and burst into tears as he took the girl from her arms.

It was one of the hardest things he had ever done, taking a child away from a parent figure but he knew the child would die soon if he did not do it. In addition, he had a feeling that Mrs. Collins was sick also. Her breathing and her general continence told him that she probably had a lung disease and would not live much longer. He had tears in his eyes and a lump in his throat as he put the little girl in the front car seat. That was the hardest part of being a doctor; making the occasional life and death decision or in this case a heart-breaking act to save a life.

The little girl's only possession was the dress that she was wearing and a cornhusk doll that Mrs. Collins had made for her. On the trip to town he gave her some cornbread and milk which she devoured between coughs. She smiled, and jabbered most of the way home until she fell asleep on the front seat with her head on his leg. Occasionally she would cough or whimper and he would put his hand on her back. A gentle pat would let her know that someone was there and then she would fall back asleep.

When Doctor Williams pulled into the driveway of his house his wife walked out to the car to meet him and looked at the little girl.

"John Williams, what do you have there?" she said with a quizzical smile.

"Martha, her name is Mary, and if I hadn't taken her.... well, she was in a situation where she wouldn't have lasted another two weeks, maybe less."

"Oh, John, she's so skinny and she's absolutely filthy. Oh, but look at that smile."

Martha took her inside, placed her in the kitchen sink and gave her a warm bath. Mary laughed and played in the water. Martha scrubbed the dirt, grime, snot, and Lord knows what else off her smeared face and hands.

"John, run next door and ask Joan if they will let us have some of little Betty's old baby clothes."

Martha was drying Mary off when John returned with some clothes.

"Here's some for right now. Joan said that she would bring some more in a little bit. She can't wait to see the little girl."

Martha dressed the little girl and watched in delight as the baby looked at the new dress they had put on her. She fingered every piece of bright color on the dress. In between bronchial coughing fits she would rub each color with her finger, look up at them, and prattle on about it, as if she had something to say about each and every color.

They could not help but fall in love with her, as did their eight-year old son, who accepted her as his little sister and protected her as such.

35

Under their care she soon became healthy. Martha read to her every night and Mary absorbed everything they put in front of her. She could read by the time she was four-years old. She was gifted and excelled in school. The doctor thought that the girl's natural mother had to have worked with her, because if she had not been socialized and worked with at that young age, then she would never developed as she had. *She had to have been a good mother*, he thought.

Doctor Williams was only able to take Mary to see her grandmother a couple of times. She became sick and died after that first year of sarcoidosis, a disease that inflames the lymph nodes and lungs. A sickness common to the people of the Saharan and Mediterranean regions and seems to plague many of the people of Melungeon descent in East Tennessee.

A spell turned into a year and a year into a teenage girl.

Mary did well in high school and she was not stigmatized and looked down upon as many of Melungeon descent were. Although she was dark-complected with an olive-colored skin, and coal black hair, she did have Caucasian features. She was attractive and many people thought she was Italian. She married after her senior year of high school to Barry Sexton. He was well-liked, intelligent, and he eventually took over and did well with his father's insurance business.

Mary had trouble conceiving and she and Barry thought they were not destined to have children, but on Mary's thirty-ninth birthday she discovered that she was pregnant and in April of 1987 a little girl was born, whom they named Sudie Sexton.

Sudie was a fireball. She was into everything. Her parents were gifted and intelligent, so the genes that coursed through her body made school a breeze. She challenged herself in school work and she was very competitive in athletics. If you were a young athletic girl in East Tennessee then you were destined for girls' basketball. She was a good point guard and a smart playmaker.

She was very pretty and enjoyed the attention. The boys called her "Sudie Sexy-ton". As a pre-teen and teen she had hated the implications of her last name along with the combined alliteration of her first name but Sexton was a common East Tennessee Melungeon name and she eventually got over it in high school as she learned to appreciate her sexual looks. She had the Melungeon olive skin and coal-black hair. She kept it short, almost pixie-style. She was likable and had many girlfriends, although, as always, some were jealous of her. She did not want to get married too early. She wanted the college experience and she went for the brass ring, an Ivy-League education. Her father, dreading the expense of an Ivy League college, groaned when he heard this, but he did not have to worry. Sudie wrote a masterpiece of a letter, asking for admittance to Yale. She pulled on their heartstrings about her Melungeon heritage and how, if Yale wanted diversity, she would be the perfect candidate. Of course, excellent scores on her entrance exams helped too. Because of her ethnic background and good grades she got a full academic scholarship.

She maintained a 3.6 GPA at Yale and learned to speak Spanish fluently, which for some reason came easy for her. She participated in several sports but her passion turned to sky-diving when, one weekend, a boyfriend took her to a nearby airport and got her started in the sport. It was almost a sexual experience for her; the rush of falling out of the plane, the sudden explosion of the chute opening, and then the slow descent downward. She loved it, joined a sky-diving club, and jumped out of an airplane every chance she got.

There must have been someone at Yale, possibly one of her advisors, looking for people who fitted a certain profile that the CIA looks for, because one day a CIA recruiter, a woman in a grey suit and skirt, approached her as she was sitting in a quiet corner of the student lounge, studying.

"You're Sudie Sexton, aren't you?"

Sudie looked up, a little surprised that this professional-looking woman wanted to talk to her. "Yes, I'm Sudie."

"Sudie, this may surprise you, but over the last two months

we've been checking out your background, grades, what you like and dislike, your hobbies, and your language skills. All this to see if you fit our profile for a special job that very few people get offered."

"What kind of job?" Sudie asked, almost in a whisper.

"A job with the CIA. You would go through our training and if you are accepted at the end of it, our trainers will evaluate you and make recommendations as to what job suits you best, but I'm thinking you would make a good field agent and I'm rarely wrong. Do you think you would be interested?"

"Of course, I'm interested." She could not imagine anyone not being interested.

"You graduate next month. In the meantime, I'll send you some applications to fill out. Mail them in as soon as you can. You'll receive instructions on when and where to report for training. By the way, try not to talk about this too much to your friends."

"OK, but will I have time to go home and see my parents after graduation?"

"I'll see if I can get them to give you a week or two before reporting. I can't promise it though." She stood up, waved a little good-by to her and started walking off.

"Wait a minute, you don't have my address", Sudie shouted.

"I know everything about you", she said over her shoulder, as she walked away.

The recruiter was also thinking to herself that with her looks and language skills she could be used in various parts of the world. She could be American, Cuban, South American, or from the Middle East, and various other regions of the globe. Her Melungeon-English heritage had given her the right combination of dusky looks that made her look like she could come from almost any part of the world. As far as her good looks, she had won the genetic lottery, which could be a curse or a blessing in this business, depending on the assignment.

Chapter Four

Beking drove to a nearby strip mall, parked, and opened the trunk. A small, wheeled suitcase was in the trunk. He stood and looked around to make sure no one was nearby to see him check out the trunk. The suitcase revealed three stacks of money wrapped in cellophane, a new driver's license, three different passports, and a small box of matches. They all had his picture with three different names, and three different nationalities. Finally, there was an envelope with instructions and a pack of matches.

He tore into one of the money packs, grabbed a couple hundred dollars, snatched the envelope with his instructions, and got back in the car. The instructions were short and simple. It read:

• *Empty your wallet and pockets of all identifying documents and burn them.*

• *Drive until you reach your contact point. Do not pick up any supplies. Do not stop!*

• *Drive to Oriental, NC ASAP. It is pre-programmed in the GPS unit on the dash.*

• *Go to Gordon's Marina and find a 47 ft., Robertson and Caine catamaran with the name **Oriental Flyer** on the back of the boat. Ask for Buddy. He is your contact and will get you out of the country by sea. Follow his instructions and do whatever he says.*

• *Spend your money carefully; you may need it toward the end of your trip.*

• *Leave the car unlocked in the marina parking lot. Place the keys under the floor mat. It will be picked up within a couple of hours of your arrival.*

• *AGAIN. Burn this letter along with all of your identifying documents.*

Beking took a deep breath and thought; *I can't believe this is happening to me. Where will I end up, Asia? Will I have to learn a new language? Will the CIA be looking for me for the rest of my life?*

He shook himself out of his thoughts and turned on the GPS. He drove until he found an isolated side road in the country. It was an unpaved, sandy, dirt road and after a couple of turns he was hidden from the main road. He threw all of his documents and the instruction letter into a pile in the center of the road. He struck a match and watched the pile burn until it went out. He took a stick, stirred the ashes, and then took his foot and mixed the ashes into the sandy road.

The next five hours of driving was the most nerve-racking of his life. As he traveled the back roads through small towns, he felt every person in those towns was eyeing him. Local police, parked along the road, brought on waves of anxiety. Once, a North Carolina State Trooper raced up behind him, siren wailing and then chattering. He knew it was over with and that he had been caught, but the trooper passed him and disappeared down the road.

Early that evening Beking arrived in Oriental, NC. He put the car in park, turned off the engine, and looked at the sign which said, *Welcome to Gordon's Marina.* He laid his head back against the headrest and took a deep breath. *I made it,* he thought. He got out of the car and stretched. His legs were wobbly and he was hungry. He had eaten a breakfast bar as he left for work this morning and nothing else. It was about 7:00 pm and the marina was closed, which was good; no one was here to see him.

Inside the marina, the owner was going over some paperwork at one of the tables near the snack bar, when he noticed a man, pulling a small, wheeled suitcase. The man looked around for a minute and then went down the walkway and boarded the *Oriental Flyer.* He went back to his paperwork thinking, *That must be Buddy's new charter.*

Buddy Miller watched the man coming down the walkway. Ever since he had gotten the phone call, he had been on edge, waiting for this trip to begin. He knew this was no ordinary charter and that his passenger was wanted by the U.S. Government, but the financial rewards were great. All expenses paid, plus $500,000. This would pay off the *Oriental Flyer* and then some.

He and his black crewman, Mack, had been provisioning the boat most of the day. That included food items, MRE's from the Army/Navy surplus store, first aid supplies, and filling the diesel and water tanks to capacity. Just last week he had replaced his old navigation charts with the latest available upgrade. He also had all the latest Pilot Books for many of the islands of the Caribbean. He had double checked his GPS system and felt ready to go. He would be gone for at least two or three months. He had let the marina know that he would be gone but told them as little as possible. When they, in casual conversation, inquired about his destination, he had replied, "Mexico."

He had done a charter to Mexico once. It had been in early fall and dozens of migrating hummingbirds had perched on his rigging and rested for a short time before continuing on their trans-gulf flight from Texas to Mexico.

"Are you Buddy?" Beking asked.

"Yep, you Beking."

"Yes, I'm David Beking."

"Come on aboard. We'll be casting off in a few minutes."

Buddy wanted to get out of the harbor and out to sea as soon as possible. Getting through the Outer Banks can be a little tricky at night, but with the aid of a full moon and a GPS unit, it should be no problem.

Beking looked at the little harbor town of Oriental as they motored out of the harbor, raised sails, and turned toward the outer banks and the open sea. It really was a pretty little harbor town with all the old houses and boats. He walked down the hatch-type door to the living area and found that it was really quite luxurious. Four separate rooms for sleeping, a bathroom, and a common kitchen/living area. *If the seas aren't too rough I might actually enjoy this. I hope they have something to read*, he thought.

It took about four hours to get out past the Outer Banks and turn south by southeast. It was much more beautiful than Beking had anticipated. The moon made every wave sparkle. It looked like an ocean full of diamonds. After resting and calming down a bit, he walked over to where Buddy was piloting the boat and started a conversation.

"Can you tell me where we're going and how long it'll take?"

Buddy thought for a moment and said, "Your final destination is Venezuela. My instructions are to get you to Grenada with as few stops as possible. There, a decision will be made as to whether you will be flown to Caracas or we finish by boat."

"Why don't we go to Cuba? Wouldn't that be quicker?"

"The waters around Cuba are carefully watched by the U.S. Navy and they have no problem boarding any boat near it. Now, on the other hand, the waters around the Caribbean Island chain are pretty much an international boater's playground. The Navy would have to have a damn good reason to stop and board a boat there. Besides, there're so many sailboats running up and down the islands that we'll blend in nicely without raising any suspicion."

"Oh, so we have to go the long way."

"It's the safest way."

Beking thought about it for a while and then asked, "Will we stop and sleep at nights?"

"No. No stops, or at least, very few. Mack and I will pilot the boat on six-hour shifts. The route is programmed into the GPS and autopilot. We're going to sail to the east side of the Bahamas and bypass them. There's too much chance of getting spotted there by the CIA. It'll take about two or three weeks, depending on the weather and seas. We'll also bypass the U.S. Virgin Islands. Our first stop will be Anguilla. So, prepare for hard running for at least two weeks."

"Is there anything I can do to help, maybe help me pass the time?"

"No, not really. Mack and I can handle everything. We do have an e-book reader. I loaded it with several books I thought you might enjoy. When we get to some of the more electronic-savvy islands, you may be able to download some of your own choice, but stay away from any book about Asia, spies and such. You never can tell what might give you away.

"Won't they be able to trace your credit card if I download a book?"

"No, it should be safe. It's under another name and untraceable to me. Oh, one other thing. When we get near Anguilla, you're to dye your hair. Change your brownish-blonde hair to black. Don't shave either, grow a beard. You need to change your appearance as much as possible."

"Oh, ok", Beking said. He took a moment to let it all sink in and asked, "Is Mack trustworthy?"

"Yes, of course. Although he doesn't know who you are or the real reason for this trip. That's for his own protection. Don't tell him your last name; just refer to yourself as David. He has been my first mate for three years now and knows how to pilot the boat using the GPS and autopilot. He also keeps the boat clean and cooks, as he would on any charter."

The FBI had instructed Eric Dawkins to start in Manteo, NC and work his way south and not to miss any marina on the North Carolina coast. It was actually an enjoyable assignment. The marinas were usually located in scenic spots. The towns were quaint, historic, and the seafood was good. No one at any of the marinas had seen anyone who resembled the person in the photo that Eric was asking about.

Today he was at the waterfront in New Bern, NC. He had walked around the marina showing people Beking's photo. No one had seen him. He ambled back on the marina's walkways which lead to the benches on the waterfront. It was a little after five o'clock in the afternoon and he was tired. He sat down, took out a map, and started planning his day for tomorrow. He intended on spending the night in New Bern and start out early tomorrow.

"Hello, Eric", a female voice said from behind him.

Now that voice sounded familiar. He twisted his head and shoulders around to see who was behind him. *I thought so*, he mused.

"Sudie, what are you doing here?" Then it hit him; she was his CIA contact.

"What do you think I'm doing here?"

He looked around to make sure no one was within earshot. "I guess you're my shadow."

"Well, they said to keep close contact with you."

"Even at night?"

She came around the bench, sat down beside him and wrapped her arm tightly though his. "Especially at night", she grinned.

They had met a few months ago. He had finished at the FBI Academy and was taking advance training in Washington. She, also, was taking advance training after her acceptance in the CIA. Friends had introduced them and the attraction for each other was hot, hot, hot. Every weekend they went off together to some romantic beach cottage, but as regular assignments started to separate them the romance was put on hold. They kept in touch by email and both had intentions of getting back together but events always seemed to keep them apart until now.

This is going to be a great assignment, he thought.

That evening they had a wonderful meal at a great seafood restaurant, which provided a romantic view of the marina and the ocean sound. After dinner they walked along the waterfront, and then went back to the hotel where they had adjoining rooms.

Eric had finished his shower and was sitting on the bed with a towel wrapped around him, watching television, when the door between their adjoining rooms flew open. Sudie walked toward him with nothing on but thong panties. He was sort of shy, but she had almost no inhibitions. She was beautiful, knew it, and enjoyed flaunting it. She stopped in front of him, held her arms slightly out to her side, and did a quick torso shimmy, making her breasts shake and jiggle, and then laughed at the astonished look on his face. She pushed him backwards on the bed and fell on top of him. It was on again; right where they had left off a few months earlier and as hot as ever.

Eric was looking at his folded map beside his breakfast plate when Sudie joined him.

"Got our day planned out?" she asked.

"Oh, hi, good morning. Yes, I think we'll make a loop around the Pamlico Sound area. It should be a full day; there are dozens of marinas."

"Let me look at that map." After a while she said, "Humm, that's a funny name for a town."

"What's that?"

"There's a little town here called, Oriental. You think it's full of Asians?"

"NO! It's named after a boat that shipwrecked there back in the late 1800's. It's a quaint little town and they claim to be the sailing capital of North Carolina. Lots of sailboats and big marinas. We'll have to check that one out carefully."

Sudie ordered oatmeal with fruit and continued to look at the map.

It turned out to be another grinding day. They hit one marina after another without success. He did learn one thing though. Sudie could get those crusty old marina-types to talk a lot better than he could. He could only get "yep, nope", and, "can't help you", out of them. Sudie could start a conversation, smile, bat her eyes and you could hardly stop them from talking. *I believe they would have given up their social security number if she had asked,* he thought.

They arrived in Oriental around six o'clock that evening and found a bed and breakfast that had two rooms available. They had a light supper and crashed in their rooms. They were both worn out, from the tiring day and their activities from the night before.

The next day they pulled into the parking lot of Gordon's Marina in the early afternoon. It was a well-kept, modern-looking marina with all the necessities. They walked the docks and asked marina employees and boat owners if they had seen the person in the photograph. As always, the response was negative. One of the employees suggested that they talk to the owner and operator of the marina, a Mr. Gordon.

Mr. Gordon was behind the counter working the cash register, selling nautical accessories to customers. When the customers left,

Eric and Sudie approached him and asked for a minute of his time. He was very reserved at first and even Sudie could not get much out of him. Finally, Eric showed him his FBI identification and, as an ex-navy man and patriot, Mr. Gordon opened up.

"Mr. Gordon, take another look at this photo and see if you can remember anyone like him", Eric said.

"It doesn't ring a bell   " His mind flashed back to a man pulling a suitcase down the walkway toward Buddy's, *Oriental Flyer*.— "Wait, this could be the guy that chartered Buddy Miller's boat, the *Oriental Flyer*. I'm not sure by any means, but it could be him."

"What kind of boat is the *Oriental Flyer*?" Sudie asked.

"Are you an FBI agent too?"

"Yes, I'm a government agent."

"Come over here and look at this poster", Gordon said, motioning them to follow him over to a bulletin board with posters on it. There was a nice size poster advertising the *Oriental Flyer* as a charter boat, capable of cruising the Eastern seaboard, the Gulf of Mexico, Mexico, and the Caribbean. There were color pictures of Captain Buddy, the boat, and its semi-luxurious interior. Because it was a catamaran it boasted of its speed and comfort.

"When did they leave?" Eric asked.

"Last Tuesday I think. Yeah, four days ago."

"Did he say where he was going?"

"No, not specifically, but I got the impression it was Mexico."

"How long would it take a boat like that to reach Venezuela?" Sudie interjected.

"I would say two or three weeks if they pushed hard, but it would normally take five or six weeks for most charters since they don't push that hard. They make stops all along the Caribbean chain, enjoying the scenery, food, and people."

Sudie took out a digital camera and took a picture of the poster, featuring Captain Buddy and the catamaran.

Eric took out a business card and gave it to Mr. Gordon and said, "If he contacts you let me know where he is, but don't tell him someone is looking for him."

Gordon looked at the card and asked, "Is Buddy in some kind of trouble?"

"Let's just say, we're more interested in his passenger."

Eric turned to Sudie as they walked toward the car, "What do you think? Possible lead?"

"Possibly. It's thin though." Suddenly she stopped.

"Eric, there's surveillance cameras everywhere. Let's go back in for a minute."

"Mr. Gordon, how long do you keep your video surveillance records?" Sudie asked.

"It's on a hard drive and runs continuously. It overwrites itself after a while, but I can usually go back about two or three weeks."

"Can we look at the evening when Buddy's charter arrived?"

"Sure, but I don't know how well you'll be able to see with that particular camera, at that distance."

The video showed a man pulling a suitcase toward the docks. It was hard to make identification. Eric and Sudie downloaded twenty seconds of video to their flash drives. They would send it to their respective agencies for analysis. Their forensic labs could do great things these days.

"I'm going to call this into FBI headquarters in Washington and see if they can put a rush on developing anything on Buddy Miller and any foreign government.", Eric said.

"And I'll tell our agents in the Caribbean to be on the watch for a catamaran called the *Oriental Flyer*", Sudie added.

They spent the next two weeks working their way toward the South Carolina border, checking out every marina. By the time they reached Sunset Beach, NC, near the border, they were both worn out. They were checking out a few small marinas near Sunset Beach when Eric got a call from Washington.

"Hello, Eric Dawkins speaking."

"Eric, this is Wayne. Where are you?" Eric's boss said.

"We're down to our next to last marina before we hit the South Carolina line."

"Listen, we haven't been able to make any connection between

47

Buddy Miller and any foreign agency, but you may have given us a lead. The forensic lab enhanced your video and we were able to get a 71% positive recognition factor on the person in your video. We think it was David Beking."

"You got a 71% factor on just one side of his face?"

"No, we got a front shot. There was one moment where he turned his head toward the camera, when he looked back at his car, and we were able to get a full frontal view of his face.

It was a little blurred but we were able to work with it."

"That's great. What do you want me to do now?"

"Check out those last two marinas and then catch a flight to St. Thomas in the U.S. Virgin Islands and check in with the FBI field office there. I'll email you your contact information and instructions."

"OK, I'll call when I get to the field office in St. Thomas. Bye."

While he had been talking to his boss, Sudie's phone rang with similar information.

"We got a 69% recognition factor. What did you get?" Sudie asked.

"71% and I have to go to St. Thomas immediately."

"So do I. Let's knock out these last two marinas and get to the Myrtle Beach Airport and see how soon we can get there." Sudie paused a moment and said, "Eric, you know we won't see much of each other when we get there. I'll be with my people and you with yours. This might be our last night for a while."

"Oh, God, that's right. Well, we'll have to make the most of it; ....maybe find a wedding chapel in Myrtle Beach?"

"Are you crazy? We're not getting married. I mean I *do* love you, but I want to be a field agent with all the excitement that goes with it for the next few years. This is exciting and I'm having fun!"

Eric had been half-kidding but decided to play it a little further. "You mean you want me to wait on you for the next five or ten years!"

"Yes, I do, I expect it. You go and have some little flings but don't get serious on me."

"And what if I start to get serious about someone else?"

Sudie turned in her seat, leaned toward Eric, lowered her voice, and said, "You be careful. I'll always *know* where you are and what you're up to. I *assure* you that I'll come and break it up."

Eric was a little stunned by her seriousness. He felt like he had been checkmated and didn't know what to say. He knew she was capable of doing it. She had the looks and smarts to follow through on her threat. She could intimidate other women; she certainly intimidated him.

"Eric, just let me know when you're down, lonely, or in need of sex. If at all possible I'll come take care of you."

"I can't believe you want to stash me in a cupboard somewhere, so no one else can get to me."

"That's exactly what I want. When I get my fill of this job as a field agent and move up the ladder, then I'm going to pull you out of that cupboard, and *then* we'll get married and have a family."

Eric could only shake his head and sigh.

Sudie reflected on their conversation for a few moments and then thought to herself, *I wouldn't really break it up if he was really in love and I thought the girl was good for him, but, if she wasn't...*

They spent one last *glorious* night in Myrtle Beach. They had a room near the top floor of a high-rise hotel, facing the ocean. The next day they caught a morning flight to Miami, and then on to St. Thomas.

Chapter Five

God, I'm tired of the open sea, thought David Beking. They had been at sea for fourteen days, circling east and then south of the Bahamas and the Virgin Islands. He had occasional bouts of sea sickness at first, but seemed to be getting his sea legs now. His stomach had not been queasy since the fourth day out. The sea sick patches had helped. He had spent yesterday afternoon dying his hair a darker color. It matched his emerging beard.

"Captain, when do we get to Anguilla and this restaurant you've been talking about?" Beking asked.

Buddy sighed; it was the third time he had asked today. "We should reach Anguilla and that particular bay around 6:00 pm, a couple of hours before sunset. There's a fantastic restaurant there. It's right on the beach with an open deck veranda. The food is wonderful."

"Is it part of a hotel?"

"No, only a restaurant. We'll have to use the dingy to get in and then back out to sleep on the boat. Oh, take your e-reader with you. You'll probably be able to pickup Wi-Fi in the restaurant. You can download some more books, and bring some of your money; the chartering party usually treats the crew at the restaurant."

"OK, I will", Beking said, wondering if that was really true. "What about tomorrow?"

"Tomorrow morning you should take a walk on the beach and stretch your legs. Mack and I'll be going to a chandlery to pick up some marine items."

"What's a chandlery?"

"Sorta' like a marine hardware store."

Beking strained his eyes out over the bow, hoping the island of Anguilla would appear. *Man, I can't wait to get off this boat*, he thought. The e-reader had been a lifesaver, but his eyes were becoming blurred from reading so much. It had helped when Captain Buddy showed him how to increase the font size. The trip would not be so bad if other people had been aboard to talk to, but being the only passenger, he could only read and maybe watch a DVD movie from their limited selection.

"What do we do after you get back tomorrow?" Beking asked.

"Have lunch, pull up anchor, and head south."

"So soon?"

"It's for your own good. Certain people will spot us if we stay in one place too long."

"Yeah, I guess you're right."

"Damn straight, I'm right. You could be sitting in a Washington jail right now if people hadn't acted quickly for you."

Yeah, OK, you're right, Beking thought, trying to curb his narcissistic tendencies.

Sudie looked out the window of the turboprop puddle-jumper taking them into St. Thomas. She could see the runway, but it was disappearing as the pilot turned toward it.

She looked over at Eric and shook him, "Wake up baby, we're about to land."

Oh, crap, he thought. He didn't think he would ever recover from last night. *I probably need an IV drip of some sort.* Sudie had been insatiable all night long, and on top of that she woke up bright and cheery. *What was it she kept yelling at him last night during sex? Oh yeah, "Come on baby, pop my Chute!"—God, I didn't know she had some weird in her.*

Eric felt like a zombie walking through the airport. It had been cold in Washington; cool in the Carolinas; warm in Miami; and it was downright hot here in St. Thomas, but it felt so good. *All I want to do is sit on that bench, over there in the shade, and let the warm breeze wrap around my body.*

"Eric! Snap out of it. Your luggage is here."

He took a deep breath and grabbed his luggage.

51

"Here come our agency people. Baby, we probably won't see each other for a while. I'll contact you when I can. Bye now, love ya", Sudie said. The last part in a sexy southern drawl.

"Bye", was all Eric could get out. He knew she was right about contacting him. The FBI could only operate in the U.S. or its territories, but she had free license to roam the world. He would never know where she was. *I need time to recover anyway*, he thought.

The ride from the airport to the CIA agency house was exciting for Sudie. It was her first time in the Caribbean. The agency's house was twenty minutes from the airport, outside of the main part of town, about half way up a mountain. The house had a veranda and a view of St. Thomas and the harbor. The full beauty of the harbor was hard to capture on a postcard.

One of the agents showed her to a room and said, "Use this room. It has a private bath and a view. Come to the situation room downstairs in thirty minutes. There's a staff meeting to discuss the David Beking spy case; where he might be, all the things we're doing to find him, and what your role is in all this. By the way, my name is Chris and I know you're Sudie." He held out his hand and they shook hands. She knew better than to ask for his last name. Spooks gave out as little information about themselves as they could.

Thirty minutes later Sudie walked downstairs. It was more of an underground basement than a lower floor. The room reminded her of what the interior of a submarine looked like in the movies. It was wall-to-wall electronic equipment; obviously, this also functioned as a National Security Agency listening post.

"Why do we have a listening post here in the Caribbean? It doesn't seem to me like there's anyone in the area that we need to spy on."

"There's not", Chris said. "But here, we're clear of a great deal of electronic interference from North America's east coast. It makes for a much better signal from Africa, Central, and South America."

Oriental Flyer

The location of the house makes great sense, she thought. They were within a hundred yards of the telephone company's antenna yard. Their antennas blended right in with the agency's' antennas and no one would suspect a thing, except maybe the telephone company.

"The phone company doesn't mind us being this close?" Sudie asked.

"Nah. Remember, we don't broadcast, we only listen; besides, we give them a lot of cast-off equipment. They love us."

Sudie observed the activity in the room for about ten minutes. Some were listening to Africa, a few to various South American frequencies, but most of the operators seemed to be concentrating on Venezuela.

"Sudie", Chris called to her. "Come in the conference room; we want to begin."

Chris introduced the different team members to her by first name only and what their general area of expertise was.

"Ok, let's get started", Chris said. "In front of you is a two-page synopsis of the main file sent down from Washington concerning the David Beking spy case. I believe everyone has read the main file, except for Sudie, but I'm sure she can do that later today or tonight."

The team talked for about forty-five minutes before Chris ended the general discussion and turned to Sudie.

"Sudie, we have talked about this for several days and everyone has their own theory on where Beking could be and how to catch him. We would welcome your thoughts."

She knew they were testing her. Could she come up with a plausible theory on what his escape plan was, and how to intercept him? She decided to tell them what had been going through her mind for the last two weeks.

"I think there are three main routes he could follow. First, he could drive down to Key West and find a boat to Cuba, but that theory is weak, because I don't see how he could get past us in Florida. Second, he could take a boat out of the East Coast and head for Cuba which is also weak because of our naval presence there. The third route and this is the one I like best. He could take a sailboat out of the East Coast, sail around the Bahamas and the Virgin Islands, head south down the Caribbean chain, making as few stops as possible, and then sail to Venezuela. From there, he could take the "terror flight" from Caracas to Tehran.

"Very good Sudie, I think you have fallen in with the main consensus of thinking here. Where do you think he would make his stops, if any?"

"I think he might stop at Anguilla or St. Kitts; then possibly Dominica, maybe Grenada, and then on to Venezuela.

"Why Dominica?"

"It's the least developed and least visited island. It's almost undiscovered by the tourists. If it were me, I would find a place along the East Coast of Dominica to put in and rest for a couple of days."

"Hum… maybe so. Sudie, we already have agents at each one of those islands. I want you to also cover those four islands. Work with our agents there. Go up and down that chain until you exhaust all possibilities. If you find him, don't try to apprehend him yourself. You will assist the agent there in the arrest or we will send in a team to take him into custody. It'll depend on the situation.

Sudie, remember, the agent you'll be working with is experienced, you're not. Work with him, don't be a hot dog; that's how young agents get killed."

"No sir, I won't."

"Read your material, talk to the people around this table, and learn as much as you can the rest of the day. Tomorrow you fly to Anguilla."

The crew of the *Oriental Flyer* had been admiring the coastline of Anguilla for the last hour and was eager for Captain Buddy to get the dingy in the water. They could see *The Flaming Tangerine;* the restaurant that Buddy had been bragging about. It was almost 7:00 pm and they were starved for something besides the food they had on the boat.

"Come on guys, jump into the dingy, let's get ashore", Buddy said.

They didn't have to be told twice. They were all eager to get to the restaurant that was about thirty yards inland from the shore. When they walked into the open-veranda section of the restaurant one of the waiters recognized Buddy.

"Captain Buddy, so nice to see you back."

"Thanks, Lorenzo, can you find us a quiet table on the other side of the veranda?" That side tended to be less crowded.

"Certainly Captain, follow me."

They ordered several seafood appetizers; surf and turf entrees, and desserts that were specialties of the chef. They continued the evening in the bar where they got a good buzz on, but no one got drunk. Beking spent a half an hour downloading books to his e-reader. It was nearly 11:00 pm when they returned to their boat and sacked out for the night.

The next morning Captain Buddy and Mack took off for the nearest chandlery and Beking took a long walk on the beach. He finished his walk at 11:00 am, just as the restaurant was opening for lunch. He took a seat in the veranda and ordered a Bloody Mary while waiting for the Captain and Mack to return.

It was noon before Captain Buddy and Mack joined him on the veranda. By then Beking was working on his third Bloody Mary and feeling no pain. Buddy made sure they had a quick lunch and hurried his crew back on the boat. They had to steady Beking a couple of times to keep him from falling in the water.

Captain Buddy weighed anchor and set a course that would continue on around Anguilla and out to the east, and then south on the windward side of the Caribbean chain of islands. He set the GPS and autopilot for a waypoint on the eastern side of the island of Dominica. It would take three or four days to reach Pagua Bay, his favorite spot in the Caribbean.

Under the circumstances he should make a straight run to Grenada or Venezuela and finish his charter, but he loved this particular little bay, the bar and grill upon the hill, and a special little Dominican lady there. He felt he could safely spend a day or two there. Dominica, especially the eastern side, was remote, and for the normal tourist you really had to make a special effort to get there. *Surely the CIA won't find me there*, he thought.

Sudie and her scraggly-looking Anguilla field agent, Jeff, were making the rounds of all the chandleries on the island. It was her third day there and they were about two-thirds of the way around the island.

"What's the name of this one?" Sudie asked.

"Mainland Chandlery."

"Let's check it out."

Once inside, it took a few minutes to get to the manager and ask if he recognized any of the men on the flyer. The manager looked at the pictures of Captain Buddy, Mack, and Beking for a moment and said he did not recognize them but they could ask the two other clerks if they wanted to.

Sudie took one and Jeff the other. Sudie walked over to the female clerk and said, "Excuse me, do you mind looking at this flyer and seeing if you recognize any of these men?"

"Oh, yes, that's Captain Buddy and his crewman. I think his name is Mack. They were in here about—maybe three days ago."

"You're sure."

"Oh, yes. Captain Buddy comes in here several times a year. I know him."

"They didn't happen to say where they were anchored or where they were going, did they?"

"No, they didn't say where they were sailing to, but I think they were anchored nearby."

"Why's that?"

"They were walking when they left here."

"Which way?"

"That way", she said, pointing a finger.

She motioned Jeff over and said, "Come on, we've got a hit. My clerk said they were in here about three days ago and they left walking in that direction."

56

It took them about an hour before they found the restaurant that Captain Buddy and his crew had eaten. Several waiters and a bartender all recognized them in the flyer.

"Damn it!" Sudie said. "They were anchored right here, thirty yards off shore."

"Well, the waiter said they headed west, at least we know that much", Jeff said.

"Probably headed in the wrong direction, trying to throw anyone off who asked. Hand me the satellite phone; I have to report this to Chris in St. Thomas."

Sudie punched the pre-programmed button for the St. Thomas field office, then the button to activate the scrambler. Someone answered and she asked for Chris.

"Chris, this is Sudie. They were here three days ago. They anchored one evening and had an expensive dinner at a restaurant on the beach. The next morning they walked to a nearby chandlery and did some shopping, and then pulled anchor and left at noon. We got positive recognition at both the chandlery and the restaurant. Witnesses also indicated that his hair is darker and he is growing a beard."

"OK Sudie, good work. If they left three days ago I think it's already too late for St. Kitts. Catch a plane down to Roseau, Dominica. That's on the western side of the island. You'll have to get over on the eastern side. The agency has a shell company there doing aircraft charters and our agent is the pilot. That will be very convenient for you since under normal conditions getting across the island would be a long and arduous trip by vehicle.

"It's almost too convenient that we have an aircraft charter business there," Sudie said.

"For that island, it's a necessity. Quite profitable, too."

Long have they passed, long lapsed—faces...
Long through the carnage I moved...
away from the fallen
Onward I sped at the time.
But now of their faces and forms at night,
I dream, I dream, I dream.

-Walt Whitman
"War Dreams"

Chapter Six

Jay and Howie were attending to Captain Nehemiah Cross. Howie got him into a sitting position and Jay was trying to give him four aspirins. It was the only pain medication that Dr. Duc could get for them. Nehemiah was in the last stages of cancer and he was in constant pain.

"Come on Neha, swallow your medicine. It'll help you sleep", Jay said.

Neha looked at the pills in Jay's hand and said, "Sometimes I wann'a sleep and sometimes I don't."

Jay knew what he meant. He welcomed the peace of sleep but the dreams wore them out emotionally. It was that way for all the men.

Jay had the pills on a small green leaf and moved it toward Neha's mouth. He opened up and Jay poured the pills on his tongue. Howie reached around from behind him with a cup of water and put it to his lips. He had difficulty swallowing them but managed to get them down without choking. They laid him back down on his cot.

The men had made an addition in length to Neha's cot. He was six-foot, four inches tall; a black man who had played college basketball at Memphis. He had wanted to be a fighter pilot but his height did not allow it. A man that tall would have his legs amputated at the knees, by the cockpit, if he ever had to eject from a jet fighter. He was good at math and electronics so the Air Force made him an Electronic Warfare Officer in a B-52 bomber. He had been shot down during the last two weeks of the war over Hanoi.

Jay and Howie walked across the room, sat down, and gazed at Neha.

"How long do you think he'll live?" Howie asked.

"Can't be long or at least I hope it's not long. I hate to see him suffer so."

"Do you think that we could get the guards to help with his grave? I don't think there's anyone left that has the strength to dig a grave now."

"I'll see if Dr. Duc can get us some help."

"Look. He's already asleep. Look at his eyelids flutter; he's dreaming."

His nights were always filled with dreams but this one dream happened almost every night.

"Evening, Nehemiah", the bouncer said.

"Evening, Charles."

"Nita's just starting on her second set of the evening. She'll be glad to see you."

Nehemiah nodded and entered the night club. It was a Memphis jazz club and Nita was the finest jazz singer he had ever heard. He was prejudiced, of course, since she was his girlfriend. He had dated Nita Fisher since he was a senior and she was a sophomore in college. She was the most beautiful girl in school and he couldn't help but wonder why she ever fell in love with him. She was about five-foot, four inches tall, with a dainty frame and hands, but behind that dainty frame was a powerful voice, made for jazz.

He found a seat and watched as she belted out a ballad. She spotted him about halfway through it and made sure her eyes and hand movements were for him. At the end of the set she came over to his table and gave him a kiss.

"When did you get back in town?" she asked.

"Today. I got through with the basic portion of the Electronic

Warfare training this week and have to report out west for advanced training next week, but I do have a week off for now."

"You're going to spend it with me, aren't you?"

"Yes, you and my parents."

"Have you seen your Momma and Daddy?"

"This afternoon, as soon as I got in town."

"How are they?"

"Oh, they're the same. Dad's still teaching math at the University and Mom's working in the administrative office; but you know that, they said you come over quite a bit."

"That's right. I've got to stay in the good graces of my future in-laws."

"I think you're doing fine. I believe they would rather see you than me."

"I doubt that, but I do enjoy talking to them. Your Mother is so sweet."

The dream started to move in fast motion…scenes of lovemaking…going together to the church picnics where he was raised…Electronic Warfare flight training…the night he gave her a ring…evenings watching her sing…Electronic Warfare school graduation…their last evening together…her tears when he left the Memphis airport for assignment at Guam AFB in the Pacific.

They were planning to get married when he returned from his tour of duty in Guam. He was fairly certain that he could get a job with one of the electronics companies that outfitted the B-52 with electronics. He knew the plane's electronics backwards and forwards and already had some ideas for improvement. He could see himself with a good job in California, a pretty wife, a nice home, and the fun they would have touring the western states. She would be near the recording companies and maybe, just maybe, she might get a recording contract with a jazz label.

The atmosphere in Guam was a great deal tenser than it was in the training command. A few B-52's had been shot down in the preceding weeks and the flight crews were not as cavalier as the ones he had seen in the states. They were much more serious and everyone seemed to have that small knot in their stomach, worrying about the possibility of getting shot down.

Part of their training and practice was the triangle-three formation of planes. By flying in a tight triangle and turning on their counter-electronic defense mechanisms they were, theoretically, able to defeat the SAM missiles coming at them. The electronic shield made the radar in the head of the missiles think that their formation was further away than it really was, thus flying past the formation before exploding. Some pilots had a hard time believing it, they just had to go on faith that it would work.

Six weeks after he arrived in Guam he was on his twentieth mission. It was a long boring trip from Guam to Hanoi, but terrifying once you got there. They were making their bombing run when he heard his pilot say, "Where's number two going? He's getting wide on his formation. Damnit, we'll lose our electronic barrier!"

"Number two, close back in formation", his pilot said."

"Oh, ok, guess I drifted a bit. Coming back."

Nehemiah heard a loud explosion from the back of the plane. The plane lurched to the left and after a few moments of panic the pilot called for everyone to bailout of the plane.

He landed on the outskirts of Hanoi and was immediately captured with most of his crew. They were marched through the streets of Hanoi to a prison. People jeered and threw things at them. He seemed to be a special target. Most Vietnamese had never seen a black man before, much less a six-foot, four-inch black man. If racial prejudice was bad back home, it was miserable here.

As soon as they found out he was an Electronics Warfare Officer he was separated from the other prisoners and sent to another prison away from Hanoi. Over the next five years he was tortured many times. He contemplated suicide, but the thought that there might be a slight chance of getting home to Nita one day kept him going. Years turned into decades and now he found himself dying of cancer in a God-forsaken prison camp in North Vietnam, an old man. *Nita, I pray that you're happy*, he thought. He wondered what her life was like.

Chapter Seven

Eric Dawkins had been called back to FBI headquarters in Washington as soon as the CIA passed on the word that Beking had already bypassed any U.S. territories. He was trying to doze on the plane back to D.C. but something kept nagging him. He tossed it around in his mind but there was no other answer. Somehow the Chinese Embassy had found out that American Intelligence knew about Beking spy activities and they had alerted him that he had to run. *But how did the Chinese Embassy find out? Only the FBI or the CIA knew. Do we have a mole? Surely someone else must be thinking the same thing.*

He wondered how and who to approach about the subject. For all he knew he could be reporting his fears to the mole himself. He would have to play it by ear when he got back to headquarters and see if there was an investigation already under way, but if not, figure out who to approach.

Eric spent the next two days filling out reports about his search activities along the North Carolina coast, spelling out what he found out and what his conclusions were. He didn't hear a thing about a search for a mole.

At lunch that day he took his sandwich to a bench outside. He sat there thinking about Sudie, Beking, and if there was a mole in their midst.

"Agent Dawkins?" a voice said.

"Yes sir", Eric said looking up. *My God, it's the Director!"* he almost said out loud.

"Read your initial reports. Good work.

"Thank you sir."

That video clip you gave us was a good lead. At least, now we know where he's headed. The CIA should be able to catch him."

"I hope so", Eric said, wondering if Sudie would be in on the takedown.

There was silence for a moment and then the Director spoke, "Does anything about the David Beking escape seem odd to you?"

Eric took a deep breath, gathered his courage and said, "Yes sir, it does. Who told the Chinese Embassy that we had found out that Beking was a spy and then tipped him off?"

"Exactly. We need to find out who it is ASAP, because it could endanger the CIA operatives' lives who are working this case in the Caribbean."

"Oh God...Sudie!" Eric blurted out before he could help himself.

"Yes, I understand she's a good friend of yours", he said with a slight grin. "We're forming a small task force to flush this mole out. Would you be interested in joining us?"

"Yes sir, I would", Eric said, knowing that an opportunity to work on such a case so early in his career would be a rare opportunity for any young agent."

"The task force will consist of three high-ranking agents from the CIA and three from the FBI, or least at first. Maybe more later on, but you've been chosen not only because you're bright, but because we have to have someone to do all the paperwork, set things up, busy work, the junior man so to speak."

"That's OK. I still want to do it." *That way I can help Sudie*, he thought.

"Good. I'll tell your supervisor that you're on a special assignment. Wayne will be a little curious of course, but I'll talk to him. He'll be OK. We're going to meet this afternoon at three o'clock in my office. Can you get your present paperwork squared away to start working with us, this soon?"

"Yes sir. I finished my final report right before lunch. I'll give it to Wayne as soon as I get back from lunch. Is there anything I need to bring to the meeting?"

"Just a notepad to keep notes on. It'll mostly be a brainstorming session."

Eric gulped down the remainder of his sandwich, headed back to his office, typed a cover page to his report, and took it into Wayne's office.

Eric got a quizzical look from Wayne when he entered his bosses' office. "Is that the report?" Wayne asked.

"Yes, but I need to tell you some…", Eric said before he was cut off.

Wayne held up his hand and said, "Don't say anything more. I don't want to or need to know. The Director has already called and said you would be on a special detail for a while."

"Thanks, Wayne. I feel sorta' funny keeping a secret from you."

"Don't. If it's what I think it is, then it will be a great opportunity for you to get some exposure to the big dogs upstairs, and if you happened to actually help solve the case, then you will be on the fast track, my friend. Do your best."

"Thanks Wayne. I'll be sure and let'um know who trained me."

Wayne smiled and waved him out of the room.

At five minutes till three, Eric reported to the Director's office. He was shown to a conference table in his large office. Three other senior agents were there but they had to wait ten minutes for the CIA agents to be escorted to the office.

"Gentlemen", the director started, "we have a mole, a traitor, in our midst." For the next two hours they reviewed each step of how they discovered there was a mole and where he might be working. Various methods of how to set traps for spies were discussed. No concrete method of approach was agreed upon at this meeting but they would settle on an approach at their meeting tomorrow. They did agree on lie detector tests for anyone remotely connected with the case, starting with themselves. Some people think it is possible to beat a lie detector, and to a certain extent, it is, but many times what really shows up, is that the test is determined to be "inconclusive". In further tests, as the old saying goes, "the clean get cleaner and the dirty get dirtier."

"Eric", the Director said as everyone was leaving.

"Yes sir?"

"Spend a few minutes summarizing your notes, put them in a

folder, and then put them in that file case over there. Don't let them leave this office. It's a brand new file cabinet and only information about our meetings and search will be kept there. I will have the only key."

"No problem sir. I'll be glad to leave them here. One less thing I'm responsible for."

Eric paused and asked, "Sir, can I ask a question?"

The Director cocked his head and paused. He sensed that Eric wanted to ask an off-the-wall question by the look on his face. "Certainly. I don't know if I can answer you, but I'll listen to your question."

"Sir, I knew we were chasing a Chinese spy and that there was probably a mole among us, but today is the first time I've heard about the photos and the prisoners still in Vietnam. Are we going to try to rescue them?"

The Director did not like to talk about this subject; it was potentially a career-ending topic. It turned his stomach and there was nothing he could do about it. It had nagged at him for years.

"Eric, I doubt it. The early administrations did not want to pay the ransom; sets a bad precedent. Each country should return prisoners after a war as stated in the Geneva Convention. Every succeeding administration did not want to deal with it. It was too explosive politically. They all denied that the prisoners existed; said it was a fantasy that people wanted to believe."

Eric let the Director's thoughts sink in for a moment and said, "That's a damn shame, sir."

"Yes. It is."

Jay Carter's eyelids were fluttering as he entered REM sleep. He was in the North Carolina hill country, walking up the front path to his grandparent's house. His dog, a terrier named Rebel, was walking with him. Rebel was a faithful companion and slept at his feet every night. The house was a white two-story farmhouse built on a hillside. The pump house and the storm cellar were still nearby. He could hear music coming from inside the house.

He entered the front door and stepped into the living room. There was no furniture in the house except for some straight-back cane chairs that some of the musicians were sitting on and they circled the pot-bellied stove. They were playing a mixture of country and gospel songs. No one seemed to recognize him except for one of his uncles who gave him a quick wink of the eye. There were two fiddle players, two guitarists, one bass fiddle, and one female singer. She looked like his sister Tancy, but this lady was a mature adult, maybe in her late fifties. She smiled at him but continued singing.

There was an empty chair with a guitar in the corner. It looked like his guitar. He wanted to join the group and play his guitar, but the dream would not cooperate. He stood there and listened to them play until dusk. Rebel slept with his head resting on the toe of Jay's shoe. Jay sang along softly as he listened to them sing an old country song.

> *"The other evening,*
> *As I lay dreaming*
> *I felt you lay against me.*
> *I reached for you*
> *But you were gone.*
> *With head in hands*
> *I cried myself to sleep again."*

He woke up and looked at his fellow prisoners sleeping around him. He tried to resist it but a muffled sob broke through. It had been forty plus years. He was so tired and emotionally drained; he knew that someday he would welcome death with open arms. *Oh, please God, have mercy. Send that chariot for me.*

Eric had followed this one low-level Chinese Embassy staff member for a week now. He knew where he lived, where he liked to eat lunch, that he liked American baseball, and that he had an Asian-

American girlfriend who worked at the Library of Congress. He did not see any spy activity going on, although he did made a mental note to check out the girlfriend at the Library of Congress and get a photo of her for his file.

The mole hunt had expanded to several surveillance teams that were following almost every Chinese Embassy staff member. They all reported to him and no one had seen anything suspicious as of yet.

Eric followed his target to lunch and saw that he was meeting his girlfriend at a popular deli. *Good*, he thought, *now I can get a picture of her.* He took out his camera with a zoom lens, turned the polarizing filter to take out the glare of his car windshield, and snapped a few shots of her. He doubted anything would come of it, but it would be in his files anyway.

His earpiece crackled in his ear and another team said, "Agent Dawkins, another target is coming up behind you."

Eric looked in the rear view mirror and was surprised to see Mr. Wu walking on the sidewalk. He was going to walk right by his car. He rushed to put the camera equipment away and tried to look like any other businessman waiting in his car. He looked straight ahead in the most nonchalant manner he could.

Tap, tap, tap.

Eric looked to the passenger window. Mr. Wu was bent over and knocking on his window.

Eric lowered the window a couple of inches and said, "Yes?"

"Agent Dawkins, may I speak with you a moment?"

Eric put his voice transmission device to the open-mike position, unlocked his car doors and said, "Yes, Mr. Wu; what can I do for you?"

Wu made a big production of getting comfortable in the car, smiled at Eric and said, "This is a fine car that the FBI gives you to track our staff. You know, we make fine cars now, too.

"Yes, I know. You've stolen and copied almost everything that we produce."

"And improved on them."

"What do you want Wu?"

67

"Oh, nothing, nothing. I thought since we're going to be in close contact for a while that we might want to get to know each other; become friends."

"Oh, please", Eric said sarcastically.

"Have you found out who your mole is yet?"

"What makes you think we have a mole?"

"Oh, come on now, Agent Dawkins. We have our ways, besides the FBI seems to have an increased interest in our staff lately."

"It takes vigilance to make sure our secrets stay secret."

"A free piece of advice, Agent Dawkins. Concentrate more on protecting your cyber secrets through the internet. That's where the good stuff is."

"Thank you, Mr. Wu. I'll pass that along, but I believe I'd rather catch you red-handed in spy activities."

"You would do me that favor? I miss my home and family, and with my diplomatic immunity I would have a quick trip back to China."

Eric glared at him. *Asshole.*

"Well, time to go. I see I've overstayed my welcome. I've enjoyed chatting with you so much. Oh, is this your lunch bag; an apple and a sandwich? You don't mind if I take it, do you", he said getting out of the car. "It's so symbolic anyway. You know, the way China is eating America's lunch."

Crap, Eric thought, *he's screwed me.* Wu had now cast suspicion on him. He had gotten into his car, talked for a few minutes, and then left with a bag belonging to FBI Agent Eric Dawkins. He would spend hours, if not days, explaining what happened, what was in the bag, all over essentially nothing. Wu had done it just to play with him, throw suspicion on him, and make his life a little bit more complicated and miserable.

The team, a few cars back, came over the radio, "We could hear the conversation over your open mike. He got you good. He left laughing and smiling."

Eric did spend the next two days explaining what happened. He had to write reports, go through interviews, and take more lie detector tests. Thank God for the open mike recording. The Director talked to him about it after all the interviewing and testing was done.

"Eric, you did fine; don't worry. It's a mind game the spy masters play. They get in your head. You get so pissed off; it throws off your game. He took advantage of you. He knows you're a young agent. Listen, this is Thursday; take tomorrow off and have a long weekend. Relax and get your mind right. Come in fresh Monday."

"Yes sir", Eric said, getting up to leave, but was thinking to himself, *I can play games too.*

Eric drove to his apartment, trying to forget the day and also trying to plan something to do over the long weekend. *I wish I could fly down to the Caribbean and spend the weekend with Sudie*, he thought, but he had no idea where she was.

Sudie put the binoculars down and rubbed her eyes. She was constantly looking across the bay of Roseau, Dominica for catamaran sailboats. The CIA, as always, had a house high up on a mountain where they had a good vantage point to keep an eye on everything. There was no listening station here but the extra altitude helped on electronic reception and transmissions when communicating with the regional offices in Puerto Rico and the Virgin Islands.

Once a day she and Godfrey, the company's lead agent on the island and pilot, got in the company's plane and flew up the west coast of the island to Portsmouth, the second largest city on Dominica. They watched for sailboat traffic along the coast and checked out the harbor at Portsmouth for catamarans. At first they were not checking the east coast of the island, but eventually agreed, at Sudie's insistence, to fly down the east coast. They agreed to do it every other day to keep the cost down, due to the price of aviation fuel.

It seemed strange to Sudie that there was an airport on the west side of the island at tiny Melville Hall that was larger than the one at Roseau, the capital. *Maybe they're trying to encourage development on that side of the island or maybe it may have been the only place on the island with land flat enough to have a runway*, she thought.

Roseau was boring for Sudie. There was not that much to do. The tourist industry was small and not that many people visited the island, which puzzled her since the island was such a garden spot. It had more rivers and waterfalls than any other island in the Caribbean.

She read more than she had since college days and last Sunday she went to a soccer game. Roseau had a nice sports stadium and she could get into watching the soccer games but the cricket matches had no appeal to her. Back home, even the baseball games bored her, but cricket put her to sleep.

Too bad Eric can't fly down for a few days. He could join us on the flights and maybe we could spend a couple of days at one of those little cabana hideaways, overlooking a bay, on the west side of the island, she thought.

Today after reaching Portsmouth, Godfrey turned the plane east so that they could go down the east side of the island, looking for catamarans. They had just passed the Melville Hall Airport when Sudie said, "Look at that place overlooking the bay. I bet it's one of those little places that have nice cabanas and a restaurant."

"Yes, it is; I know it", Godfrey said. "They have nice rooms, a bar, and grill. You ought to try it sometime. I'll fly you over some Friday afternoon and pick you up on my Sunday afternoon patrol. It's only five or ten minutes from the airport. You can sun on the beach or play in that river down there; it's shallow enough to wade in. Some locals like to take their dogs down there and play in the river."

"Sounds like an idea. What's the name of this place?"

"Pagua Bay and that's the Pagua River."

Eric could not remember when he had been in a worse fistfight. He and his partner had followed a target into an old warehouse that was, for the most part, unused except for a small section that was used by the telephone company for storage. As soon as they entered the door they were jumped by five young thugs. He had gotten in a few good licks but soon both he and his partner were being held and used as punching bags. Eric was beginning to wonder if he was going to make it out alive when a voice boomed out over a speaker. "That's enough. Empty their guns; keep the bullets and throw the guns across the room."

Eric strained to see where the voice was coming from. It looked like a surveillance camera with a speaker. The men searched them, emptied their guns and threw them across the room. They threw Eric and his partner on the floor, and left.

"Get your guns and leave", the voice said.

Eric thought that it might have been Wu's voice, but under the circumstance he could not even come close to being sure. They got their guns and walked outside and checked each other over. They both were going to have shiners. They had cuts on their hands and face, and Tommy, Eric's partner for the day, was having trouble breathing; probably broken ribs.

"Come on, let's report this and then go to the agency's first aid clinic", Eric said.

He was sitting on a table at the clinic with an attractive nurse cleaning and disinfecting the cuts on his face and hands. The treatment was a little painful, but he could not help but think how much he enjoyed the soft female touch. *Must be from childhood; a mother thing*, he thought. He was thinking about starting a conversation with the nurse when one of the senior FBI agents on the special team walked in.

"You ok, Eric?"

"Yes, I think so, but I'm going to have a really good shiner tomorrow."

"Yeah, it looks like it. Wear it like a *badge of honor*; everyone will think that you're a real hot shot field agent."

"I doubt that."

"Eric, why do you think those men jumped you? Were they young thugs or were you getting too close to something?"

"I have no idea, but I do know that they were disciplined, either as street fighters or foreign agents. They obeyed the stop command as soon as it came over that camera surveillance sound system....You know, there was something familiar about the voice. I would like to tell you that it was Wu's, but it could have been any Asian male voice."

"I realize that you were in a fight almost as soon as you got there, but after they left, could you see what was in the other side of the building?"

"No, not really. I vaguely remember some rolls of wire and a couple of antenna dishes. Everything else seemed to be in boxes."

"We're getting a search warrant and we should be in that building in an hour or two. Go home and get some rest."

"No way! I want to be in on that search", Eric said.

The senior agent sighed and said, "All right, but let my men do the searching, you just observe and take notes."

"No problem."

Ninety minutes later they were in the warehouse with a team of agents. It was already evident that someone had been in there in the meantime. The cameras and wiring to support it were gone. It appeared by the dust marks on the floor that someone had been moving things around. Agents were tearing through boxes and Eric was being kept busy taking notes and photos.

"Eric, come here. Looks like somebody forgot something. What do you think of this?", the senior agent said.

"I don't know, sir. It looks like electronic circuitry to me."

"It is; and pretty damn sophisticated electronics too. "

Eric looked at him, impressed by his knowledge of electronics.

The agent smiled and said, "I was almost an electrical engineer before I switched to law enforcement and I've had a lot of technical field experience."

"What kind of electronics is it?" Eric asked.

"Components for listening devices and telephone switching gear. Surveillance type of electronics."

"You think the phone company knows that it's here?"

"I doubt it."

"So how does this relate to our mole search?" Eric asked.

"I don't know. We'll have to box it up, take it back to technical forensics, analyze it, and then determine if and how it could relate to our search."

Eric stayed in his apartment as much as possible over the weekend, mainly because everyone who saw him took one look at his face and asked, "What happened to you?" He told them they didn't want to know, ended the conversation, and scurried back to hide in his apartment. He spent most of the weekend doing guy things; watching sports channels, football, eating popcorn, ordering delivery pizza—"Man, who clocked you?" the pizza guy had asked. The rest of the time he watched his two favorite TV channels, *The History Channel and The Military Channel.*

Monday morning, as he was looking into the mirror, tying his tie, he wondered if he should try to put some makeup on to cover his eye. It was as good a black eye as he had ever seen; swollen and purple-black. He decided against make-up because it would have taken enough make-up to make him look like a clown. *Just deal with it,* he thought, *take the stares, take the ribbing. Do your job. Where are my sunglasses?*

The Director opened the committee meeting promptly at 9:00 am and after thirty minutes concluded the meeting by saying, "Gentlemen, we don't seem to be getting anywhere. The lie detector tests are negative, the snitches are quiet, shadowing the embassy staff doesn't seem to be turning up anything. I think they are well aware of our increased surveillance and are behaving until we decide to back off a bit. The only excitement or lead we've had is when Eric went charging into that warehouse and got the crap beat out of him. Eric, I don't want you doing that again. A more senior field agent would have been a little more cautious about entering that building without proper backup."

"Yes sir", Eric said.

"Now the search of the warehouse did turn up some interesting objects. What they mean, we don't know yet. We have some people in the forensic lab researching it. As for now, everyone continue with their assignments, shadowing and so forth.

"Eric, sometime this week, I want you to interview that Chinese Embassy's staff member's girlfriend, the one who works at the Library of Congress. Probably won't turn up anything, but do it anyway."

"Yes sir", he said again.

"All right, that's it, let's get to work", the Director said, waving everyone out of the room.

Eric took a few seconds to finish his notes and was putting them in the file cabinet when the Director said, "Eric, how's Tommy?"

"He's going to be out for three or four weeks. He did have some broken ribs and the doctor is afraid that if he does any physical activity one of the ribs could puncture his lungs."

"Well, it happens every now and then, but be careful, let me warn you again, not to enter buildings like that without proper backup."

"No sir, I've learned that lesson."

"Good, now go find me a mole."

Chapter Eight

The *Oriental Flyer* was approaching the northeastern portion of the Caribbean Island of Dominica. It had taken Buddy longer that he had anticipated. The weather had been bad and he had to tack into the wind most of the way. He was staying far enough away from the islands so that he could not be spotted from land or any aircraft flying along the beach. It made the trip boring, but safer. The bad weather also meant less chance of getting caught in the cross-hairs of a satellite. In about thirty minutes they would be at his favorite place in the Caribbean, Pagua Bay.

If the Pagua River was high enough and the tide was high, he could walk the catamaran into the mouth of the river for about a hundred yards and tie her up next to the shore which would provide foliage cover. If he took the sails down, the *Flyer* would be very hard to see from the ocean or the air. *If they've had enough rain lately I shouldn't have any trouble getting her in there*, he thought. *I can't wait to see Maria."* He was close enough to get cell phone reception and had called her to let her know that he would be there soon.

Luckily there had been enough rain lately to make the mouth of the river passable so that Buddy and Mack could maneuver the catamaran into the mouth of the Pagua River. They cut the motor they used only for navigating in marinas or tight places, and jumped overboard into the waist-deep water and pushed the catamaran up the river for about a hundred yards. There was a small notch in the shore line where someone, years ago had made a place for their boat. It was perfect for hiding a boat from prying eyes from the ocean or air. The trees spread out over it and shaded the entire boat. They had a small problem getting the mast by some tree branches but they soon worked that out.

He wanted to stay two or three days. He had sent a message to the small hotel to reserve cabana #4 for him. It was the cabana that was the most remote of all on the property. No view, but lots of privacy, and a running stream right next to it, which made for great sleeping. Mack would stay on the boat and guard it. Mack knew Buddy had a girlfriend here and he didn't want to be in the way, besides Buddy would do the same for him when they got to Grenada, where he had a girlfriend.

Buddy grabbed the cell phone that the embassy had provided him and walked back to the road where he hitched a ride to the cabanas.

"Captain Buddy, so nice to see you again", the receptionist said.

"Hi Phyllis, do you have my favorite cabana ready?"

"Of course and there's someone already there waiting for you."

"Maria's already here?"

"Yes, she is."

"Well, in that case, can you have the bar send a pitcher of rum punch to the room?"

"Certainly. Here's your key. Enjoy your stay. Oh, Captain Buddy, will you be dining with us at the restaurant tonight?"

"No, I think most of our meals will be room service."

"That's not a problem. We'll be glad to do that."

It was Friday afternoon and Godfrey had agreed to drop Sudie off at the Melville Hall Airport while on their patrol flight. He would take over the patrol duties for the weekend and pick her up on Sunday afternoon. *Poor girl*, he thought, *she hasn't had a real day off in weeks*.

Sudie was enjoying the short flight over from Portsmouth. There seemed to be a different river or waterfall every few minutes. Looking ahead, she could already see the ocean and the vague outline of the Melville Hall Airport. She had made her reservations at that little cabana hotel on the hill overlooking the bay. All she wanted to do was rest in the sun, swim, and order umbrella drinks; if only the weather would clear up.

"You got your satellite phone?" Godfrey said as he was taking her bag out of the cargo hold of the airplane.

"Yes, I've got it."

"This is one of the few places on the island where your cell phone will work."

"Oh, really, that's nice. Maybe I'll call my parents and boyfriend."

"Keep your cell phone on Sunday afternoon and I'll try to let you know when I'm an hour away from the airport. If that fails, I'll use the satellite phone."

"Ok, see you Sunday afternoon."

Sudie walked into the small terminal and the man at the desk arranged a ride to her hideaway cabana hotel. It took about fifteen minutes to reach the cabanas. She paid the driver and walked in to register.

"Hi, I'm Sudie Sexton. You should have a reservation for me."

"Yes Ms. Sexton, we do. It's just like you requested. Gorgeous view of the ocean from both your bedroom and deck, air-conditioned, satellite television, and amplified cell phone reception."

"It sounds wonderful."

"Here's your key and since this is your first time here, I'm giving you credit at the bar for one free drink that can be used at the bar or restaurant. We make a great rum punch."

"Don't worry, I'll use it."

"By the way, there is a special event around 7:30 tonight on the restaurant's deck. If I were you I would plan my evening meal around that time."

"What is it, a band?"

"Can't tell you, it's a surprise."

"Sounds nice. I'll do it."

Sudie turned the key to her room, looked in and thought, *This is better than I thought it would be.* The room was spacious; it had a wide-screen TV mounted on the wall, a small kitchenette, a nice bathroom with a jetted tub, a spacious tiled shower, and a terrace with a wonderful view of Pagua Bay. Someone had a nice sailboat anchored in the bay Sudie noted with interest, but it was not a catamaran.

She unpacked and changed into some clothes that were more suitable for lounging and dinner tonight. She walked back to the bar and used her coupon to get a rum punch drink. She returned to her room and sat on the terrace, sipping her drink. She watched the fishing boats as they cruised in and out of the bay and soon fell asleep. She awoke at 7:00 p.m. and walked to the restaurant for dinner. She passed one of the staff taking a dinner tray to one of the bungalows. *Why would anyone order room service when there is such a wonderful view available at the restaurant? I wonder what the surprise is*, she thought as she entered the restaurant.

The waiter brought out Sudie's blackened grouper and Phyllis, the owner and operator of the facility, walked over to Sudie's table.

"Hello, Ms. Sexton, how is your fish?"

"Wonderful. You must have a great chef."

"Well, yes. He's my husband."

"That's nice; a husband who cooks."

"Did your room suit your taste?"

"Oh yes. It's very nice. The view is stunning."

"And speaking of stunning. Here comes our surprise", she said, pointing out to the ocean.

Sudie gasped at the sight of a full moon rising out of the sea. It seemed bigger than she had ever seen it and it was yellow, like an old harvest moon that you see in paintings and illustrations.

"All you need now is a boyfriend", Phyllis said.

"Oh, I have one. I wish he were here."

"By the way, the moon will do the same thing tomorrow night, only an hour later.

"Well, save me a table."

I will, but now I have to go and check on my other guests. Enjoy your meal."

Sudie spent that night and Saturday sipping on rum punch drinks and laying out in the sun on the beach. She would read awhile, sleep a while, and then take a dip in the ocean. She did not want to think about work. She met some other guests at the hotel while on the beach and they invited her to join them the next morning, Sunday.

They were going to take a thirty minute walk to the Pagua River and wade in it. It sounded like a fun thing to do and she accepted the invitation.

The next morning Sudie met her new friends at the restaurant for a late breakfast and then they started following the road to the Pagua River. As they got nearer to the river some of the neighborhood dogs started following them.

"Are those dogs safe?" Sudie asked.

"Don't worry about them, they're friendly. They follow us because they think we'll play with them when we reach the river, and they're right. We always do. They love to play fetch with sticks we throw in the water."

"Hmm, ok. That sounds like fun. I like dogs."

When they reached the river the dogs became very excited and rushed in and out of the shallow river. One found a stick and laid it at their feet for them to throw. Sudie watched them for about ten minutes when finally one of the dogs brought the stick to her. She grabbed it and threw it as far as she could up stream. The dogs bounded after it in a race to see who could get to the stick first.

As soon as the stick landed in the river, Sudie froze. A catamaran was tied up on the far bank, almost hidden by the trees. She sat down on the bank and wondered if it was possible this was the boat she was seeking. The dogs returned with the stick and she gave it to her friends and told them she was going to wade upstream a short distance.

She left her backpack that had her satellite and cell phone on the bank with her friends and started wading up the river. It was an easy walk. The bottom was mostly rock and sand and it never got more than waist deep.

When she got abreast of the catamaran she could hear music coming from the inside, indicating that someone was aboard. She sank down into the water with only her head sticking out and worked her way toward the catamaran. It was deeper where the boat was anchored and she had to change to a silent breast stroke. When she got behind the boat where she could see the name she found that it was covered by part of the sail. It looked as if they were deliberately hiding the name.

She was scared now. These could be desperate people. Did she have enough nerve to go lift the sail and peer under it to see the name?

She gathered her courage and swam the five yards to the back of the catamaran using a quiet breast stroke. She pulled the sail back just far enough to read the name.

ORIENTAL FLYER
Oriental, NC

She gasped and thought her heart would beat out of her chest and that anyone within twenty yards should be able to hear it. She backed away and started toward her friends. As she got to the front of the boat she heard someone come out on deck. She was in the middle of the river by now and when she looked toward the boat a black man was looking at her. It was Mack, Captain Buddy's first mate. She smiled and waved and he waved back. Hopefully he would think that she was only some tourist having fun in the river.

It took all the composure she could muster not to rush back, grab her backpack, and run. When she reached her backpack she calmly picked it up, walked into the foliage near her friends, pulled out the satellite phone, and called Godfrey in Roseau on the other side of the island.

"Hey, Sudie. Is that you? You're early."

"Godfrey, go to scramble mode."

Uh oh, I wonder what's wrong, Godfrey thought, pressing the scramble button.

"OK, I'm scrambled. What's up?"

"They're here! The *Oriental Flyer* is here! It's anchored about a hundred yards up the mouth of the Pagua River."

"They haven't seen you, have they?"

"No. They don't suspect anything"

"Are they all on the catamaran?"

"Mack, the first mate is. I don't know about the rest. They could be at a hotel nearby. For all I know they could be at the same place

I'm staying at." An image flashed though her mind of a hotel staff member taking a tray to that last remote bungalow. *Oh God, I wonder....*

"Sudie, stay put. Keep an eye on the *Flyer*. I'll call this into Washington and then assemble a team to come over there. I should be at the Melville Hall airport in sixty to ninety minutes. Don't let them see you and don't do anything foolish."

"OK. I'll wait for your team. Bye"

A storm was approaching and her friends left to go back to the hotel. They tried to get her to go with them but she told them that she wanted to stay and play with the dogs awhile longer. They shrugged their shoulders, a little baffled, and left her with the dogs.

"If you're not back by dusk, we'll send someone after you", they shouted as they were walking away.

She waved back her acknowledgement and huddled under some broadleaf foliage that protected her somewhat from the rain that was beginning to fall. She opened her backpack and checked her gun. It was where she could easily get to it. She checked the clip and made sure the safety was on.

Forty-five minutes later a jeep pulled up to the mouth of the river and two men jumped out and started running up the side of the river as far as they could and then they waded the rest of the way to the *Oriental Flyer*. She recognized Captain Buddy and Beking, although Beking dyed his hair and was growing a beard.

They called out to Mack to lower a ladder. They scrambled onto the catamaran and made preparations to get out of the river and into the sea.

"How in the hell do they know that they've been spotted? Man, we've got a bad leak somewhere." Sudie whispered to herself. *Should I try to stop them?* she wondered. Then Chris' words came to her mind, *That's how young agents get killed.*

The dogs had huddled beside her for warmth during the rain but they were little comfort as she watched Buddy and Mack push the catamaran past her toward the mouth of the river and into the ocean. As they passed by her Buddy looked at the strange women sitting by the river near the tree line. Dogs were huddled against her and she was using a light coat as protection against the rain. He turned his attention back to the business of getting out to sea. Luckily, it had rained hard last night. The combination of a high tide and a river that was higher than normal meant that he would have no trouble getting the boat out of the shallow mouth of the river and into the ocean.

They used the motor on the catamaran to get about a half-mile out and then they set the sails. With full sails the *Flyer* reminded her of an athlete that had been warming up and was now on a full run. She had not realized how fast a catamaran could sail. The *Oriental Flyer* was out of sight and into the cover of a storm within five minutes of leaving the mouth of the Pagua River.

She picked up the satellite phone and dialed. "Godfrey, they're gone. Someone apparently let them know that they'd been spotted. They came running down to the boat and were gone in ten minutes. They sailed south under cover of a storm."

"I don't see how they could have known", Godfrey said. After a long pause he added, "There's something bad wrong in Washington."

"I think so, too", Sudie confirmed. "I just saw proof of it."

"Go back to the hotel, check around and see if they were there in the same hotel you were in. Then get packed and catch a ride to the airport. I'll be there in twenty minutes to pick you up. But take your time, I'll wait until you get through checking out of the hotel and catch a ride to the airport."

"See you soon", Sudie said.

Sudie thumbed a ride back to her hotel and packed as fast as she could. When she was checking out at the front desk she pulled out a picture of Captain Buddy, Mack, and Beking and asked, "Have you seen these men?"

Sudie could tell by the look on Phyllis' face that she recognized the men but was probably struggling with some privacy issues. "Listen, these men are wanted for questioning. I need to know what you know about them." Sudie slapped down an official Dominica Government ID card that Godfrey had given her for such circumstances. It was phony, of course, but it looked official and it worked.

"That's Captain Buddy Miller", she said, pointing to one of the pictures. "They've been here for two or three days. Came in Friday morning. That's his first mate, Mack, but I didn't see him this time. The other man signed in as Doug Smith. Buddy came in about an hour ago and threw down ten one hundred dollar bills, said he was in a hurry and ran out. Said to give any overage to Maria or he would settle up next time if he owed anything. He doesn't though, a thousand dollars was more than enough."

"Who's Maria?"

"That's his local girlfriend. Here she comes now."

"Don't tell her who I am. Ask her where Buddy was headed."

"Hi Maria. You leaving?" Phyllis asked.

"Yes, I guess so. Buddy left in such a hurry. I don't know what got into him. He got a call on his satellite phone and from that moment on he couldn't get out of there fast enough. Sorta' hurt my feelings."

"Well, I'm sure it wasn't you. Did he say where he was going?"

No, but I heard that other man say something about Venezuela. Can you get someone to take me home?"

"Certainly. Here, Buddy left this for you", Phyllis said, handing her an envelope with what was left from the thousand dollars; there was three hundred dollars in it. "He said to get your roof fixed."

"Thanks", Maria said, looking into the envelope. "Lord knows my roof needs fixing; that last hurricane about ruined it. I got leaks everywhere."

Sudie cut in. "Maybe that driver can take me to the airport after he drops Maria off?"

"I'm sure he can", Phyllis said.

Thirty minutes later Sudie was at the airport getting into the plane with Godfrey. "Have you contacted Langley yet? Do they know that someone alerted them?"

"Yes, they know now. I sent it encrypted. Someone may hear it but they won't be able to decode it. There's got to be an electronic leak somewhere. There was no time for a mole to contact the Chinese and then the Chinese to get a message to them. They had to have intercepted a message internally at one of our agencies; either CIA, NSA, or FBI. Someone was listening and let Captain Buddy know, probably by satellite phone."

"I shared a ride with Maria on the way over here. She said he did have a satellite phone."

"Learn anything else from her?"

"No, she has no idea what he's involved in."

They flew in silence for a few minutes before Sudie spoke again, "Do you think we can find them by air tomorrow?"

"I doubt it. The weather is going to cover him up for the next two or three days."

"Crap!", Sudie said, as her satellite phone rang.

"This is Agent Two, Dominica", Sudie said, answering in a way not to identify herself.

"Agent Two, this is Agent One in St. Thomas. Get to Grenada as soon as you can. They'll be expecting you." Sudie halfway smiled. Even Chris was using coded identification. Everyone was realizing that there was a serious electronic leak somewhere.

She looked over at Godfrey and said, "I have to get to Grenada as soon as possible."

"I'll fly you to St. Lucia tomorrow morning and you can catch a puddle jumper to Grenada from there. It's a good thing I'm instrument rated. It could be rough. Bring your air sickness pills."

Great! thought Sudie.

Captain Buddy estimated that, at best, it would take thirty-six hours to reach the vicinity of Grenada. They were already six hours into the voyage when Mack brought the satellite phone from below.

"Phone for you, Captain", Mack said, handing it to him.

"Thanks, Mack."

"Hello"

"Listen carefully", the voice on the other end said. "Opposing forces are closing in on you. You will be engaged if you port in Grenada. A seaplane will meet you at Pickup Point #2. Call pre-programmed #4 on the satellite phone when you are two hours from Pickup Point #2. From there, you are on your own, but expect to be met and questioned at any American port you come to. Also, your package is waiting for you at your post office box. Good Luck." The phone went dead. The package was his payment money that was waiting for him at a bank in the Cayman Islands.

Mack looked at Buddy's worried face and said, "What's up Captain?"

Buddy took a deep breath and said, "We're going to anchor at Sugar Loaf Island and wait for a seaplane to pick up Beking. You remember that place, don't you? It's just off the northern tip of Grenada."

"Captain, what's this all about?"

"Mack, you don't want to know. The less you know the better off you are."

"Who's chasing us?"

"The CIA—Listen, Mack. I can let you off at Grenada or you can go with me to the Cayman Islands where I get paid; from there I'm not sure where I'm going, maybe South Africa, Rio De Janerio, India, or even Hong Kong. One thing's for sure. I can't go back to the states for a few years."

Mack looked at his Captain. He had never seen him so worried. He thought about it for a minute or two and said, "Captain, I think it might be best for me if you let me off in Grenada. I have friends and a girlfriend there."

"I know you do. I think it's probably a wise choice. Now listen, in a few days I will arrange to have $25,000 transferred into your bank account in Grenada. I will write you a letter of reference for First Mate. That should settle you down in Grenada for a while, but if you ever go back to the states or any of its territories, expect to be questioned."

"Thanks Boss. That's a lot of money."

"You deserve it. I may have messed up your life for a while."

"Captain, what should I say if I ever get questioned?"

"Tell the truth. You haven't done anything wrong and I haven't told you anything that will get you in trouble. Your knowledge of this is only that of a First Mate. You can say that the whole voyage seemed strange and the passenger was quiet and hardly ever spoke, which is true. Tell them I threw you off at Grenada and you don't know where I went from there."

The next day Captain Buddy picked up the satellite phone and punched the pre programmed button #4. A voice answered on the other end. Buddy told them that he was two hours away from Rescue Point #2. The voice acknowledged his message, told him that the CIA knew who he was and was pursuing him, and then hung up.

"Go tell Beking that I want to talk to him", Buddy said to Mack.

When Beking came on deck, Buddy asked him to sit down.

"What's going on Captain? How much longer until Venezuela?" Beking asked.

"I'm not taking you to Venezuela. In two hours we'll be anchored off the northern tip of Grenada. A seaplane will meet us and take you on board and fly you to Venezuela. You'll be in Caracas in three to four hours."

"Wow, so soon?"

"Go pack your bags. You're to give me all the money given to you except for $2,000."

"I've hardly spent a dime, so that means I need to count out about $8,000 for you."

"Sounds about right and don't worry there'll be plenty money waiting for you in Caracas."

Beking was practically giddy. *I'm going to make it. Once I land in Caracas, I'm practically home free*, he thought.

Two hours later they were anchored in shallow water near Sugar Loaf Island. They had been waiting about twenty minutes when they heard the seaplane approaching.

"There it is, my ticket to freedom", Beking said.

They all shook hands and Mack rowed Beking to the seaplane in the *Flyer's* dingy.

Captain Buddy watched as the seaplane turned away with a smiling Beking looking out the window. He wondered what damage

Beking had done to the United States. What had he done to his own country? He had been willing to do almost anything to pay off his boat and get a good charter business going. His boat would be paid off soon but there was no chance of a charter business now, or ever in the United States. *There's always a catch to easy money*, he thought, as a small sense of remorse started to nag at his conscience.

Chapter Nine

Eric was in the Tuesday morning briefing session with the team that was trying to track down the mole. His black eye was getting down to the point that a touch of makeup and a pair of sunglasses could keep most people from asking what happened. The Director started talking while sitting in his chair. He usually stood up.

"Gentlemen, for those that don't know, here's what's happened over the last seventy-two hours. Sunday afternoon, a CIA agent spotted the *Oriental Flyer* and her crew on the east coast of Dominica. The agent, a new female agent, was off duty and was in no position to apprehend Beking or the crew."

Sudie, Eric thought.

"NSA intercepted several messages to Captain Miller on the *Oriental Flyer*. Almost immediately after the agent called in the sighting a phone call was sent to the *Flyer's* satellite phone, warning them that they had been spotted. After the intercept, NSA put a tag on that satellite phone number and we overheard two more calls. One instructed them to anchor on the northern tip of Grenada, and the second was to a seaplane pilot with instructions to pick up Beking.

We can safely assume that Beking is in Caracas and will be flying out on the "Terror Flight" Thursday night to Tehran"

Eric couldn't stand it and interjected, "You mean he's gone and we can't do anything about it?"

The Director paused and held up a hand for Eric to let him continue. "The CIA has the ball and there will probably be an assassination attempt on Beking's life. I hope they can pull it off, because it's tricky."

"How tricky?" Eric said.

"Very. The CIA will brief us at the end of this meeting. Now, however, we have our own problem. The directors of the CIA, FBI, and the NSA met last night. We are all in agreement that the swiftness with which the Chinese warned the *Oriental Flyer* confirms that the leak has to be an electronic leak within our own facilities. From this point on, there will be no communication about anything to do with this team, except by verbal communication. No telephone conversations and no email messages are to be sent.

"I WANT THIS LEAK FOUND IN THE NEXT FORTY-EIGHT HOURS!" the director shouted. "Let the CIA take care of Beking, we have to find a leak that's damaging our national security."

The flight to St. Lucia was rougher than Sudie expected. She had filled her air sickness bag which was unusual with all her experience with flying and parachuting. It was as rough a flight as she had ever been on. She started feeling better when the plane touched down on the runway.

As soon as Godfrey reached the parking apron and cut the engine a CIA field agent ran out and opened the door for Sudie.

"Ms. Sexton, come inside and call Chris in St. Thomas. There's been a change in plans.

Sudie grabbed her bag, ran to the first private place in the terminal that she could find, and called Chris on her satellite phone.

"Sudie!" Chris exclaimed. "I'm glad I finally got you. Go to scramble."

"OK, I'm scrambled. Go ahead."

"Sudie, there's a Pentagon jet on its way to St. Lucia to pick you up. It will take you to Whiteman Air Force Base."

Uh oh, Sudie thought, *that's where the B-2 stealth bombers are.*

"What am I going to do there?"

"It'll be explained to you on the flight to Whiteman. Sudie, you're being handed a dangerous and difficult assignment. Your unique background, your looks, your language skills, and your parachuting experience makes you a perfect choice to carry out this assignment. I can't say anymore. Try to rest; you're in for a rough week."

"Jeez, Chris, what's going on?"

"They'll explain it to you. Good Luck."

Sudie stared at the phone receiver, listening to the dial tone for a moment before she came to her senses and punched the off button. Godfrey and the local field agent were staring at her, wondering what was going on.

She looked up at the other two agents and said, "I'm to wait here. There's a Pentagon jet on its way for me. I guess that's all I should tell you."

"I'll wait here with you," Godfrey said. He told the other agent he could leave.

She sat there and thought about what Chris had said. After a few minutes she turned to Godfrey and said, "I think this mission could be dangerous. I'm a little scared."

"Try not to think about it. Remember, on this mission, you may be the tip of the sword, but there's a whole blade behind you. Meaning, there will be a lot of support people around you, seen and unseen."

"I hope so."

An hour later a sleek-looking corporate-type jet landed. Refueling trucks rushed out to it and started refilling it with aviation fuel. An agent exited the airplane and ran into the terminal and spotted Godfrey and Sudie. He walked over to Sudie and held up a picture of her to help him identify her and said, "Come with me Ms. Sexton. We've got a lot of ground to cover, both literally and conversationally."

"Yes sir, I'm ready", was all she could say.

"Hi Godfrey", the agent said, acknowledging his presence.

"Hi Dan. Take care of Sudie. She's a good one."

"I'll do my best, but after the drop it'll be out of my hands."

What drop? thought Sudie

Thirty minutes later they were screaming down the runway, headed for Missouri. The inside of the jet was luxurious in a business-type of way. Nothing gilded with gold, but it had every luxury one would need for a high-powered business meeting.

"Sudie, my name is Dan and I'm going to give you your preliminary briefing on the flight to Whiteman Air Force Base." You'll be briefed in more detail once we reach Whiteman."

"OK Dan, let's have it. Tell me what I'm about to do."

"I'm to give you a quick outline of your proposed mission. I say, proposed, because after I brief you, you will have the choice of accepting or refusing the mission. It's a dangerous mission. If you succeed your future in the Agency will be assured. If it blows up in your face, whether it's your fault or not, you could spend years in a foreign prison, or worse, be killed."

Sudie's face blanched a bit, which was hard to do with her dark olive complexion. Dan noticed it and said, "Do you want me to continue?"

Sudie took a deep breath, summoned her courage and said, "Yes, go ahead. I want to hear what it is you want me to do. Then I'll determine for myself if I have the training to accomplish this mission."

"Sudie, it's not so much whether you have the proper training as it is that you're the only agent we have that can pass for being a Latin-American, speak Spanish, have wingsuit-parachute training, and can also pass for someone from the Middle East. To train you properly would take weeks, but we don't have weeks. We only have until tonight to get you in position in Venezuela."

"You don't have anyone else that can do a wingsuit jump?" Sudie asked.

"Sure I do. I have dozens of Delta Force men or SEALS who can do it, but I can't squeeze them into a stewardess uniform. I also have plenty of female CIA agents who could pull off the stewardess bit and a few of them can speak Spanish, but none of them can jump out of an airplane and fly ten miles in a wingsuit."

"I'm beginning to see your point. All right, explain it to me."

Dan turned on the big screen TV and a picture of a B-2 stealth bomber popped up on the screen.

"Here it is in a nutshell. This is called Operation Bamboo Splinter and your code name is Oleander.

"Oleander?"

"Yes, Oleander. It's a beautiful flowering bush, but poisonous if ingested."

"Uh oh, I think I know where this is headed."

"We're going to suit you up in a wingsuit and tonight a B-2 bomber will fly you to within eight to ten miles of Venezuelan airspace. You will be placed in the bomb bay and dropped out over the ocean at 32,000 feet. You will glide to a specific point just outside of Caracas.

"How far have you glided before?" Dan asked.

"Out at Yuma, I once flew almost nine miles from a 30,000 foot drop."

"Good. You will have a military-type of GPS guidance system on your left wrist and an altimeter on your right. You will follow the GPS to your landing spot. You should be about five to seven thousand feet at that time so you'll have to lose altitude and pop your chute at 2,000 feet and then glide toward the red flares. Your helmet will have a night-vision sighting system. That will help you see the heat source from the flares and the team waiting for you on the ground."

"This doesn't sound too bad, so far. It actually sounds like fun," Sudie said.

"I'm sure it does, but once you land the dangerous part begins. The team will take you to an apartment in Caracas. You will be fitted into a Cuban Airline stewardess uniform so that you can pass as part of the flight crew on the Venezuelan "Terror Flight" to Tehran, Iran and contrary to popular wisdom it has not been discontinued. It only flies as needed. While on that flight you will poison David Beking, who will be a passenger." Dan watched for Sudie's reaction.

I'm to assassinate…to kill him?"

"Yes, do you have a problem with that?"

Sudie had to think about it for a moment. "No, I'll do it. I know the damage he's done. He needs to pay for it", she said, falling back on her Tennessee mountain code of justice. "But why do I have to pretend to be a Cuban stewardess? Shouldn't I be a Venezuelan Airline stewardess?"

Oriental Flyer

"The Venezuelans and the Cubans have an exchange program for their stewardesses. The Venezuelan stewardesses would recognize an imposter so you have to go as a Cuban stewardess. Tomorrow night is the first night for this particular Cuban stewardess. A team will take her down and give her a shot that will knock her out for a couple of days. You'll take her place and you will have to bluff your way into her job as a stewardess. You'll have all the proper ID's and documentation of course. Also, your Spanish dialect is nearer to Cuban than Venezuelan."

"You're right, my language instructors at Yale were mostly Cuban exiles, but I don't know anything about being a stewardess."

"There will be people at Whiteman AFB to work with you on that this afternoon. Sudie, you're going to have to go in there with an air of confidence to pull this off."

"I know, but how do I poison Beking?"

"You'll be given three sugar packets laced with poison. You'll also be given a small vial of poison. Both contain a special blend of Thallium and Ricin that one of our CIA labs has concocted. Use the liquid if you can.

"In the last few years other research labs have come up with an antidote to Thallium, but I doubt that it will work on this special blend. If the Thallium doesn't get him then the Ricin will. It's designed to be slow activating but once it does, well, there's nothing they can do. Hopefully you can slip it into one of his drinks. A word of caution, don't let any of the liquid touch your skin, not even a drop."

"What happens if a drop does touch my skin?"

"With one drop, it would take a while but you would eventually get sick. The longer you go, the sicker you'll get. Fortunately, we do have our own antidote for this particular blend. It's lab protocol. If you make a poison, you have to make an antidote."

"What happens when we land in Tehran?"

"You'll get your bag, go to a ladies restroom, put on a Muslim-type of dress and put on a headscarf. Use the lower part of the headscarf as a veil until you exit out the front door of the terminal

and get into your team's car. A team will be in place looking for you
and they will get you out of Iran.

"Use it as a veil? Why?"

"It'll keep the cameras at the airport from getting a good picture
of your face. Wouldn't hurt to wear sunglasses too. You'll also have
a large red dot sticker on your suitcase to help our people locate you.

"Now, I want you to look at each picture as I put it on the big
screen. The first one is what Caracas looks like at 30,000 feet from
ten miles out at sea. The bright lights are Caracas, of course. Do you
see the red dot to the left of the lights of Caracas, just inland?"

Sudie nodded yes.

"That's where your team will be waiting for you. They'll get
word from the B-2 when you've left the aircraft. They'll wait two
minutes and then light three red flares. Anything other than three red
flares means trouble. Don't land there. Mission aborted. You'll be
given alternate instructions later on today in case that happens. Here,
read this mission synopsis."

"Someone did some fast typing to get this ready."

"We plan for everything. We've had variations of this mission
planned out for a long time. We had to tweak it a bit to fit you and
your special talents."

Sudie read the mission plan during the flight and occasionally
engaged Dan in conversations about particular details. She was given
a couple of hi-protein energy drinks. They were to replace the fluids
that she lost during her rough morning flight. She managed to get
them down before they landed at Whiteman AFB in the early
afternoon.

She was briefed all afternoon. To keep her rested for the evening
mission they made sure that she was either sitting or reclining in a
lounger. They would have liked for her to have taken a power nap
but no one, including Sudie, thought she could go to sleep. A
sedative was briefly considered but just as quickly dismissed. She
needed to be at her sharpest for the complicated mission.

Oriental Flyer

In Washington, Eric was leading a team that was sweeping FBI headquarters looking for an electronic leak. They had spent most of the day finding nothing and now they were in the basement where all the telephone equipment was installed. Eric had thought all day that this might be the spot where they would find something but so far, everything was as it should be.

The team was mostly techies with various areas of electronic expertise. The two with the most telephone tapping and surveillance experience were leading the search here in the basement. The room was row after row of computer-like towers with miles of wiring. As he watched them trace down all the spaghetti-like wiring he wondered, *How in the world can they tell if anything is out of the ordinary.*

They had been over everything twice when he heard one of the men say, "Hello. What do we have here?" Everyone rushed over to look at what he had discovered.

"What is it?" Eric asked.

"I don't know. I've never seen anything quite like it. It's so small and inconspicuous I almost missed it."

It looked like a flash drive, but it was about three times bigger than an ordinary one. It was screwed neatly to a plywood board along with other equipment, making it look official. A normal telephone wire with a clip was plugged in from one side. It came from the central telephone exchange board. The other end was hard-wired with a wire running out of it. It soon integrated itself with a bundle of other wires running along the wall and out of the building with the other wires.

One of the techies clipped a device on the out-going wire and Eric ran outside with the other techie where he tried to locate the wire by clipping on to different wires. Soon his device beeped, indicated he had found the corresponding wire. They followed it to where it ended within the bundle. The end had a six-inch metal antenna. It was on the edge of the bundle but still far enough inside of it as not to be easily seen. The antenna was exposed enough to where it would have no problem sending a signal.

Eric and the techie went back inside and discussed with the team what they had found.

"Should we unplug it?" one of the team members asked.

"No! Not yet. Let's get some experts down here to figure out what it does first. Hell, who knows, it could be some of our own stuff", Eric said.

Within thirty minutes a new team was in place examining the device.

"This is not good", one of the senior techies said.

"What is it?, Eric asked.

"The best I can tell it can listen to any telephone in the building through the central exchange. It can record a conversation, compress it into a file, and send it out in a static blip, like the submarines do."

"What's a static blip?"

"Well, that's my terminology for it. It was designed years ago for our submarine fleet. A sub can compress all of their message traffic into a compressed file or a series of files, rise to the surface, raise their antenna, and broadcast their messages. If anyone was listening it would sound like ordinary static, but the Navy or the NSA could receive, unzip the files, and read the messages. The subs can receive in the same manner.

Eric sent everyone away except for the two senior techies. He wrote a hand-written note to the Director, asking for him and the mole team to meet him here in the basement, as soon as possible. He sealed the note in an envelope and had one of the departing search party members to hand deliver it to the Director. Fifteen minutes later everyone had arrived and Eric briefed them on what they had found.

"What or who is it listening to?" the Director asked.

"I can't tell without taking it apart and analyzing it?" the techie said.

"Damn. I wish I knew who it was listening to. If I was doing it, it would bug me."

The techie thought for a moment and said, "I can tell you one thing. It's not a device that can do widespread monitoring. It's sort of like using a telescope to read the newspaper. It can probably only

96

listen to one line or person at a time. If they were listening to you, Mr. Director, then they probably had to search a long time to find your line, but once they did, then they could hear every conversation you have."

"Damn it. That's how they know", the Director said.

"Should I unplug it?" the techie asked.

"No! Wait a minute", Eric said.

Everyone looked at Eric, wondering what he had in mind.

"Maybe we can set a trap. Instead of unplugging it, can we make it send signals intermittently? Make it seem as if it is becoming defective. They might send someone to see what's happened to it. Then we could either turn them to work for us or follow them to their source."

The Director shook his head slowly and said, "Yes, that's what we should do. Let's go to the third floor conference room and decide how we are going to proceed. I don't want to meet in my office anymore."

It was 4:00 pm and Sudie was being tucked into her thermal suit and then her wingsuit. There was fabric under her arms and between her legs that would make her glide like a flying squirrel. She had a helmet with a night-vision device mounted to it. She also had an oxygen mask that she would need until she got below 10,000 feet. A military GPS guidance device was strapped to her left wrist and an altimeter to her right wrist. They would put the performance parachute on her once she was in the airplane. With a performance chute she could glide and land exactly where she wanted to.

At 4:30 pm the B-2 stealth bomber took off for its six-hour trip to the coast of Venezuela. If everything went as planned, Sudie would be dropped out of the bomb bay at 10:50 pm and she would land on the ground a little before 11:00 pm. There was a pilot, a co-pilot, and three people who continued to brief Sudie. After two hours of briefing Sudie knew everything that she could possibly absorb in such a short amount of time. The hum and vibration of the aircraft made her sleepy and she was allowed to sleep until forty-five minutes before her drop time.

At 10:05 pm Sudie was awakened and given a small cup of coffee and a power bar. At 10:20 pm she started breathing nitrogen for the next thirty minutes. Being dropped from such a high altitude she would need the nitrogen to prevent the possibility of getting the diver's bends. At 10:45 pm she positioned herself on the edge of the bomb bay doors in a sitting position. Instead of lying flat in the bomb bay, she had elected to sit on the frame around the bomb bay doors and push herself out from a sitting position.

At 10:50 pm the flight crew signaled Sudie and her advisors that it was time for her to drop and they would be opening the bomb bay doors in ten seconds. One advisor smiled and saluted her. Dan blew her a kiss.

She smiled back at them and the doors opened with a rush of wind. She pushed off hard from the bomb bay frame to make sure her parachute cleared the structure.

The wind and the sub-zero temperature almost took her breath away. She threw her arms into a touchdown signal position with a 90 degree bend at the elbows and arched her back and legs. This stopped her tumbling and got her into a position where she could spread her arms and legs so the wingsuit could take effect and begin her glide toward land. She was glad they had made her put on a thermal suit under the wingsuit, otherwise she would be frozen by the time she got down to 10,000 feet.

She spent a moment orientating herself and then headed for Caracas at about 30,000 feet. She was eight miles out. Her GPS unit indicated that she was headed toward the correct coordinates. It had an arrow pointing in the correct direction and a mileage countdown until she reached her target.

It was exactly like the briefing photo they had shown her of Caracas from ten miles out to sea at 30,000 feet. It was like looking at a city at night from an airplane window seat, only better. *It's beautiful*, she thought.

She kept checking her GPS unit to make sure she was heading in the right direction, but she didn't really need to. She was concentrating on that dark patch of land slightly east of Caracas. After two minutes she pulled down her night-vision goggles and started looking for the flares. She actually watched the flares light up from where she was. One, two, and then three red flares awaited her. She was three minutes into her five minute flight when she realized that she was going to be high so she pointed herself down at a slight downward angle to lose altitude. She gained speed but she lost the altitude. A mile away from the flares and at 2,200 feet she flared out to lose some airspeed and then pulled the cord on the parachute. She felt the drag chute come out and then the sudden jolt of the parachute opening. *Easy, so far*, she thought.

She could see the three men on the ground looking to the north, trying to spot her. She did a slow circle around them and by flaring out her landing she was able to land about ten feet behind them in a gentle standup landing. The men were startled when they heard her chute hit the ground behind them.

There she was, hands on her hips in a sort of space like outfit, looking at them. They had never seen anything quite like her before and didn't know what to say at first.

"You can never tell what kind of Goldfish will fall out of the sky," she said, offering her coded introductory sentence.

"We've never seen it rain fish before," was their coded response.

"Come, we have to get you to a safe house in Caracas", one man said.

They gathered her parachute, wingsuit, and other gear and packed them in a large duffel bag. To keep from looking like she had just dropped in from outer space, Sudie went behind a bush and changed into a dress more appropriate for local attire.

The men pulled out a satellite phone, went to scramble, and reported that they had caught their rabbit.

Forty-five minutes later they were in the safe house near the airport. A seamstress started taking Sudie's measurements for the stewardess uniform that she would have to alter for her. She would work through the night on the uniform. Besides the seamstress, there were three other CIA agents in the house working in support of the mission. One agent was a former Venezuelan stewardess. It was her job to turn Sudie into a stewardess that no one would be suspicious of, with only a few hours of training.

Sudie stayed up until 2:00 am being fitted for her uniform. During the whole time she was constantly briefed on how to fit in with the Venezuelan stewardess crew without arousing suspicion. At a little after 2:00 am she was allowed to go to bed. Sudie was awakened at 8:00 am the next morning when her briefings began again. They would continue until 5:30 pm that afternoon when they would leave for the airport. The flight was scheduled to leave at 7:50 pm.

Late that afternoon another CIA team was parked in a van outside of Consuela Alvarez's apartment. She had arrived from Cuba a day ago as part of the Cuban-Venezuelan stewardess exchange program and was staying in a small house that the airline used to staff their crews. She had yet to meet her new crew. Two men dressed as telephone repair men got out of a van and walked to the house's side door and knocked.

"Yes?" Consuela said, answering the door.

"Excuse us senorita, but we've been told that your telephone is not operating properly", one of the men said, knowing that they had disabled the phone two hours ago.

"Yes, it was working this morning but now it does not have a dial tone."

"If you would show us the phone, we'll see what we can do."

As Consuela turned to lead them to the phone one of the men grabbed her from behind and put a chloroformed handkerchief to her mouth and nose. She struggled, but was unconscious within a few seconds. The second man pulled open a small case and gazed at Consuela's body, trying to estimate her weight. He filled a syringe with what he thought would be the correct amount and injected it into her arm. She would sleep for two days.

The men signaled for the van to back into the driveway and closed the security fence so no one could see them. They fixed the phone, loaded Consuela into the van, and drove off to a safe house where they could keep her under observation for a couple of days. After Sudie's flight landed in Tehran and she had ample time to get away, then they would take Consuela back to her house, put her in her bed, and leave before she woke up. The lead agent, who had helped brief Sudie that morning, gazed at Consuela's face and was amazed at the fact that Sudie looked very much like Consuela. *Pure luck*, he thought.

Captain Buddy always enjoyed tying up in the George Town harbor in the Cayman Islands. The buildings around the harbor were quaint and colorful. *I can't dally around though, I have to hurry or I'll be spotted*, he thought. He secured the *Flyer* and caught a taxi to the bank that Mr. Wu had specified. He wore a broad-brimmed straw hat and sunglasses just in case his face was caught on a surveillance camera somewhere and it was run through a facial recognition process. The CIA was sneaky; a camera could be hidden in any window of the buildings around the bank.

Buddy sat down in a chair where a sign said "Customer Service". In America, entering a bank with a big hat and sunglasses would immediately alert security and make all the tellers nervous, but here they were used to customers who were trying to hide their identity.

"Sir, can I help you?" a well-tanned customer service rep asked.

"Yes, I would like to withdraw my money and close the account. I would like the money in Euro's. Here is the account number and I'll give you the appropriate passwords when you're ready."

"Certainly, sir. Come in my office and we'll get the process started."

Buddy followed him into his office and the man typed the account number into his computer. Buddy saw the man's eyebrows arch.

"Anything wrong?, Buddy asked.

"No, no. There's nothing wrong. It's only that this is a sizable account. We'll hate to lose it."

"I wouldn't think that $500,000 would be very much to a bank like this", Buddy said.

"It's not, but 2,000,000 euro's is a lot of money, even for us."

"WHAT?" Buddy said, confused.

"Here's an envelope with a message for you Mr. Miller. It was recently attached to this account. Maybe it will enlighten you."

Buddy opened the envelope and unfolded the note which read:

> *Dear Captain,*
>
> *If you are reading this then you have been successful in your mission. The $500,000 was for a successful mission and with the understanding that you could return to your normal life. You cannot. You will have to live abroad in hiding. We reward our agents who succeed and are loyal; therefore we have deposited 2,000,000 euros to your account. This will help you have a comfortable retirement wherever you may choose. If you ever make it to Asia, say Hong Kong. Look us up.*
>
> *Good Luck,*
> *Your handler.*

"Do you have a shredder?" Miller asked.

"Why yes, I have a micro-shredder. Would you like to use it?"

"Yes, please", Miller said, as he stood, walked over to the shredder, inserted the note and envelope, and watched it turn the note into fine bits of confetti.

"How do you want your money? I know you said Euro's, but do you want it all in cash or in a certified check, or a combination of both?"

"Do you have a branch bank in Hong Kong?"

"We don't have a branch bank there, but we do have associations with banks that we can work with. We can setup whatever you wish."

"I would like 75,000 in Euros, 25,000 in dollars in a briefcase for my immediate use and the rest deposited to an account in a Hong

Kong bank of your choice. I also want you to pay off the mortgage on my boat before you transfer the money. Here is the lender's information along with the payoff amount. Oh, one more thing. I would like $25,000 deposited to this account in Grenada—No, wait a minute", Buddy said, think of his increased reward. "Make it $40,000."

"That will be no problem sir, but it will take a couple of hours. Would you like to walk around town for a while, or if you like, we have a lounge where you can relax, watch TV, read, and have some snacks."

"I'll wait in your lounge, if you don't mind." *I have some thinking to do. I certainly don't want to walk the streets where I could be spotted and recognized*, Buddy thought.

Buddy's mind was reeling. The extra money opened up a whole new realm of possibilities. He would like to settle in Australia but that was out of the question. They worked too closely with the United States. Chances were that he would eventually be discovered.

Thailand was a possibility but too many Americans were living or visiting there. India, maybe? The only real safe plan for the moment was to get to Beijing. Settle there for a while. Maybe get a little plastic surgery and then see if the Chinese Government would help him get settled in New Zealand under a new identity. *Hawkes Bay, on the North Island. I would love to live there, maybe have a small vineyard or orchard. It's a laidback country. I think I could blend in there without getting caught. I'll have to wait a couple of years until this blows over*, he thought.

He was thinking about Maria when the bank representative came for him. *I'll never see her again*, he thought and that saddened him.

"Mr. Miller, we're ready for you. Could you follow me to my office?" Once seated, the bank representative continued, "We have transferred your money to a new account in Hong Kong and have made the deposit to that account in Grenada. We have kept enough to give you the cash you requested and we have also kept enough to pay off your boat. I can't seem to find your loan account number for the boat on this paperwork. Do you happen to have it?"

"Oh yes, here it is. I'm sorry. I thought it was attached to the other paper."

"Very good. I'll make a phone call to see if we can make this happen."

"No, wait a moment, please."

"A problem, Mr. Miller?"

"No, not really but I would like for you to wait three weeks before you contact the mortgage company and pay off the debt. Would that be a problem for you?" *The FBI could be monitoring that account*, he thought.

"No, of course not. I can do that", the bank representative said, wondering if Mr. Miller had something to hide.

"Very good. If you could do that for me then I'll take my cash and be on my way."

Buddy opened the briefcase that the bank had put the money in and gazed at it. He had never seen so much money and it was a nice leather briefcase too, but he was sure he had paid for it, one way or another. He gave the bank representative a quick nod and walked outside where the bank had a security guard with one of the bank's cars ready to drive Buddy to his boat.

Buddy got out of the harbor as quick as he could. He pointed the boat toward South Africa. He was tired. He had been sailing almost non-stop for weeks now with very little shore time. The last few days had been especially tiring without having Mack to swap shifts with, but he had to get out of the Caribbean, an American controlled pond.

It took Buddy two or three days to get out of the Caribbean. At first he kept close to the South American shore line so that he could make a stop and restock his boat for the trip to Asia. He spent one night ashore where he got a good meal and a solid nights rest before sailing toward the middle of the Atlantic. Once well out to sea he would trust the autopilot and get some rest.

Chapter Ten

One of the agents briefing Sudie had obtained a taxi cab somehow and was driving her to Caracas' Simon Bolivar Airport. In a few minutes she would be completely on her own until she landed in Tehran where another team would take her in tow. Conversation was sparse but about ten minutes from the airport he started talking on one last topic.

"Sudie, one last thing. We suspect that the exchange program between Cuba and Venezuela is to share information so that Cuba can share in the flights between this area and the Middle East. I wouldn't be surprised if they gave you free rein of the cabin so that you can learn as much as you can."

"That would be nice. It would make getting to Beking much easier."

"Do you have your camera pin on?"

"Yes, loaded and ready."

The CIA had done an outstanding job of taking the wings pin on her uniform cap and making a camera out of it. There was a tiny button to activate it and it would take a digital picture every thirty seconds for an hour before it filled up.

"Try to find a time after the initial takeoff rush to activate the camera, walk through the cabin, and talk to each person. We would love to know who else is on that flight. Give the wings to our Tehran agents as soon as you make contact there."

"Don't worry. I'll get it to them—if I make it."

"You getting scared, Sudie?"

"A little, but don't worry. I don't see why this shouldn't work."

"It should, unless there's a leak somewhere. Let's hope they've plugged everything in Washington."

"Oh, God. I wish you hadn't said that."

"I wouldn't let that worry you. I know they're taking

105

extraordinary measures, verbal messages only, to keep this mission quiet."

Five minutes later he dropped Sudie off at the main entrance of the airport terminal. According to the layout she had memorized she should make a left and find Room 163 which was a small lounge where the aircrew gathered.

Two minutes later she found the door and tried to open it. It was locked. She knocked and waited.

The door opened and a stewardess opened the door and smiled at her, "Hello. You must be Consuela. Come in and I'll introduce you to everyone."

Introductions were made and everyone seemed to be genuinely friendly. She listened to them make light conversation for about fifteen minutes before their driver came to the lounge. They all followed him out to a passenger van. He then drove them to a secluded loading dock where a Venezuelan Airbus plane was waiting for them.

Once inside the plane a stewardess name Abril took Sudie under her wing and showed her around the cabin and galley.

"I hope I can be a help to you and not embarrass myself, Sudie said.

"Do not worry, Consuela. It is a long flight, almost fifteen hours, but it is an easy flight. We have a pilot, co-pilot, and four stewardesses. I have never seen more than fifteen people on this flight. Just watch and learn. Seems like a waste with such a large airplane."

"Maybe you will let me serve drinks and coffee to the passengers?"

"Sure, No problem. Why don't you check the overhead storage bins and see if they have pillows in them."

Forty-five minutes later the passengers started boarding. They were a swarthy looking group. Mostly Middle Easterners, but David Beking was easy to spot even with his beard. He looked just like his photo. He took a seat over the wings. All of the passengers were seated in the middle section of the aircraft to make it easier for the stewardesses to service the passengers. The plane looked like it could hold at least 300 people. Abril was right. It did seem like a waste, but she knew why they used the Airbus. During her briefings they explained that the Airbus had a range of 6,000 – 9,000 miles. That meant it could fly from Caracas to Damascus and Tehran, non-stop.

Fifteen minutes later the plane taxied out on the runway and took off. As soon as the captain turned off the seat belt sign the stewardess started working the cabin. There were only twelve passengers so there was one stewardess for every three passengers and Beking was not one of Sudie's.

An hour later when Sudie and Abril were in the galley together, Sudie asked her, "Who is the well-dressed man up front on the left? He keeps staring at me; it's kind of unsettling."

"Oh, Consuela, be careful. He is secret police. His name is Victor. I do not know his last name. He keeps a protective eye on the passengers. If he continues to stare at you it means he is interested in you…well, how do I say it…?"

"Sexually?" Sudie said.

"Yes, I'm afraid so. He tries to have sex with all of the stewardesses. Most submit because they are scared of the secret police; others are able to refuse him because their families are powerful enough to protect them. Be careful, Consuela."

"Do not worry. Uncle Fidel will protect me."

"I hope so. You may need it."

Three hours into the flight, after everyone was settled down, Sudie asked Abril if she could make a walk-thru of the cabin and talk with the passengers.

"Sure, go ahead. It's a long flight and I'm sure they will enjoy talking to our new and very pretty Cuban stewardess. Be careful of, you know who."

Sudie walked behind a curtain and activated the button over on the back of her wings to start the camera. Instead of a push on-off button, it was a sliding on-off button. That way she could tell if the camera was actually on.

The next thirty minutes was pleasant enough. About half of the passengers were from the Middle East and could only speak a smattering of Spanish, but they appreciated the effort and they usually had an animated conversation for a couple of minutes. The Spanish speaking ones were a different story. They would have talked for an hour each if given the opportunity. They were all eyes for Miss Consuela.

When she approached David Beking, she pretended to speak a broken mixture of English and Spanish, just enough to communicate. He seemed happy and nervous at the same time. She asked if she could get him anything to drink but he said not at this time.

The last passenger was Victor and presently he was sitting behind the other passengers. She had noticed that occasionally he would do a slow walk-thru of the passengers and alternate sitting in front of them and behind them.

"Good evening, sir," Sudie said. "Is this your first flight?"

"Oh, no! I have flown this flight many times, but I believe this is your first time, is it not?"

"Well, it is not my first flight. As you can tell by my uniform I fly for a Cuban Airline, but, yes, this is my first flight on this airline."

"Your accent sounds Cuban but just a bit off."

"That is probably from exposure to so many Europeans that my parents associated with. They were university professors in Havana and always had guest professors in our home."

"They are retired?"

"Yes, they have retired, although my Father has passed away. My Mother still lives in her little apartment near the university", she said, hoping what she had just said was true, at least, that is what the briefing had said about Consuela. If he was any kind of security police worth his salt he probably knew her background. She hoped he had not looked too close at Consuela's picture, although her teammates back in Caracas said that the similarity in their looks was uncanny.

"Have you been to Tehran before?" he asked.

"No. This will be my first time."

"If you like, I would love to show you around. There are many interesting sights to see there.

"That would be nice. I might enjoy that", Sudie said, knowing that she would not be there and would not have to fulfill on her implied promise. She shuddered as she walked away from him. He gave her the creeps. His hair was oily, his skin was greasy, and he carried an air of arrogance. She did not want to talk to him again if she could help it. She walked back to the galley, which was empty, and switched off the camera.

She was beginning to worry. Beking asked for very little in the way of drinks and that compounded the problem of him not being assigned to her. How was she going to be able to accomplish her assignment? It was getting late in the evening and most of the passengers were falling asleep for the night. *I have to do something tomorrow morning*, she thought.

She found a chair in the back near the galley and made it recline so that she could go to sleep. They would not arrive in Tehran until nine or ten o'clock in the morning. She was snuggling in under her blanket when she felt a presence above her.

"Need a little company?" Victor asked.

It took her a moment to recover from his boldness. "I am sorry. I do not think that I would be very good company right now. I am so tired"

"Oh, I think I could energize you."

Sudie could hardly believe his arrogance. No wonder the other girls disliked him so much. "Why do we not save it for Tehran?" she said with a telling smile.

"Tehran it shall be."

As Sudie watched him return to the passengers, she could not help but think, *What a creep.*

At 6:30 am the next morning Abril woke the other stewardess and they started preparing breakfast for the passengers. Sudie was getting desperate. She could not figure out a way to get to Beking. She was helping Abril in the galley when Beking's seat number showed up on the information board.

109

"Do you want me to go see what he wants?" Sudie asked.

"Yes, please. I am so tied up with these breakfast trays that I could use your help."

Sudie walked to Beking's seat and said, "Señor Beking, what can I do for you?"

"Some coffee, please."

"I would be glad to do that for you", she said in broken English. *If he only knew.*

Abril was leaving the galley as Sudie entered. Sudie took down a tray and placed a coffee cup on it. She took a quick glance out the galley door to see if anyone was coming and then took the vial of poison out of her pocket. As she poured the contents of the vial into the cup, the plane hit a small bit of turbulence and a drop spilled on her finger and ran down the length of it. She gasped, put the vial down, grabbed a towel, and wiped the liquid off her finger. She forced herself to concentrate on her mission. She poured coffee in the cup, picked up the trey, and walked to Beking's seat.

"Here is your coffee, Señor Beking. I hope you enjoy it."

He nodded and smiled.

As she walked back toward the galley Victor put out his leg in the aisle to stop her. He leaned forward and put his hand on her knee and said in a very sexual way, "Do you not have any sugar for me?"

Sudie could feel her anger rising. She knew her face must be turning red, and it took a lot to get her olive skin to flush. She fought to regain her composure.

"I sure do. Here", she said, pulling one of the poison packets of sugar out of her pocket. "Have some special Cuban sugar", she said suggestively.

He opened the pack, poured it in his coffee, stirred it, and sipped it. "That is much better. Cuban sugar is very sweet."

"Oh, you are right, Cuban sugar is the best. You will taste the sweetness for a long time."

He removed his leg for her to pass and Sudie walked back to the galley. She took one of the vodka mini-bottles out of the liquor cabinet and poured it over her finger and scrubbed it with soap and water. She then walked back to one of the lavatories and flushed the vial and other sugar packets down the toilet. *Don't panic,* she thought, *they have an antidote.*

An hour later they landed in Damascus, Syria and three passengers left the plane. They stayed on the ground for about thirty minutes and took off for Tehran.

During the flight Beking stopped Sudie and asked, "Do you know what time we will land in Tehran?"

"9:55 am, Tehran time, is what our schedule says and our pilot says we are on time. We will land at the Mehrabad Airport in Tehran." Landing there was unusual for international flights. This airport was normally used by domestic air traffic flying within Iran. All others flights used the new international airport thirty-five miles south of Tehran.

"Good. I have another flight later in the afternoon."

"A vacation, perhaps? What is your destination?"

Beking paused a moment. He did not know if he should tell the truth or not. Finally he said, "Asia, on business."

"We have enjoyed having you on this flight. Have a pleasant trip."

He nodded and she walked to the galley. As she passed Victor he hardly looked up. He looked a little pale and was pulling at his necktie. *Wow!* she thought, *that sugar packet must have been particularly strong.*

The landing was non-eventful and after twenty minutes of straightening the cabin and closing down the galley the whole crew walked into the terminal toward a lounge. When they reached the door to the lounge Sudie whispered to Abril, "I will join you in a moment. I need to go to the ladies room."

"You passed it. It is about ten meters back", she said, pointing with her finger.

Sudie walked into the ladies room and entered a stall. She pulled a muted green knee-length coat out of her bag, called a manteau, along with matching pants and a headscarf. The manteau covered her body from her neck down to her knees and was in line with the hejab code of dress for women. In Iran, the women wear a headscarf that completely covers their hair with maybe only a wisp of hair framing their faces. Although most women do not wear a veil, Sudie pulled part of the headscarf over her face as a veil to keep airport cameras from getting a good image of her. In less than ninety seconds she had transformed herself, placed a red sticker on her bag, put on sunglasses, and was walking toward the front entrance of the terminal. *This has been easier than I thought it would be*, she thought.

She avoided the taxi line and walked about twenty yards away from the taxi stand. Within a minute a car pulled up to her with a driver and a female passenger in the front seat. The passenger held out a small piece of cardboard with a red sticker on it. "Get in", she said.

"Are you Navid's cousin?" was Sudie's coded question.

"No, I am Navid's English teacher," was her coded response.

Satisfied that this was her contact team in Tehran, she opened the back door of the car, threw her small rolling suitcase to the other side of the back seat, got in the car, and then pulled the headscarf away from covering the bottom half of her face.

The driver checked over his shoulder and merged into the traffic leaving the terminal. The female passenger with the red sticker, turned and said, "Miss Sexton, I am Shaheen. I have been assigned to get you out of Iran." Pointing to the driver, she said, "That is Jafar. He is part of our team and can be trusted."

Sudie was sitting in silence and only nodded her head. It was hard to believe that she had pulled off the mission and was apparently getting away without suspicion.

"Did you accomplish your mission?" Shaheen asked.

"Yes, I did. Beking was poisoned and here is the camera that is hidden in this wing pin. You should have good photos of every passenger on board. Get it to Langley as soon as possible."

"Anything else that we should know about?"

"Well….I also poisoned a Venezuelan Security Air Marshal."

"Why!"

"He pissed me off."

"Oh my God! He was not sanctioned. That could cause repercussions."

"I'm not sorry. He needed killing", Sudie said softly, looking out the window, thinking of the other Venezuelan stewardesses.

Eric leaned back against a tower bank full of computers while watching a couple of high level techies from either the CIA or NSA. They were working on the flash drive that someone had planted in the telephone bank at the FBI. They had looked at it yesterday morning, x-rayed it, and had come back the next evening a little after midnight. They wanted to pick a time when whoever was observing it would not be so heavily focused on listening to it. It was not unusual for either the computer or telephone system to be shut down in the middle of the night for maintenance.

One techie shut down the system and the other removed the oversized flash drive and started opening it. It took about ten minutes of careful cutting with a very small cutting device before they could pull it apart. They studied it and talked about it for about a quarter of an hour. They started working on one small wire where they added a small circuitry part of their own which would make the device work intermittently. They pushed it back together, resealed it, and pulled the device's rubber covering back in place.

One of them turned to Eric and said, "That should do it."

"Can you test it?" Eric asked.

"Not until tomorrow morning, when the Director first talks on his phone. Don't worry, we'll be on it. We'll let you know as soon as we can verify it."

The next morning Eric decided to interview the girl at the Library of Congress. This was the girl that was dating a low level Chinese staff member at the Chinese Embassy. It would give him something to do while waiting for the techies to verify their work.

113

Eric entered the Library in his overcoat carrying his briefcase, looking very FBI-ish. At the main desk he showed his credentials and asked for Ms. Amanda Taylor.

"I'll take you to her office. Follow me, please."

They walked down a long hallway, made a couple of turns, and entered an office.

"Ms. Taylor, a gentleman from the FBI is here to see you."

Amanda Taylor looked a little surprised and puzzled but said, "Please, come in. Sit down. What can I help you with?"

Eric flashed his ID, smiled, and started his interview.

"Ms. Taylor, we are doing a routine check on all Chinese Embassy personnel. I understand that your boyfriend works at the Chinese Embassy."

"Yes, he does, but I can assure you that I am not giving any secrets to him, nor am I in any position to have knowledge of any state secrets, unless Thomas Jefferson has some here in some of his old books."

"No mam, I'm sure you're not giving away any state secrets, but I am interested in any other embassy members that you might happen to know."

"I really don't know anyone else; unless you count some of the embassy people that my cousin invited to a family gathering we had a couple of weeks ago."

"Tell me about that."

"My cousin, Donnie Ling, invited a Mr. Wu to the party that we had for my parent's twenty-fifth wedding anniversary. I think he is very high up in the embassy. My parents considered it a great honor for him to attend."

Eric's attention perked up at the mention of Mr. Wu. "Tell me about Donnie and how he knows Mr. Wu."

"I'm not really sure but I think he knows him through his job at the telephone company."

"The telephone company? He works for the phone company?"

"Yes, he's a specialist in hi-tech telephone equipment. The phone company is always putting him on special projects and jobs."

114

"Has he ever talked to you about Mr. Wu?"

"No. I was introduced to him at the party. That's the only time I've ever had any contact with Mr. Wu."

"So, Mr. Wu was invited to your family function by Donnie."

"Yes. Here's a picture of the event with family and friends", she said pulling a newspaper from a stack of papers behind her desk. The picture was from the society page of one of Washington's prominent newspapers. Eric noted the date and page number. He could get a hard copy from the newspaper.

"Thank you, Ms. Taylor. This has been a very routine interview and nothing should come from it, so I would appreciate it if you would not mention this to anyone. It might cause someone like Donnie some undue anxiety", Eric lied convincingly.

"I won't. I hope I answered your questions. This is the first time I've ever been questioned by any of our police or intelligence agencies."

"Oh, don't worry about it. It's strictly routine. Good day Ms. Taylor", Eric said and left her office.

Eric walked out of the Library of Congress feeling like he had possibly hit the jackpot. Here was a link between Mr. Wu and someone at the telephone company. *I need to find out if Donnie Ling has ever worked on the FBI's phone system where the flash drive device was located,* Eric thought.

When Eric reported his findings to the mole team at the FBI, a flurry of activity commenced. They started a file and investigation on Donnie Ling, records were checked to see if Donnie had ever entered the building, an FBI contact at the phone company was alerted, and a tail was put on Mr. Ling. His phones were not tapped for fear he might, with his expertise, realize that someone was listening to him.

Almost immediately they found out that a Mr. Donnie Ling had worked in the FBI's basement on the phone system. He had been down there six times over the last eighteen months.

Eric placed a work order with the phone company to check out supposedly faulty equipment in the basement. The phone company said they would have a technician in there, within two days.

An intelligence officer knocked on Mr. Wu's door and entered.

"Yes, what is it?" Wu asked.

"Sir, we seem to be having a problem with the device that we planted in the FBI's telephone system."

"What kind of problem?

"The device is still working but it is intermittent. We're getting about every third word."

"Do you think the FBI has found the device?"

"I've thought about it and I think it is only a bad piece of circuitry. If they had found out about it I believe they would have removed it."

"I don't know, Wu said, "they're not dumb."

"We've had problems before with this type of circuitry. It's in such a small and tight package that sometimes the heat buildup shortens the life of the unit. It nearly always starts out with an intermittent signal and then soon after a failure occurs."

"All right. I'll meet with my contact and have him to check it out", Wu said.

Wu waited for the officer to leave his office and picked up the phone and dialed a cell phone number.

"Hello", Donnie Ling said.

"Meet me tonight. Six o'clock at site three."

"I'll be there", Donnie said.

I wonder what this is about. I bet he wants me to go back to the FBI's basement again, Donnie thought.

Donnie did not mind doing this for the Chinese government. His father had instilled in him a great sense of honor and allegiance for the homeland of China; unlike Amanda's family who had accepted the American way of life. He would see what Mr. Wu wanted him to do mainly because Wu was very generous with his money.

Tommy was sitting in his car with another FBI agent tailing Donnie Ling. This was the only type of duty that they would assign him until his ribs healed. Donnie had pulled near the edge of a convenience store parking and stayed in the car. *Unusual*, thought Tommy. Five minutes later another car pulled up and much to Tommy's surprise Mr. Wu got out of his car and got into Donnie's car.

"What's up, Mr. Wu?, Donnie asked.

"Just a minute. I want to watch the traffic for a minute and see if I see anything suspicious. Like someone tailing me."

"God, I hope not. That would make me a suspect."

"Don't worry. I've driven around for thirty minutes making sure I was not followed."

Wu looked around for a while and when he felt comfortable he said, "The device that you planted at FBI headquarters is failing. It's giving out intermittent signals. Do you think you can get back in there?"

"Yes, actually I'm scheduled to go there tomorrow to check out some phone problems they've submitted a work order on."

"Do you think they will let you work alone?"

"Yes, they always have in the past. They usually escort me down there, stay with me a few minutes, and then go to the other side of the room and sit until I'm through."

"Can they see where the device is?"

"No, it's behind some computer towers."

"Good. Here's a replacement part for the unit that's going bad. Just replace it. We'll know if it's a success or not by its broadcast signal, but I want the old unit back. Our technical people want to examine it. Call me when you get out and we'll set up a meeting place", Wu said, and then got out of the car.

Ten minutes passed before Donnie got out of the car and went into the convenience store, bought a drink, and left.

"Did you get good video on that?" Tommy asked his partner.

"Sure did. It looks like we've caught ourselves a little spy. Too bad we didn't have a listening device to catch their conversation from the vibrations off the car windows."

At 8:30 the next morning the Director convened the mole team.

"Gentlemen, we are making progress. Based on a lead that Agent Dawkins developed we have found out who planted the device in the phone system. It appears to be a phone company technician. A Mr. Donnie Ling."

"Are we sure that this is the person?" one agent asked.

"We should know for sure later today. The phone company is sending a repairman to fix some telephone equipment in the basement. We have cameras hidden in the basement around the device to see and record what he does. I'll bet you this month's pay that it will be Mr. Donnie Ling, our person of interest."

Donnie Ling was allowed into FBI Headquarters at 1:15 that afternoon. He was escorted to the basement by one of the FBI's technical services people. There the FBI tech rep followed him around for a while, talking about what he thought the phone problem might be. After fifteen minutes the tech rep left Mr. Ling to his investigation in the jungle of telephone wires and equipment. He walked to the other side of the room and sat down to wait until Mr. Ling had finished.

Donnie searched around for a while and found the dummy problem that the FBI's technical reps had setup for him to find. He fixed it and continued moving around the towers of equipment until he got to the wall where the spy device was located.

He walked to the end of the row of equipment and peered around to see if the agent was still sitting at the door. He was still there reading a magazine. He returned to the wall where the device was mounted and started removing it so he could replace it with the new one.

Eric and several other agents were in a room near the entrance of the basement door watching Donnie's every move on camera which was recording the event.

Donnie installed the new unit on the wallboard and then proceeded to take the old one apart. A few deft cuts and the device slid open.

Donnie's eyes became very large. "Crap!", Donnie whispered

loudly. He immediately recognized the fact that an interrupter has been added to the device. He felt someone's presence behind him and slowly turned to look behind him.

"Put the device down slowly and raise both hands in the air", Eric said, as he rounded the corner of the equipment towers nearest Donnie, gun in hand.

"I didn't know what it was, so I decided to check it out. I didn't put it there", Donnie said, becoming very scared.

"Oh, come on Donnie. We know what you've done. We even have you on video, meeting with Mr. Wu last night."

Donnie deflated. He knew it was over with. "Can I make a deal of some sort?"

"Maybe. We'll have to see how helpful you are during your interrogation."

Donnie spilled his guts during the afternoon briefing. He agreed to wear a wire when he was to meet Mr. Wu again. Eric was smiling. Mr. Wu had humiliated him and caused him to have the beating of his life. It was time for a little payback for Mr. Wu.

Later that afternoon Eric had Donnie to place a call to his contact number. Donnie made the call and left a message. A few minutes later Mr. Wu called back.

"Hello."

"Yes?" Wu answered carefully.

"The repair has been made."

"Yes, I know. We are already receiving messages."

"I have the old device. Where do you want to meet?"

"Meet me at site two at eight o'clock tonight."

"Will you have something for me?" Donnie said, trying to be as natural as possible.

"Yes, of course. Do I not always have something for you?"

"Yes, thank you. Goodbye", Donnie said and hung up.

"How much does he usually give you, Donnie?" Eric asked.

"$2,500 each time."

"Was it worth it?"

Donnie could only hang his head.

"You know the only chance of ever seeing daylight again is to work with us. You had better not do anything tricky. I'll become very suspicious if Mr. Wu doesn't show up tonight."

Donnie looked up at Eric and swallowed hard, "Don't worry. I'll cooperate."

Eric was looking forward to this meeting. He wanted to see the expression on Wu's face when he arrested him for espionage. Of course, everything had to go just right and Wu would probably be out of the country in twenty-four hours on his diplomatic immunity but Eric was sure that this would put a dent in Wu's career.

The meeting place was a parking garage near the Chinese Embassy. Ling was parked on the third floor. The FBI team was in a vehicle disguised as a painter's van several cars away from Donnie's car. The van was packed full of recording equipment including a listening device that could hear what was being said inside Donnie's car by focusing a laser beam on his car window and picking up the voice vibrations. The laser probe and the receiving antenna were disguised in the ladder hung on the side of the van. The cameras were equally well disguised.

Promptly at eight o'clock Mr. Wu walked onto the third floor of the parking deck. As he approached Donnie's car he slowed down and looked around. The painter's van would have normally raised his suspicion but that van had been parked there every time he had been to this location. He had actually seen painters getting in and out of it with their equipment. He figured that it belonged to the parking deck's maintenance crew or a nearby hotel's crew. He stopped at the back of Donnie's car and looked around one more time and then got into the car with Donnie.

Mr. Wu settled himself in the passenger seat and looked at Donnie, "Did everything go OK?"

"Yes, of course, there were no problems. Why?"

"Nothing really. We are receiving good transmissions. It just seems—"

"What", Donnie asked.

Wu sighed and said, "We don't seem to be getting the high quality intelligence conversations that we're used to getting. Maybe it is my imagination but the director seems to be avoiding certain topics. Anyway, do you have the old device?"

"Yes, here it is", Donnie said, handing the device to Wu.

Wu looked it over carefully and said, "I will turn this over to our technicians and see what is wrong with it." Wu continued to look at it.

"Do you have my payment?" Donnie asked.

"Yes, of course." Wu reached into his pocket and pulled out an envelope and handed it to Donnie.

"Thanks", Donnie managed to squeak out. He knew that once the exchange had been made that the FBI agents would pounce on them.

Wu looked at Donnie, wondering if something was wrong and then followed his gaze to the window next to his right shoulder. FBI agent Eric Dawkins was bending over staring through the window. The color in Wu's face drained.

Eric tapped on the window with his gun.

Wu's head snapped back toward Donnie with a look of anger.

"I had to. They caught me red-handed. I had no choice!"

Wu looked straight ahead, took a deep breath, and opened the door.

Eric treated Wu rather respectfully. He did not slam him down on the hood or anything approaching roughness. Instead on his own accord, Wu put his hands on top of the car while Eric searched him.

"Wu, you are under arrest for espionage. You will be taken to FBI headquarters for questioning."

"You will not get anything out of me. You know I will be out of the country within forty-eight hours because of my diplomatic immunity."

"That's true, of course, but your colleagues will also wonder what you told us while being held at FBI headquarters. Might put a little damper on your career", Eric said. He was loving this. It was just the right amount of payback.

Wu was questioned the rest of the day and part of the next before he was handed over to the Chinese Embassy staff. As expected they got nothing out of him but now he was *persona non grata* and was to be out of the country within twenty-four hours.

Donnie was taken to jail where he was to be charged with espionage, although to a lesser degree because of his cooperation.

Eric sat at his desk, grinning with self-satisfaction. All morning other agents had been coming into his office to congratulate him. He was on the fast track now. He would always remember the way Wu looked at him with disdain as he got in the car for the Chinese Embassy. It felt good. In the midst of all the good feelings, Sudie popped into his mind. He had not heard from her in weeks and the CIA was saying nothing. He was worried about her.

Oriental Flyer

*I'm going home to see my father
I'm going there no more to roam;
I'm just a-going over Jordon
I'm just a-going home.*

Folksong-Spiritual

Chapter Eleven

It was a warm evening in the prison camp and Howie was sitting on his cot. He was watching Neha as he slept on the floor. Neha had said he wanted to be put on the floor because it was cooler, so they laid out a mat and he and Jay had helped him to lie down on the mat. Jay was sleeping at the other end of the hut.

Howie almost never slept. The nightmares and dreams from years of torture were too dreadful for him, so he chose to sleep as little as possible.

When he was shot down over downtown Hanoi, he had been trying to evade a SAM missile by going straight up and then turning downward to try to confuse the missile. He did not quite finish the maneuver. He was at a very high forty thousand feet when the SAM exploded near enough to his aircraft to break it apart. He ejected and immediately his head felt like it was going to explode. At that altitude there was very little air and every blood vessel surrounding his eyeballs ruptured due to decompression.

When he landed in a residential section of downtown Hanoi he was bent over with pain and could hardly breathe. Several women ran to him and started beating him with brooms and sticks. Finally one of the older ladies made the other women quit hitting him. The women watched as Howie, gasping for breath, removed his helmet which revealed his long (or at least as long as the Navy would allow it) white-blond hair. When he pulled the blonde hair from his eyes they saw a man with royal blue eyes, surrounded by a solid red sclera, commonly known as the whites of the eyes, due to ruptured blood vessels.

123

They had never seen anything like it; blond hair, blue eyes, and blood dripping from a solid red sclera. They yelled *"katash wei' vorki"*, meaning *Fire Witch*, and beat him unmercifully for another fifteen minutes until the military arrived. The soldiers protected him but they too were stunned by his looks. His eyes healed over during the next few weeks but he endured another two years of torture and isolation until they finally let up on him. Much of the torture ceased after Ho Chi Minh died, but the torture had done its damage; he could never sleep peacefully.

He might get two hours of fitful sleep at night and always woke up terrified. He would catch a few cat naps during the day and Jay would watch over him and wake him up when REM or dreaming started. It was never over fifteen minutes of sleep. Sometimes he was so sleep deprived that he hallucinated. In the back of his mind, somewhere, he knew that he was hallucinating, but it did not matter. The torture from days past gave him vivid and agonizing nightmares.

Neha's chest would rise and fall with each breath. They seemed to be getting farther apart. *Go ahead Neha, it's ok to leave. Rest. You won't have to suffer anymore*, he thought.

Howie's head dropped and he fell asleep for about five minutes and woke again with a jerk of his head. He watched Neha's chest take a deep breath and then no more. *It's ok Neha, fly away.*

A tear ran down his face. He could only look at his body. He was frozen in place. The guards would come and take him in the morning. Hopefully by tomorrow afternoon they could have his grave dug for his funeral service.

As he looked at the body he fell into an open-eyed trance. After a minute, two small orbs appeared on each side of Neha's body. They grew bigger and brighter over the next few moments. They took the shape of two beautiful females, kneeling beside Neha. Their whole bodies glowed. They were dressed in glowing white toga-type miniskirts. One of them was white with golden-blonde hair, falling down her back. The other was a black girl with a pixie-type haircut. He had never seen anyone as beautiful as they were. *Are these angels?*, he wondered. *But they don't have wings.*

124

As soon as he had that thought the black girl looked at him, smiled, winked, and then returned her attention to Neha.

They seemed to be whispering in Neha's ear. In a few seconds a mist came out of his body that morphed into a whispery form of Neha. They grabbed him by the arms and whisked him through the ceiling of the hut.

Howie was transfixed, looking at Neha's body. Suddenly the blonde angel returned and sat at his side. She spoke to him with her mind, telling him to lie down. As he did, she put her hand on the brow of his head and then ran her hand through his close-cropped, now grey-white hair. He fell asleep and slept a healing and peaceful sleep until the morning. There were no dreams.

In Memphis, Nita Fisher awoke from her nap. She was in a rocking chair on the front porch of her sister's house. She thought she had heard Nehemiah calling her name. *Foolish dreams*, she thought, but it was nice to hear his voice again, even if it was a dream.

She was living with her sister now. Her health was not good. Even now her chest was hurting, but it did that a lot lately. When Nehemiah did not come home from the war she really did not care if she lived or died but her family talked her into going to Los Angeles to try singing in jazz night clubs, in hopes of a record contract. She was good enough to find steady employment as a night club singer which led to a couple of small record contracts with some small jazz labels, but she was forty years too late for the big jazz era. People wanted to hear the pop music of the seventies and eighties, not jazz.

Men were available too. She had many chances to marry but could never get Nehemiah out of her mind, and she did not think it was fair to marry someone else when her heart was not in it. When she was fifty she had had enough of Los Angeles and returned to Memphis to live with her youngest sister, a nurse. She had watched after her sister's children while her sister and her husband worked. She sang in the choir at church and on special occasions she would sing jazz ballads at night clubs, but they were always one-night stands. She enjoyed the singing engagements but that was all she wanted. She would rather be home with the children. She had become a much beloved aunt.

She enjoyed sitting on the front porch in the rocker. The slight exercise of using her feet to rock was about all the doctor would allow. He said her heart was too fragile. Another sharp pain went through her chest. She closed her eyes and took a deep breath. The pain eased somewhat. When she opened her eyes Nehemiah was standing in the driveway next to the porch. He held out his hand to her. He wanted her to come take his hand and go with him somewhere. She rose out of the rocker with surprising ease and ran to him. They embraced.

"Darlene, go tell your Aunt Nita that supper's ready."

"Yes mam", Darlene said, and skipped to the front porch to get her Aunt Nita.

"Aunt Nita, wake up. Momma said it's time to eat."

Darlene shook her Aunt's arm a couple of times and then walked back to the kitchen and said to her mother, "Aunt Nita won't wake up."

Nita's sister gasped, ran to the front porch, kneeled down by the rocker, and felt for the pulse in her sister's wrist. There was none. As tears rolled down her face she noticed that Nita was smiling.

Chapter Twelve

Akbar's head was swirling. As a department head of Iranian Intelligence in charge of subversion, he knew something was going on. He could not quite put it together though. It was as if an international plot of intrigue and murder had landed right at his feet. The plot was hard to figure out with pieces of the puzzle missing, but they had been coming in fast and furious for the last two days.

Forty-eight hours ago the Aviation Minister had called him.

"Akbar, I know this sounds crazy but a stewardess working with the Venezuelan Airline is missing", the minister said.

"Interesting, but sounds like a problem for the police."

"Not quite. This stewardess was an exchange stewardess with Cuba. The problem is that Venezuelan officials found the real Cuban stewardess at her home coming out of a drug induced coma. Someone else took her place on the flight from Caracas to Tehran. One of the stewardesses that was helping with the investigation said that the imposter looked remarkably like her; so close she could have been her sister, except she does not have a sister."

"The airlines do not know what happened to the imposter?"

"No. One minute she was walking down the airport corridor with the rest of the crew and the next, she is nowhere to be found."

"What about airport security video?"

"Nothing, except a picture of a woman coming out of a restroom wearing sunglasses and her headscarf pulled over her face like a veil. Completely unusable for identification purposes."

"I will check with my people and their sources and see if there is any talk about it," Akbar said.

Twenty-four hours ago he got a call from one of his people at a hospital in downtown Tehran.

"Akbar, the Venezuelan Air Marshall that landed on the flight from Caracas is in the hospital. He is very sick and the doctors cannot figure out what is the cause of his sickness. The doctors say that if they cannot figure out what is wrong with him and treat him soon that he will be dead in a few hours."

"They cannot diagnose out his disease?"

"No. They think it might be poison but they are completely puzzled."

He was on the same flight that the fake stewardess was on, Akbar thought.

"Stick with him and keep me posted on his status."

Twelve hours ago he received a call from the local Chinese Embassy.

"Yes, Mr. Ching, what can I do for you?" Akbar asked.

"Are you familiar with the flight that originates in Caracas and terminates in Tehran?"

"Yes, of course. Why?"

"We had a special passenger on that flight. We had gone to a great deal of trouble and expense to get him out of the United States, on to Venezuela, and back to China. Now he is in one of our best hospitals in Beijing with what we think is thallium poisoning."

"There is an antidote for thallium poisoning now, is there not?"

"Yes, but this is a particular derivative of thallium; surely made in a very special lab. There are also traces of ricin. The antidotes are not working. Did anything unusual happen on that flight?"

"Yes, something very unusual happened." Akbar laid out the events of the past forty-eight hours. "This smells of an assassination hit by the CIA."

"Yes, I think you are right. You have to find that imposter stewardess", the embassy official said.

"Yes, we are searching for her, but she already has a two or three day lead on us."

An hour later Akbar was conducting a briefing to the other

department heads of the intelligence agency about what had happened in the last three days. It was generally accepted that the CIA had planted an imposter on the flight to Tehran to kill the American spy, but they could not come up with any reason why the Venezuelan Air Marshall had been poisoned. Someone suggested that he might have become suspicious of her; she had recognized his suspicions, and poisoned him too.

The Director looked at Akbar and said, "How do you think they will try to get her out of the country?"

"Well, I do not think they will go to the Afghanistan border. Too dangerous, even our own military is wary of that region with all the smugglers. Besides, Al-Qaeda would love to get their hands on her. The easiest way is to get to Turkey like that elderly American did a few years ago when he rode horseback over the mountains, but I already have men guarding every mountain pass and road in that region. I do not think they will try that route. That means escape by a southern route to a port along our coast. They may try to get to the American Navy in the Persian Gulf."

The Director said, "Akbar, spare no resource or expense to find this Medea."

They had given the operation and the foreign female agent the code name of Medea, after the Greek Goddess who murdered Glauce with a poisoned dress.

In Memphis the elderly parents of Nehemiah Cross were sitting at their small kitchen table for lunch. Mr. Cross had retrieved the mail and was sitting down to thumb through it while Mrs. Cross finished putting the food on the table.

"Anything interesting in the mail?" Mrs. Cross asked.

"No, doesn't seem to be." , Mr. Cross said, while flipping through all the bills, advertising, and begging letters. "Humm, what's this?"

"What is it dear?"

"It's a letter from the Department of Defense."

Mrs. Cross throat tightened. After Nehemiah had become missing in action they would get letters periodically from the Air Force about Nehemiah and his classification of missing in action. She did not like to read them; they always upset her and even now she was choked up and could hardly talk.

"What does it say?" she managed to get out.

Mr. Cross opened it up and read it slowly. Finally he looked up at his wife and said, "They've changed Nehemiah's classification from missing in action to killed in action."

Tears rolled down Mrs. Cross's face.

Mr. Cross put the letter down, pulled off his glasses, and looked at his wife and said with exasperation, "Why—why— after forty-plus years would they go to the trouble of changing his status? Did they find out something or are they just tidying up their records?"

Mr. Cross threw the letter down in disgust, looked across the table, and watched his wife's tears roll down her face as she took a sip of sweet tea.

Jay and Howie walked back to their hut from the graveyard. They had been tending to Neha's grave. It had been two weeks since his burial and they had raked out the top of his grave to make it smooth. Jay reached up to the edge of their low-hanging roof eve. He pulled down Neha's grave marker. The shingle read:

Captain Nehemiah Cross
US Air Force
1945-2013

It had rained almost every day lately making the humidity very high and it had taken almost five days for the paint to dry to a hard finish. The paint that the guards had given him had been a cheap oil base paint that took forever to dry. He would make a cross, attach the shingle, and put it on his grave tomorrow.

Howie sat on the edge of his cot and picked up a basket that he was weaving out of reeds. He thought back to his college days. He had never gotten married but he did leave a trail of broken hearts through high school and college. That is, until the summer between his junior and senior year in college. He had fallen hard for a girl during summer school. The romance was hot and heavy for four or five weeks but then she abruptly broke it off, telling him that she was already promised to a boy that was getting out of the Navy in a few weeks. Her family, friends, and everyone at her church expected her to marry him. She said she had worked too hard to get him and she was going to marry him. It broke Howie's heart. She was on his mind constantly for a couple of years. It was not until one day when he was sitting in his jet on the flight deck, waiting for his turn to launch, when a ten minute delay occurred. It gave him a chance to relax and think, and then it hit him. He had not thought of her for three or four months now. He was over her. The tight knot in his stomach had disappeared. The relief was tremendous. He wanted to shout.

There had been no one since her. He had been too busy during flight school. The Navy moved him so many times that he never had time to get involved with anyone else so he never got married. No one was waiting for him back home. His parents were probably dead; remembered only by his sister and maybe a few family members.

"Howie, what are you thinking about? You've stopped weaving.

"Nothing…. Nothing."

By the way, how come you're not taking naps anymore? You don't seem to be as tired as you used to be", Jay said.

Howie paused before he answered. "I don't know if I can tell you. You won't believe me."

"Try me."

Howie sighed. "You remember the night that I was keeping watch over Neha when he died?"

"I remember it"

"Well, you only remember the morning when you woke up and found out that Neha was dead. What you don't know is what I saw that night. I mean the moment Neha died."

131

"What do you mean?"

"I don't know if I was dreaming or hallucinating or what. It seemed so real. Just as real as you and me, right now."

"What happened Howie?"

"I saw two spiritual beings or maybe angels come and get Neha's soul. They were beautiful. They flew out the roof of the hut with him. Then one of them came back, told me to lie down, put her hand on my forehead and told me to sleep. I slept until the next morning. The best sleep I've ever had. No dreams or nightmares. I've slept all night, every night since."

Jay thought about what he had said for a few moments and said, "God, I hope you're right. That gives me hope. Hope for something better when we finally leave this camp. Neha was lucky. He suffered but he was lucky to leave this place."

"Jay, you know, I never gave the afterlife very much thought until now. If it had only been the sight of the angels and Neha's soul I would still be wondering if I had hallucinated or something. But since she touched me on the forehead and put my mind at peace, I'm able to sleep peacefully.... well, it makes me believe."

"Good for you, Howie. Good for you. You needed the rest", Jay said in a whisper.

That evening Jay could hardly sleep. He was thinking about what Howie had seen the night Neha died. He was almost jealous. Life was so dull and boring in the camp. It was the most exciting thing he had heard of or talked about in years. Eventually his thoughts turned to Amy and the baby, she would always be a baby in his mind, and then to his sister, Tancy. He wondered what her life was like.

"This evening, on *Carolina Tonight*, we are interviewing a prominent female leader in our state's industry, the furniture business. We are in the office of Ms. Tancy Carter Walker who is the owner and Chief Operating Officer of this successful North Carolina Company.

"Ms. Walker, why don't you start us out by giving us an

overview of your company?"

"I'd be glad to, Dan. First and foremost, the company's success in a distinctive, high-end niche market, is a result of my father's vision. He demanded high-quality craftsmanship and paid for the most talented people, even though it cut into the profit margins. But that paid off later on. When most furniture companies had to leave the country to maintain their competitiveness, our loyal base of customers and buyers still came to us for that quality-conscious market of people who demanded craftsmanship, high-quality materials, and a timely delivery."

"Many of us still remember your father. He was far-thinking in both business and the state legislature. Tell me, how did he train you for this business? It seems like a tough business for a lady to be in", Dan said.

"Yes, it is demanding but I have good managers, including my husband. I also have good supervisors, and craftsmen who can run the factory with very little help from me. It's maintaining the sales for the factory that's a struggle. You can have the best product in the world but if you can't make the world recognize what you have and sell it then everyone in our organization suffers. I'm pretty good at sales. Sometimes a gentle voice and a pretty smile goes a long way."

"How did your father train you for this job? Did he insist that you run the family business?"

"No. He never forced us to do anything that we didn't want to do. Now, that doesn't mean he or my mother let us run wild. We had to eat our vegetables, make our beds, clean our room, do our homework, and were expected to do well in school. What he did do, was pay attention to what we were good at. He could see that I had a good business mind and could sell people on ideas. He could tell that my brother was a leader and could talk people into doing things. My brother was very smart and a good athlete. My father wanted him to be a congressman or even a senator in Washington."

Tancy turned slightly to the bookcase behind her and pointed to a picture of a handsome young Naval Officer wearing Navy Wings.

"That's him there", she said, pointing to the picture.

"Yes, and I understand he didn't make it back from the Vietnam War."

"No, he didn't. He's still classified as missing in action. It just about killed my mom and dad, especially dad. He was never quite the same afterward. I had to learn the business quickly because Dad just didn't seem to care anymore."

"You never heard any details about how your brother got shot down?"

"We were told that only moments before he was shot down by a SAM missile that he had shot down an enemy airplane. We never heard anything more."

"Do you think the Navy kept secrets from you about him?"

"No. I don't think so. I believe that they would have told us if they knew if he was alive or dead."

"Didn't he have a family?"

"Oh, yes. He had a beautiful wife, named Amy. She's from Louisiana; a real Cajun beauty and he has an even more beautiful daughter. Her name is Jayce, named after her Father, with a feminine twist."

"Where are they now?"

"That's an interesting story. It's a sad tale but it has a nice ending.

"We love interesting stories; tell us about it."

"I'd love to. After Jay became missing in action, Amy continued to live with her parents in Louisiana. She wasn't interested in anyone or anything except her daughter.

When Jay wasn't returned with the other prisoners after the war, Amy, with my family's blessing, had him declared dead. That opened the door for some extra military benefits for Amy and especially for Jayce.

We didn't think we would ever pull her out of her depression, but about nine months after that Jay's best friend, David Ferris, became a flight instructor at the Naval Air Station in Meridian, Mississippi. I think he had promised Jay that he would look after Amy and the baby. Now I don't think he felt that marriage was part of the bargain of looking after Amy, but for the next two years he would call on her and see if she needed anything and eventually started dating her. Although, neither of them planned it, they fell in love and got married, and David has been a wonderful husband and father. He got out of the Navy and became a very successful stock broker. They live in Atlanta now with two more children in addition to Jayce."

"That's a wonderful story, but sorta' bitter-sweet."

Dan turned to the camera and said, "We'll be back in a moment and finish talking to Tancy Carter Walker after this break."

Jay finished his prayers for his family. Tonight he put special emphasis on his sister, Tancy. He had trained himself not to dwell on them too much or he would never get any rest. He turned over on his side and went to sleep.

Chapter Thirteen

Shaheen and Jafar had Sudie in a safe house within thirty minutes after leaving the airport. Jafar's driving had alarmed Sudie but she soon realized that everyone seemed to drive like that. It was a type of controlled chaos. During the trip she gathered an impression that the city was colorless because most of the buildings were plastered in a light color to reflect the sun but the streets were punctuated with vendors that displayed their brightly colored wares; a brightly colored mosque would occasionally flash by her window.

The safe house was spacious and surprisingly cool. They had a unique air distribution system, common to the Middle East, that would catch breezes and pipe them throughout the house.

Shaheen made some tea and put out cheese and fruit for them to eat. It was a little after noon and everyone seemed hungry. Sudie was not as hungry as she thought she would be; she had a slight headache and picked at her food.

Shaheen watched her and said, "Sudie, you need to eat more than that. We will have a long, hard trip for the next four or five days. You will need your energy."

"We're starting tomorrow?" Sudie asked.

"Yes, we need to get at least a couple of hundred miles away from Tehran before Iranian Intelligence figures out what is going on, and we need to do it quickly. We'll leave during the morning traffic rush to draw less attention."

Sudie cleared her throat and said, "You will need to get a message to the CIA that I have been contaminated by the poison and I need the antidote as soon as possible."

Shaheen and Jafar were stunned for a moment. They had not counted on this.

"How did it happen?" Jafar asked.

"I was pouring the poison in Beking's coffee cup when we hit an

136

air pocket. A couple of drops splashed on my finger and ran down the length of it."

"Is that enough to poison you?" Shaheen asked.

"During my briefing they said one drop of incidental contact would make me sick and if not treated would eventually kill me."

"I'll tell them", Shaheen said. "I'm sure they will get the antidote to you at their first opportunity."

"Do you feel sick now?" Jafar asked.

"I don't know if I'm tired and worn out from the trip or not, but I am a little nauseous and I feel a little flushed."

"Well, there is nothing we can do about it. Our job is to get you out of the country", Shaheen said.

"And how are you going to do that?, Sudie asked.

"Our sources say that the route to Turkey is out of the question. Too many agents guarding the roads and mountain passes and the route to Afghanistan is too dangerous to even consider. That means we have to get to the southern coast of Iran and get you out by boat through the Straits of Hormuz", Shaheen said.

"What kind of boat?"

"Probably a fishing boat." Do not worry, it will have food, beds, and radio equipment but it will be slow."

"What's our destination?"

"If we can get you on a boat out of Bushehr then you can turn north and head for the American Navy."

"Bushehr? That's where all of Iran's nuclear research and construction is going on", Sudie said, raising an eyebrow.

"Yes, that is correct but if we cannot get you on a boat there then we will have to go further down the coast to Bandas Abbas. Bandas, as it is normally called, is a large coastal city, multi-cultural, with a lot of coastal smuggling going on. It may be our best bet."

"And after that how will I meet up with American agents?"

"If it turns out to be Bandas then the best bet will be to sail south to a coastal town on the west coast of India. Agents will be looking for you and they will get you to an American Embassy and out of the country."

"I hope that's soon enough. I don't know how quickly this poison will take effect."

Shaheen did not want to promise a guarantee that she could not deliver on and said quietly, "We'll do our best."

Sudie put her head in her hands and rubbed her eyes. She finally looked up and said, "Do you mind if I take a nap. I'm suddenly exhausted."

"Of course. I will show you your room. You should sleep for a few hours and then I will show you your wardrobe and our itinerary for the next four or five days."

Shaheen woke Sudie early the next morning. She helped Sudie pick out her manteau for the day and feed their group breakfast. The group had grown for the road trip. There were now four people including Sudie.

"Why so many people?" Sudie asked Shaheen.

"We will be traveling in a savari. That is what you would call a shared taxi. Savari's usually travel greater distances than city taxis. They normally are used to travel between cities and taxi drivers never go unless they have a full load of at least four people. Any fewer and we would be subject to suspicion."

"I see."

Shaheen turned to the man on her right and said, "This is Sanjar, our fourth person. He will be traveling in the back seat with you. He will be posing as your husband."

Sudie's eyebrows arched.

"Do not worry. He is a perfect gentleman. One of Sanjar's many jobs is working as a makeup artist in the cinema business, which is a plus for us."

"Why is that?"

"Sudie, you are very attractive. You will be noticed; therefore Sanjar will be performing some of his makeup magic to make you less attractive."

"How's he going to do that?"

138

Sanjar spoke up, "Maybe a scar on you cheek; make one eye where it will only half open; give you some acne."

Sudie turned to Shaheen and said, "Are you sure this is necessary?"

"I am absolutely sure for two reasons. One, you are too noticeable; we have to tone down your attractiveness. Two, we learned during the night that Iranian Intelligence has requested Venezuela Airport Authority for security footage of you. I do not know if they will get anything but we have to assume that they will."

Sudie's heart sank. "Do you really think you can get me out of Iran if they get my photo?"

"Sure we can", Shaheen said, trying to boost Sudie's confidence. "That's why Sanjar is here. In addition, we will have another person, a scout, out in front of us. He will be anywhere from four to eight hours ahead of us, looking for checkpoints that have been strengthened or anything unusual. He will communicate with us by satellite phone, all in coded language."

"We have to go through checkpoints?"

"Oh yes. We will go through several checkpoints. They cannot be avoided but don't worry, we will get through. Now go with Sanjar so he can put your makeup on."

An hour later Sanjar was packing his makeup kit and Sudie was looking for a mirror to see what he had done to her face.

She found a mirror in the bathroom and braved a look. One eye was half closed and pulled down slightly; there was a scar running down one cheek, and a fake tooth stuck out the front of her lip that was large and half crooked. *My God! I look like Goofy*, she thought.

She charged back into the kitchen where Sanjar was and said sarcastically, "Fine job!"

He smiled back and said, "Wait until you see what I do to you tomorrow."

Boy, if Eric could see me now, she thought.

Akbar's computer beeped, indicating that he had another email.

139

He saw that it was from his intelligence counterpart in Venezuela and unlike other emails, which he ignored until he was finished with what he was doing, he opened this one immediately. He hoped it contained what he wanted.

Yes, he thought. *It has an attachment.*

When he opened the jpeg image file, a grainy photo came up showing an attractive Cuban stewardess walking down one of the corridors of Simon Bolivar International Airport in Caracas. It was not the best of photos but it was good enough. Now he had something he could hand out to his agents. *She is very attractive*, he thought. *That might help our agents find this Medea.*

A NSA agent, hunched over a computer screen, in a house, high on a hill in St. Thomas, printed out an intercepted message and an accompanying photo and gave it to Chris, the station chief.

Oh crap, Chris thought. *This isn't good!*

It was 8:30 am and Sudie was in the back seat of their savari or shared taxi, with Shaheen. Thank God, it was air conditioned. Jafar was driving and Sanjar was in the front passenger seat. The savari was actually a vehicle that was supplied by the local underground working loosely with the CIA.

As usual, the traffic was chaotic in Tehran as they approached their first checkpoint. Traffic was backed up about fifty yards. The guards waved some vehicles right on through and others were pulled for closer inspections. It took about fifteen minutes to make their way to the checkpoint. Susie's heart was almost beating out of her chest when their turn came. Shaheen reached over and grabbed her hand and squeezed it.

"Don't worry, Sudie. It will be alright", Shaheen said.

Sudie tried to manage a smile for her.

"Destination", the guard asked.

"Esfahan", Jafar said, which was about 450 miles down the road to the next big city.

The guard looked closely at Jafar and Sanjar and then turned his attention to Shaheen and Sudie in the back seat. He looked at Shaheen and then to Sudie who had her headscarf covering her face. He made a movement with his hand to indicate that he wanted her to reveal her face. Sudie uncovered half her face which showed an eye pulled downward by a scar which ran down her cheek. There was an immediate sign of revulsion and then embarrassment on his face. He recovered and waved them through. He thought, *What inhuman sort of beast would do that to a woman.* To disfigure her so. *Maybe she deserved it*, but he doubted it.

In Tehran, Akbar had several hundred copies of Sudie's face printed up and sent out to all parts of Iran. Fortunately, for Sudie, most photos were to travel by bus so she had a one-day head start on them. He really wanted to catch her. The Chinese Embassy had indicated this morning that their person in Beijing was very close to death and there was nothing they could do about it.

For the rest of the day Sudie and her band sped toward Esfahan. The countryside was like traveling in parts of America's Southwest. Nothing but sand and scrub brushes. Shaheen had offered everyone cheese, bread, and some fruits but Sudie's stomach was nauseated and she did not feel like eating. She knew that was a symptom of thallium poisoning. *Maybe, tonight*, she thought. She had to eat something to keep up her strength. The journey ahead would be demanding.

They went through one more checkpoint that day at Kashan. The guard hardly even looked at them and waved them on. When they stopped for gas Sanjar managed to buy a Coke for Sudie. She struggled to get it down with some bread. It hurt her stomach but she kept it down without throwing up.

That evening they pulled into a safe house in Esfahan. The house was not as nice as the one in Tehran but yet it was comfortable. They had some fruit and tea for supper and then went to bed. It was autumn and the air cooled off quickly after the sunset. She shared a bedroom with Shaheen and they slept with a blanket over them.

The next morning Sudie joined Shaheen and the others at breakfast. Jafar was reading the notes left to him by Adel, the scout who was always one day ahead of them. Adel would check out the next day's trip, road conditions, checkpoints and anything else of interest, and that evening someone else at Adel's destination city of the day would drive all night to deliver the information back to Jafar and Shaheen.

"What does Adel say?" Shaheen asked.

"Everything looks good for today. He did say that the guard at the checkpoint in Yazd can be difficult sometimes."

"What kind of difficulty?"

"Adel says that he is anxious to catch smugglers. Wants a promotion, so he is diligent in his searches", Jafar said.

"What about our satellite phone? Won't that arouse his suspicion?" Sudie asked.

"Possibly, but Adel has that worked out. He will have someone meet us about ten miles out from Yazd and take the satellite phone and any other pertinent items in though the desert."

"How will he do that?

"You will see. Do not worry about it. We have done this many times."

The trip to Yazd was boring. Sudie tried to sleep as much as possible. Yesterday's trip was twelve hours. Today's trip would be about eight hours and there was nothing to see except sand and scrub bushes. Later that day Sudie noticed that Jafar was slowing down to pull off the road and stop. There was no other traffic in either direction. Then she noticed a dune buggy, of all things, coming up over a rise about fifty yards off the road. Jafar and Sanjar quickly transferred some bags to the dune buggy, jumped back into the car, and took off again for Yazd. The dune buggy disappeared into the desert. Sudie noticed that the dune buggy was very quiet. It must have a great muffler system.

Ten minutes later they were on the outskirts of Yazd at the

checkpoint station. The guard looked at them suspiciously and ordered them out of the car. He lined them up and asked for their identification cards. Fortunately, they had taken a picture of Sudie with her makeup on so she did match her photograph. He looked at each one closely and then their ID card. When he came to Sudie he looked at her card. His eyebrows arched slightly and then at her. He asked her to remove her headscarf which covered half her face. He leaned in to her to study her closely.

"Shussh!" Shaheen said and waved her hand at the guard. "Do you not see that she is embarrassed about the way she looks? Leave her alone!"

The guard locked eyes with Shaheen and then shrugged, gave Sudie back her ID card and then went on to thoroughly search the car. Twenty minutes later he waved them on through.

They arrived in the late afternoon and the people at the safe house had a full meal cooked for them but Sudie could only get some fruit, a little bit of bread, and a cup of tea down. Later that evening the man on the dune buggy had made his way into town, changed his cargo to his local car, and brought all the items to the back door of the safe house.

That evening, after supper, Sudie listened to her fellow travelers talk about the political situation in Iran. They hated the current Iranian government and she could tell they did not have much use for America either.

"I don't understand. If you don't like America, why are you helping the CIA and me?"

Shaheen looked at her, thought for a moment and said, "There are many things we do like about America but there are many things we do not like. We think your government is arrogant and does not respect us. Maybe that is what we are taught to believe by our government's propaganda, I do not know. We do not want our country to become decadent and have the women to wear such revealing clothes or become immoral as they are in the West. I have actually never met an American that I did not like, but I do not like the policies of your government. The only reason we help you is that we recognize that you and your country are free and that you would like to help us become free of the tyrants that run our country now. That is why we help you."

Sudie replied, "I understand what you are saying, but even though our culture is different in what we wear and how we interact with the opposite sex it does not mean that we are less moral. Many, many people in America have strong feelings about morality. They wish to keep the Ten Commandments; they feel strongly about keeping their word; they try to help people in need whether in America or overseas. They know they have been blessed and they want to share. Americans are not as immoral as you think. You see only the sensationalism that is in the media and the movies."

"Do not the Americans mistreat the Muslims?"

"Maybe a little after the terrorist strike on the Twin Towers in New York, but you scared them. Once they realize that you are not on a Jihad to kill them and convert them all to Islam, and that you want to live in peace and worship Ali, then that's OK with the vast majority of Americans. America was founded on religious freedom."

They sat quietly for a few moments and looked at Sudie. Finally Shaheen said, "Maybe you are right, but I would like to visit America and see for myself."

Akbar's hand shook slightly as he was writing some notes. The pressure on him to find this female assassin was becoming more intense. Now his boss was bringing down someone who was going to observe his methods and possibly give him advice. The search for the American agent was hard enough without someone looking over his shoulder. His office door opened and his boss walked in with a Chinese gentleman.

"Akbar, I would like for you to meet Mr. Wu. He has just flown in from Beijing and will be working out of the Chinese Embassy here in Tehran."

"Good day, Mr. Wu. It is my pleasure to meet you", Akbar said.

"No, no, it is my pleasure. I am a guest and I only want to

observe and possibly call on our resources, such as satellites and other electronic surveillance devices, if you would happen to need them. I assure you that I am not here to critique your work or methods. I will try to stay in the background and offer our country's resources when I think that we can help."

"Thank you, Mr. Wu. I appreciate that very much."

Akbar's boss interrupted and said, "I will leave you two to your business. I have an important meeting that I have to go to."

When the door closed Akbar motioned for Mr. Wu to sit down and said, "Sit down, Mr. Wu, you look tired."

"You cannot imagine what I have been through in the last week. Four days ago I was in the FBI's custody for espionage but they had to release me because of my diplomatic immunity. I was immediately flown to Beijing, where my government debriefed me for twenty-four hours and then put me on a plane for Tehran to assist you. I have hardly slept except for what I could get on the airplane."

"I will try to make this quick so that you can get some rest before we leave Tehran tomorrow," Akbar said.

"Thanks, I appreciate that", Mr. Wu said.

Akbar paused for a moment and said, "The Venezuelan Air Marshall that we had in our hospital died thirty-six hours ago. How is your agent with the thallium poisoning?"

"I got word that he died this morning. They told me when I first reported in to the local embassy."

"So, there was no saving him."

"No. None of the antidotes or medicine that we gave him worked."

"I thought maybe the antidote, Prussian Blue, would have some effect."

"Normally it would but this was a special derivative that had a special molecular arrangement that we could not figure out in such a quick time frame. It had to be from a CIA lab. It was too complex and effective."

"Yes. I am sure you are right. Now let me brief you on what we are doing and then you can go get some rest and come back tomorrow morning.

"Tomorrow morning we will fly to Bushehr and concentrate our efforts out of there."

"If I remember correctly Bushehr is a large coastal city where your government is building a nuclear reactor."

"Yes, that is right. We think that the American assassin and whoever is helping her will try to make their escape from that area. If they can get a boat out to sea and sail west or northwest for approximately a hundred miles then they will be right in the middle of an American Naval Carrier group."

"Are there any other possible escape routes?"

"It is possible that they may try to escape from Bandar Abbas but that is much further south and a long ways away from the American Navy."

Wu thought for a moment and said, "Bushehr is the obvious choice but if I were working on the American side, I would go to Bandar and escape south to India."

"But Bardar is where our main naval fleet is anchored. We could catch anyone there."

"Maybe, maybe not", Wu countered.

The conversation died for a few moments and then Akbar spoke, "You should go to your hotel and get some sleep and then meet me at the airport tomorrow morning at 8:00 am."

Wu nodded and Akbar escorted him out of the building and helped him get a taxi back to the hotel.

The ride yesterday from Yazd to Kerman had been uneventful for Sudie and her team but this morning they had a big decision to make. Would they turn toward Bushehr and the closeness of the American Navy or would they head further south and try to make their escape from Bandar Abbas?

"Why shouldn't we try Bushehr? It's only a hundred miles from the safety of the navy and the antidote I need?" Sudie said.

"I know Sudie", Shaheen said. "It is tempting, but Adel tells us that it is crawling with agents looking for you. Jafar and I have

146

worked in Bushehr before and we know how dangerous it is. You have to realize that because of all the nuclear construction and the presence of nuclear scientists in that town there is more government eyes there than you can imagine. Adel tells us that it will be safer to leave from the Bandar Abbas area."

"But that's right in the middle of the Iran's main naval base."

"And that is the beauty of it. They will not suspect it as much as Bushehr."

"But if I can escape from there, where will I go?"

"You will sail out into the Arabian Sea, bypass the coast of Pakistan, and sail south, down the coast of India. You should have no trouble getting to an American or British consulate once you land there."

"But I need that antidote. I am getting sicker every day."

"If you get caught in Bushehr they will never allow you to have the antidote. It is best to sail out of Bandar Abbas."

Sudie sighed, leaned back in her chair and said, "OK, but let my people know where we are going and maybe they can make arrangements to get the antidote to me somehow."

"Do not worry, Sudie. You are our guest and responsibility. A responsibility, because of our culture, that we take very seriously. We will do our best to take care of you. Now let us get in the car and start for Bandar Abbas. We will drive until we get to the outskirts of town just before the checkpoint, and see how Adel plans to get us into town past the checkpoints."

Sudie finished with some bread and washed it down with tea. It was practically the only thing that she could stomach without throwing up. The fruit they gave her never had a chance on her stomach because of the citric acid. She got up, let Sanjar apply the morning's makeup, grabbed a small bag, and got in the back seat of the car with the others.

I miss Eric, she thought.

In Washington, Eric was called into the Director's office and motioned to sit down.

147

"Eric, that was good work on the Wu case. Also, on finding the electronic leak in our phone system."

"Thank you sir. It was satisfying to tag Wu and get him out of the country. Hopefully, I put a little dent in his career."

"I doubt it. He's well connected and will probably get a promotion. Anyway, I have something else for you to do. It concerns your girlfriend, Sudie."

He sat upright in his seat and said, "What's that, sir?" He had not heard anything about her in a couple of weeks. He only knew that she was on a dangerous mission.

"Sudie was sent on a mission to poison Beking. She accomplished her mission but she came in contact with the poison. Some of it got on her skin. It doesn't work as fast as it does when ingested but she's probably getting pretty sick by now. The last information that I've heard was that an Iranian team associated with the CIA is helping to get her out of Iran. There's a package that will be dropped to them tonight with instructions and some specialized equipment to aid them in their escape, but no antidote."

"Why no antidote?"

"The lab that made the poison has either lost or destroyed the antidote."

"How did that happen?" Eric said, his voice rising.

"We don't believe it was intentional. They say that they have protocols that make them destroy poisons and antidotes at specified periods. They think that they accidently destroyed the antidote last month."

"What does that mean for Sudie. She's not going to die is she?"

"No, no. I don't think so. They are working feverishly to remake the antidote. It should be ready within twenty-four to thirty-six hours."

"How do we get it to her?"

"That's where you come in. Since Beking's espionage case is still officially a FBI case, I am detaching you as our liaison to NCIS in the Indian Ocean, probably at Camp Lemonier in Djibouti."

"Where's Djibouti?"

"It's a small coastal country on the eastern side of Africa; sometimes referred to as the Horn of Africa."

"NCIS, that's Navy, right?"

"Yes, they're a civilian criminal investigative wing of the Navy. You will work with them and also, loosely with the CIA. You will take the antidote with you. From Djibouti you will either deploy to the fleet in the Persian Gulf or to somewhere in the Indian Ocean, maybe Diego Garcia. As soon as the antidote is ready you are to pick it up and report to Andrews Air Force Base here in Washington and fly straight to Djibouti. There's a C-130 on standby waiting for you and the antidote. We have to get it to her as fast as possible. The longer she goes without it the more it damages or destroys parts of her internal organs."

"Where's the lab?" Eric said, standing up to go.

It was dusk when Sudie's team arrived on the outskirts of Bandar Abbas. They waited in the car, off the road, behind a dune and a dip in the land. It was a spot that Jafar said that he had used before when having clandestine meetings. He said Adel would join them soon.

Forty-five minutes later Adel arrived in a dune buggy, also with a serious muffler system. He parked his buggy and walked toward their car, smiling. Everyone got out of the car to greet him. It was the first time that Sudie had ever seen him, their guardian and path maker. Everyone went through the greeting pleasantries and then Adel was introduced to Sudie.

"I am pleased to meet you Adel, but please forgive my looks, Sanjar has outdone himself in his efforts to make me look ugly."

"Miss Sudie, I am pleased to meet you also. You must be an important person with so many assets pulled in to aid you."

"I don't know how important I am but I am certainly a scared person."

"No, she is not!" interjected Shaheen. "She is calm and brave."

"Do not worry about your looks. I am well aware of Sanjar's abilities", Adel said. "We will have to wait here until about 2:00 am tonight. There will be a package parachuted to us from a plane very high up. It will have instructions and equipment that Miss Sudie will need to help her escape."

"Surely it will have my antidote", Sudie said, excited about finally receiving her medicine.

"Let us hope so", said Shaheen.

They laid a blanket on the ground and had a picnic supper. Sudie ate what she could but her stomach hurt, more so every day. After supper they got back in the car and tried to sleep until the 2:00 am parachute drop. Adel laid a blanket on the ground and slept there.

As the evening grew dark, the temperature dropped and Sudie became comfortable enough to sleep, although fitfully.

It was almost 2:00 am over Southern Iran and a B-2 stealth bomber out of Diego Garcia was closing in on its drop coordinates. Normally they would be dropping a Sherpa, a GPS guided parachute system, but the winds over Southern Iran, at this time of the year, were too stiff and the chance of the package landing off course was too great. Besides, the Sherpa was normally used to deliver 1,000 to 2,000 lbs of supplies and too big for a B-2's bomb bay. Tonight, the package was small, less than fifty pounds.

What they were dropping had only recently been developed and did not even have an official name yet, although the air crew called it the *supply bomb*. It was made of wood (to avoid radar) and shaped like a bomb with a door that opened to a cavity where critical supplies or equipment could be stored. The inside was coated with egg-crate foam cushioning. The supply bomb looked like a wooden JDAM bomb, a bomb that has a GPS fin-guidance system that could place it within twenty-feet of its target. The supply bomb would drop until the radar altimeter indicated that it was five hundred feet above the ground and then it would pop its chute. The chute would have barely enough time to open, slow, and then hit the ground, almost dead on target, every time.

At 2:00 am Sudie's team was leaning against the car, waiting for something to drop out of the sky. At 2:03 they heard something that sounded like a muffled pop, as if someone had shaken out a blanket with a hard pop.

A few seconds later Adel pointed and said, "There it is."

A wooden bomb attached to a parachute had landed about twenty feet from them. They all ran to it and Jafar opened the hatch on the device and started pulling out equipment. There was a GPS unit made for a sea-going vessel, a satellite telephone, cell phones, and an envelope with some instructions.

"Where's the antidote?" Sudie asked.

"I do not see it", Shaheen said. "Let me see what is in the envelope."

"What does it say about the antidote?" Sudie said.

Shaheen read for a moment and said, "Sudie, it is not here. There was a problem at the lab that makes the antidote but it will be delivered as soon as they can get it ready for you."

Sudie turned and walked back to the car. She leaned back against the side of the car and looked up at the sky. A tear ran down her cheek as she slid down by the car to a sitting position, her arms crossed on her knees, and her head down on her arms. Her whole abdomen was cramping and her feet were beginning to burn; classic signs of thallium poisoning.

Adel and the rest of the group put the equipment on the dune buggy and buried the supply bomb. Everyone got in the car except for Adel and Sudie.

"Miss Sudie, you will come with me on the dune buggy to the safe house. The rest of the team will go through the checkpoint outside of Bandar Abbas and on to the safe house", Adel said.

"I can't go with the others in the car?"

"Miss Sudie, your picture at every checkpoint now. Everyone looking for you."

"OK, she said meekly, but won't the guards at the checkpoint be suspicious of a savari with only three passengers?"

"Jafar will tell them that they let one passenger off at Kerman and the other three passengers paid for the empty seat themselves so as not to have to wait for the next day to pick up another paying passenger. It happens occasionally, especially on long trips."

The ride over the open country was painful for Sudie but she managed to control the pain. Eventually they came to the outskirts of Bandar Abbas through an open field and parked in the courtyard of a house in a residential section on the edge of town. Shaheen and the others were already there and anxiously waiting for her. They were all exhausted and went to bed as soon as they could. They slept until noon the next day. They would have to plan how they were going to get Sudie onto the fishing boat that would provide her escape.

There was a cool breeze sifting through the Vietnamese jungle tonight. Jay was dreaming about the time the family had taken a camping trip to the Outer Banks of North Carolina near the Hatteras Lighthouse. They had a large tent that they slept in. The ocean breeze was cool and made for good sleeping. During the day his mother had found a small wind break behind one of the dunes where she did a little cooking, but mostly, she made sandwiches.

He was fishing and Tancy was by his side helping him with bait and conversation. It had taken some practice but he had mastered the technique of slinging a one-ounce triangle weight with a hooked worm using the old spinning reel. He had to be careful and apply his thumb to the spinning reel with just enough pressure to not stop it, but keep it from over-spinning and fouling the reel, with a tangled mess of line. His Dad had made him practice this at home so he would be ready when he got to Hatteras, although he thought the real reason was that his Dad didn't want to spend a good part of his vacation untangling the reel.

Tancy and their mother would walk the beach looking for interesting shells and occasionally coming upon the skeleton of old shipwrecks that had washed ashore from the dangerous reefs of Diamond Shoals, a little off shore. In the afternoons, he and Tancy would swim in the ocean, although they were careful not to get more than waist deep in the treacherous surf. When they got tired they would sit on the sand and Tancy would build a sandcastle; he would build a fort around it, with a moat. When he could not keep his eyes open anymore he would go to the tent and lie down on top of his sleeping bag and sleep until supper. He always felt that it was some of the best sleeping he had ever done.

He and his dad caught Spanish Mackerel, Spot-Tail Trout, Blues, and if they were lucky, a King Mackerel. They ate sandwiches during the day but at night his mother would cook some of the fish they had caught and cleaned. He thought nothing had ever tasted better.

After supper he would help his Dad build a fire. Campers on either side of them for a half-mile would come and bring their web-strapped aluminum chairs. As a state senator, his father would hold court over the campfire. They would sit, talk politics, tell fish stories and funny jokes until midnight. He and Tancy would roast marshmallows and listen to the adults talk.

On their last day of vacation he was fishing at his favorite spot when his father walked over to where he was standing and said, "Son, it's time to put the rod and reel up. Vacation is almost over." There was a pause and then he said, "Your time here will end soon."

He had dreamed this same dream many times but his father had never said that before and that last sentence reverberated in his mind as if he was in a sound chamber, repeating itself over and over.

Chapter Fourteen

The turbulence in the small plane on the flight from Tehran to Bushehr had left Wu a little nauseous. Akbar had taken it in stride. He was used to it since he traveled all over Iran in small agency planes. They were met by a couple of his agents and were driven into town to an old office building that they used as their intelligence headquarters where they convened a meeting to get an update on the latest intelligence about Operation Medea.

"Gentlemen, please tell me you have something", Akbar said.

It was quiet around the table and Wu noted that no one wanted to make eye contact with Akbar. After a moment of silence Akbar looked at the head agent for the Bushehr office and raised his eyebrows and lifted his hands upwards, silently asking the status of the search.

The man cleared his throat and said, "Sir, we have searched every incoming savari, every bus, and every car that passed through the checkpoints into Bushehr. We have also had agents on twenty-four hour watches at every boat and fishing dock up and down our coastline for fifty miles in each direction. Agents are roaming the streets and watching known activists for anything unusual and we still have come up with nothing unusual."

"Has there been any unusual activity on the American Navy?"

"No. they are still about one hundred miles northwest of us conducting what appears to be routine operations."

Akbar though for a moment. "Maybe they are not going to try to escape from here. I would have wagered that this would be where they would try it." He turned and looked at Wu. "Have you heard anything from your embassy?"

"No, nothing. I would have thought I would have received a text asking me to call them by now, but I have heard nothing, which means they have not heard or observed anything unusual either."

"Anything at all from the checkpoints out of Tehran down to this area?"

"No sir, nothing unusual at all", one of the men said.

There was another long pause as Akbar leaned back and wondered what else he could do. Finally he said, "Do you have the photos of each car from each checkpoint from Tehran to this area?"

"Yes, here they are", an agent said placing four thick folders on the table with a photo of each car and its passengers that had passed through Esfahan, Yzad, Kerman, and Bandar Abbas in the last four days.

Akbar did not know what to do next, but to look like he knew what he was doing; he opened the file photos from the checkpoint at Esfahan and started thumbing through them. He knew it was a useless gesture but he wanted to show his men how diligent he was and how diligent he wanted them to be. He did this for a minute or two and was about to close the file when one of the photos grabbed his attention. He recognized one of the men in the picture. He knew that he recognized the face and finally the name came to him.

"Ah ha!" Akbar said. "I know this man. He works with the theaters and movie industry around Tehran." Akbar being sort of a rogue, liked to visit the theater dressing rooms and movie sets to meet and talk with the women.

"His name is Sanjar and he works as a makeup artist. What would he be doing this far south?" Akbar spread out the files and said, "See if you can spot him in any of the other folders."

Soon they had isolated his group picture at Yzad, Kerman, and Bandar Abbas. The group had four passengers until they reached the Bandar Abbas checkpoint and then there were only three passengers.

Akbar held up the picture from Esfahan, which had the best quality photo of the group, and said, "Send this back to Intelligence in Tehran. See if they can identify these four people, especially the one that is not in the photo at Bandar Abbas."

Akbar motioned Wu over to where he was sitting at the table and said, "Look at that fourth person; how unusual she looks, almost grotesque. I wonder if that is a make-up job from our friend, Sanjar, the make-up artist."

155

Wu looked at the picture. "She certainly is disfigured. She looks nothing like the photo of the stewardess sent in from Venezuela....well, maybe the eyes, or the one non-disfigured eye could be similar, but my God, Akbar, that's a real stretch."

"Maybe, but it is the only lead we have besides we will know something in a few hours. Let's fly on down to Bandar Abbas."

"Do you have a good team down there? Wu asked.

"Not as good as here. I have a couple of good agents there and a wildcard sometimes agent, named Borzoo."

"Why is he a wildcard?"

"He is sort of a free-lance agent. We call on him from time to time. He has ties with Pakistan and he claims to be loosely associated with Al-Qaeda.

"Al-Qaeda?

"Yes, he says he has ties with them, although I doubt it. He is too much of a thief, smuggler, and loose cannon for Al-Qaeda to trust him, but he does turn up some useful information occasionally."

Two hours later they were met at the Bandar Abbas airport by two of Akbar's agents. After introductions they got in the car and headed into town.

"We have some information concerning the photographs you sent to Tehran for analysis", one agent said.

"That was quick. What did they find out?" Akbar demanded.

"Three of the people are loosely associated with the opposition party, although they are not known to be radical, only sympathetic. I think it is interesting that one of them, a fellow named Jafar, is a make-up artist for the theaters and cinema business around Tehran. He could make a pretty stewardess look like a disfigured street beggar."

"Ah, yes. That is what I think also. By the time they reached Bandar Abbas they could not get through the checkpoint with all the tightened security that has been added in the last forty-eight hours. That Jafar fellow was able to disguise her through all of the other checkpoints until they got here, so they smuggled her in another way."

"This is a big city, Akbar, how will you find her?" Wu asked.

"It will not be so much finding her here in the city but by setting up tighter security at any escape point where we might have a chance to catch her", Akbar said to Wu and then turned to one of his agents. "Call Bushehr and have them send down about fifty agents."

It was dusk. Sudie, Shaheen, Sanjar, Jafar, and Adel were sitting around a table in a safe house in Bandar Abbas. Adel was explaining how they were going to smuggle Sudie out from Bandar in a fishing boat.

Adel was explaining, "Some new information has been received. They know about all five of us. They know we are here in Bandar. The city will soon be crawling with agents."

"So how will I get past them and out of this country?" Sudie asked.

"We will either, one, smuggle you into Pakistan, which is a few hours down the road, or, two, smuggle you into a fishing boat and out to sea."

"The Iranian Navy's main base is here in Bandar. Won't they come after me?"

"They will come after you with everything they have, but if we can get you out tonight and head down the coast to India we should get a good head start on them. We will not stay close to the coast line like they might expect but go further out to sea and head south and when we have gotten far enough away then we will turn East and head straight into a port in India and find the nearest English Consulate."

"So, what do you think is best? Pakistan or out to sea", Sudie asked.

"I think out to sea is best. There could be a problem at the border when we try to enter Pakistan. They could gladly turn you over to the Iranians."

"Where's the boat?

It is ten miles south of the city, waiting for us."

"Who will be on the boat with me?

157

"Only me."

"Adel, can you handle a fishing boat with sails all by yourself?"

"Of course, I was raised on a fishing boat. Now if I was actually fishing I would need a crew but from going from one point to another, I can handle that easily."

"When we get out to sea how will my people find me?"

"I will use the satellite phone and the GPS that was parachuted in to us and give them our coordinates and I have no doubts that your Navy will find us."

"God, I hope so and soon."

"I want all of us to leave now while there is plenty of traffic on the road. There is another safe house at the beach where the boat is waiting for us. We will stay there until about 2:00 am and then you and I will put out to sea."

"What about Shaheen and the rest of the group?"

"They will go into hiding. It is possible that we all may have to settle in another Middle East country. Your CIA has promised us their help in this matter. Who knows, we may even end up in the United States."

Sudie looked at Shaheen, smiled and said, "Well, you said you wanted to visit the United States. Here's your chance."

Shaheen could only smile and give Sudie a hug. She was full of mixed emotions about leaving her family, friends, and country, but she was excited about getting a chance to see the world outside of the Middle East. "Hurry, go with Adel and make your escape."

"Are all of your men in position?" Wu asked Akbar.

"Yes. They have all of Bandar's harbors and beaches covered."

"How far north and south?"

"About twenty miles in each direction."

"What about that man, Borzoo, the wild man?"

"He is not a wild man. I said he is a wildcard."

Wu looked at Akbar quizzically, not quite understanding his meaning.

"A wildcard is western slang, meaning anything goes or anything can happen."

"And you put this man in this important search?"

"He is filling in at a place where it is very unlikely that they will escape from, besides it is a remote section of the beach, hardly used."

Alarm bells went off in Wu's head. *That is exactly the place I would try to escape from if it was me*, he thought.

"Akbar, it is almost two o'clock. Would you have one of your men drive me to Borzoo's position?"

Akbar looked at Wu with some frustration but then signaled one of his men to drive Wu to Borzoo's assigned point south of town.

"Sudie, do you have enough strength to swim thirty yards out to the boat?" Adel asked.

"Yes, I think so. Is there a ladder to get on the boat with?"

"Yes, if you can get there I will help pull you onto the boat."

Adel had Sudie sit on the beach while he swam to the boat holding a bag over his head and out of the water. It held the satellite telephone, the GPS, and some other small items. That was all he needed to get on the boat as it was already well supplied with everything else they should need for a two-week long sea trip. He returned and swam beside Sudie to the boat. She was weak and had a little trouble climbing up the rope ladder, but Adel, already on board, pulled her upon deck.

The boat was not one of the bigger fishing boats that are common for that area. It was thirty-six feet long and could travel with a combination of motor and sail. These older type of fishing boats usually kept closer to the shore but it was not unusual for the poorer fishermen to take them far out into the Arabian Sea and into the Indian Ocean. Sleeping quarters were strung hammocks. Most sailors preferred hammocks because they rocked with the waves giving the occupant less motion to deal with.

Shaheen watched them leave from the edge of the dunes just before the beach area began. She felt proud of herself and her group for doing their part in helping in this escape from what she considered Iranian tyranny. She watched until the boat was almost out of sight and started to get up from the grass in the dunes when she noticed a man walking down the beach, coming in her direction.

The man stopped right in front of her and looked at the footprints in the sand leading out to the water. He cupped his eyes and stared out into the ocean. Shaheen could still barely see the boat but she did not know if he could since he did not know where to look. He took out his cell phone.

She could not make out all of the words but it sounded like, "....think I found them...sou...of town...signal is weak... call again soon."

Shaheen knew she could not let him make that second phone call. She would have to do something, anything, to stop him. She pulled her scarf off of her hair and walked toward him. She would have to pretend to be a prostitute which was abundant in Bandar Abbas.

"Sir, it is a nice night for a walk on the beach, is it not," Shaheen said.

Borzoo jumped, but recovered quickly from being startled. He knew what she was. It was two o'clock in the morning, she was walking the beach by herself, and she was not bothering to cover her hair.

"Yes, it is a beautiful night and the stars shine beautifully on your face."

What an old line, she thought.

"Would you be interested in walking with me to the dunes?" she asked coyly.

Borzoo was tempted. She was attractive. "I really have to go. I have an important phone call to make."

Shaheen stepped close to him, where her breasts were touching his chest and put one arm around him. "Are you sure? It would not have to take long."

He looked at her beautiful almond-shaped eyes. He closed his eyes and tilted his head backwards, debating in his mind whether to make love with this beauty or go make his call. He waited too long.

Shaheen had reached within her dress and pulled out a knife and plunged it deep into his stomach. He stood there for a couple of seconds looking down at her. Shaheen panicked slightly, because he would not fall, so she rocked the knife back and forth, hoping to cut an interior artery. He fell to the sand and was dead within a minute. She looked at his body and thought, *Sudie, I hope you will appreciate the fact that I have killed a man for you and by this act I may have endangered my eternal soul to hell, so that you can escape.*

She ran back to the house and told the men what she had done. It took them about thirty minutes to tie ropes to him, anchored with cinder blocks, and drag him as far as they could out in the water so he would not be discovered anytime soon. They left for another safe house where they would plan their own escape out of Iran.

Three days later some boys were playing on the beach near where Borzoo had been killed and drug out to sea. One of the boys saw something bobbing in the surf and alerted the other boys. They looked at it for two or three minutes until one boy was brave enough to wade out to it and confirm that it was what they thought it was. A dead body.

"Do not touch it! Go get the police. I will keep an eye on it," one boy said.

The boys ran off and in thirty minutes a policeman was there, confirming the boy's story. He radioed for an ambulance and an investigation team.

Four hours later Akbar and Wu were at the morgue looking at Borzoo's body.

"Has any of your men checked out the area, questioned residents, and tried to find out what kind of boat was anchored there recently?" Wu asked Akbar.

"Yes, I just talked to one of my investigators. No one saw anything and so many different fishing boats tie-up and anchor off those shores every night that the residents hardly pay attention to them, but one person said that they thought it was a smaller fishing boat, maybe with sails."

"Having sails can narrow the search down", Wu said.

"Maybe, but my investigator said the person was unsure and it could just as well not have sails. It is really not very much to go on. Borzoo could have been killed by a mugger or a drunk sailor and our assassins could be escaping through a Pakistani checkpoint; although I doubt it. That would be taking a real chance."

"The clues lead you here; nowhere else. I suggest that you use all the assets at your disposal to run down and check out every fishing boat in the Indian Ocean heading south, especially those heading down the coast of India."

Akbar could not fault Wu's logic. It was not much to go on, but he did know that they had come to this area. A man looking for them was killed, and there are plenty of boats available to make their escape in.

"Let us get back to my local office. I have to make a couple of phone calls; one to headquarters back home and one to the Admiral of the Iranian Navy."

"You can command the Navy to start the search on your own authority?" Wu asked.

"No, but the phone call back to Tehran can make that happen."

Late that afternoon Akbar and Wu were sitting in the Admiral's office. The Admiral had already received a phone call briefing him on the situation and he had received instructions to cooperate with Akbar using any and all of the Navy's resources as necessary.

"Akbar, my old friend, the Navy is at your service. All ships will leave port tomorrow to find this boat and assassin. Would you like to be on board one of my frigates, to aid in the search?" the Admiral asked.

"No, no, I need to direct things from my headquarters."

Wu interrupted. "Sir, I would like to be on the frigate that would be in charge of the search. If I can be in contact with my embassy while on board I could assist with satellite imagery."

Akbar looked at Wu and said, "Are you sure? You are not prone to sea sickness I hope."

"No problem. I was in the Chinese Navy as a young man."

"Good. Good. Your assistance with satellite imagery will be a great aid to us. The Navy would be glad to have you assist in the search", the Admiral said.

It was 8:00 o'clock Sunday morning. Eric was having a bowl of cereal and sipping on a cup of coffee when the phone rang. *God, who could be calling me this early on a Sunday*, he thought. He started not to answer it until he looked at the caller ID and saw that it was from FBI Headquarters.

"Hello."

"Eric, grab your bag. We have the antidote here at the office waiting for you", the Director said.

"Yes sir", Eric managed to get out. "I'll be there as soon as I can."

"Hurry. When you get here come to my office where you'll get a quick briefing and the antidote and then you'll be taken to Andrews Air Force Base where a C-130 is waiting for you."

"Be there as soon as I can, sir."

Eric took a quick shower, shaved, brushed his teeth, and grabbed a pre-packed bag. An hour and ten minutes later he walked into the Director's office. There was also someone there from the Pentagon, and the CIA. A small package sat on the table.

"Eric, sit down", the Director said pointing to a chair. He did not bother to introduce the other two men by name. Eric did not need to know. The Director put his hand on the package and said, "This is the antidote and there is no more for now. Guard it carefully."

"Don't worry sir, I will."

The man from the CIA spoke up, "Eric, here's what's happening as best as we can make out. We have been dependent on implanted agents for our information up to now. We know that Sudie has finally made it off of Iranian soil and out to sea, but not outside of the Iranian Navy's reach. Sudie has not made contact with us yet. We hope to get their coordinates and heading soon. She is in a fishing boat headed for the western coast of India, maybe Mumbai."

"Does our Navy have any assets in that area that can pick her up?"

"Not at the present time. Usually we have a ship in transit in the Indian Ocean either going to or from the fleet in the Persian Gulf but her escape has happened in a time frame where nothing is anywhere near her."

"Nothing at all?"

"Well, we do have a destroyer, the *USS Farragut*, rounding the tip of Africa, heading toward the Indian Ocean but it could be several days before she can get within reach of her."

"Can the *Farragut* defend itself from the Iranian Navy?" Eric asked.

"It could probably take care of itself with any Navy in the world except for the Russians, Chinese, or British. No, the Iranians will be no problem for the *Farragut*."

The man from the Pentagon spoke up, "You'll fly to Camp Lemonier at Djibouti, that's on the East Coast of Africa, and operate out of there. From there, depending on the situation, you can be flown to the Persian Gulf, the Maldives, or as far south as Diego Garcia. You will be accompanied by a Navy Seal Team. They may not be needed but they will be there, just in case.

The FBI Director joined back into the discussion. "Eric, there are instructions accompanying the antidote. Any doctor can read them and know what to do. Make sure they read them because she will have to take a series of injections at specified time intervals for the antidote to be the most effective. It may work out that a member of the Seal team may have to parachute to a ship or small boat and give the antidote to the ship's doctor or if the situation warrants, give the first injection to her himself."

"Does anyone know how far the poison has progressed in her?" Eric asked.

"No one knows for sure. We know she's feeling the effects of it. Luckily, she was only exposed to a drop or two on her skin and that was quickly washed off, but it is wearing on her. Even though it was a small amount, the poison is slowly, very slowly, working on her internal organs. Given enough time it will eventually destroy those organs.

The CIA officer spoke again. "Eric, Sudie has done a great service to our country. We will spare no expense to get her back. She doesn't know it, but the photos she took with the micro-camera hidden in the pin on her hat has helped us to expose at least two more spy rings."

"Just with photographs?"

"Yes, when we researched who a couple of those people were, it led us to people who were spying for the Chinese and the Venezuelans. So, what she did paid off big time. Whatever it takes, we're going to get her back."

The director stepped forward and said, "When you get to Djibouti you will work out of the NCIS office there. There'll be CIA personnel there also. Now, grab your bag, the antidote, and take this agency credit card and get to the airport. They're waiting on you."

"Yes sir."

"Eric? Don't get carried away with that credit card, ok?"

"No sir. I won't", Eric said, as he exited the room.

After Eric had left the room the three men sat down to discuss another matter.

"How is Operation Greyhair progressing?" the Director asked.

The CIA and the Pentagon looked at each other and then the Pentagon General said, "It's progressing according to schedule. We have an operative picked out and he is going through some advanced training. He should be on his way soon."

"Do you think he can fit in the intended environment without being noticed?"

"Yes, I believe so. He speaks perfect Vietnamese."

As soon as Eric arrived at Andrews Air Force Base they put him in a service car and sped toward the tarmac where his C-130 aircraft was waiting. As he walked up the back ramp of the airplane he could see the casual contempt in the eyes of the Seal Team members. They were courteous but still he was not one of them and they were being delayed because of this civilian.

Eric smiled at them and gave them a quick head nod to let them know that he was respectful enough to recognize their presence. He did not try to engage them in conversation except to hold up the package containing the antidote and say, "Gentleman, this package is what your mission is about. Protect it at all costs."

They looked at him; a couple of them gave him a slight nod of acknowledgement. Almost immediately the aircraft revved its engines and started taxiing toward the runway.

The flight to Djibouti took a little over twenty-four hours. Eric tried to sleep but he could only sleep so much. He took out a book and read until his eyes felt like they were going to cross, then he tried talking to different people. He talked to the cockpit crew, the loadmaster, and tried with the Seal Team with limited success. The Seal Team leader did talk with him for about thirty minutes, trying to find out all that Eric knew about what the team may be asked to accomplish.

When he stepped out of the plane in Djibouti the heat nearly knocked him down. Twenty minutes later he was in the offices of the local NCIS detachment.

Almost everyone stationed at Djibouti slept in tents, open air Quonset huts, or shipping containers. The base was at a primitive level but there was plenty of construction going on to bring it up a notch or two.

"Hi. I'm NCIS Agent Daniels. I'll be your contact here."

"Hello Agent Daniels, I'm FBI Agent Dawkins."

"Pleased to meet you. I've arranged for you to bunk at my place."

"Hope it's air-conditioned."

"You're in luck. It's one of the few places on base that is. If you can imagine a concrete shell, about the length of a small shipping container, then stack six, left to right, then another row on top, then that is where we'll be living; the most luxurious apartments on base. I'm putting you on the couch; otherwise, you'd be sleeping in a tent with your Seal buddies."

"Do you have a refrigerator where I can put this small package?"

"I guess it'll fit in the bottom of my little dorm fridge, but I'll have to give up some beer space."

"Thanks Daniels, When we leave I'll buy you a case of beer to put back in it."

It had turned into a waiting game for Eric. *Hurry up and wait*, he thought. He would spend half a day at NCIS and then the other half at the CIA's office. Some afternoons he would go with some of the other soldiers and sailors to the nearby orphanage and play soccer with the children.

The Catholic orphanage was run by the *Sisters of the Nativity* and they had two orphanages; one for boys and one for girls, which they operated on a shoestring budget. One Navy Seebee unit was so appalled by what the nuns were cooking on that they fabricated a large grill and presented it to them.

Most of the children were orphaned by parents who had died of AIDS which is prevalent around Djibouti and the Horn of Africa. The thing that touched Eric the most was, when he would visit inside the orphanage's pitiful buildings, the children would immediately hold up their little arms to be held, even if they were eating their sparse meals. Eric considered the nuns to be saints on earth.

The nuns said they were trying to keep the children alive long enough for them to be adopted, which many of them would be, by French families. Eric donated more money than he could really afford to the nuns so that they could buy food and vaccine for the children. He specified that most of the money was to go to the girl's orphanage because for some untold reason, most of the meager funds and donations they received went to the boy's orphanage.

167

Chapter Fifteen

Sgt. Trang loved the feel of a jet airliner as it accelerated down the runway. It scared some people but for him it was a feeling of raw power. It was taking him from Washington State to Vietnam where he would start his mission assignment. A few weeks ago he had been approached for a special mission. It seemed that he had unique skills for a mission that only a very few possessed. His parents had been refugees from Vietnam, therefore he spoke Vietnamese fluently. After high school he had joined the Army and had gone through airborne training. Next he tested himself by making it through Ranger training. He was proud of that Ranger tab on his sleeve. His next step in seeing how far he could push himself was Long Range Surveillance School. It was referred to as LRS and pronounced "lures". They were trained to go silently behind enemy lines and observe and report important battlefield intelligence. It was difficult training and difficult assignments, but he was accepted as a team member.

His most challenging test came when he wanted to try out for the Special Forces and become a Green Beret. His unit was reluctant to let him go, but he eventually prevailed and started the selection process. Selection lasts for several weeks and is a tremendous physical and mental challenge. He thought he could do anything since he was from a LRS unit, but the Special Forces selection process was almost inhuman and difficult to survive. He somehow managed to make it through without quitting or getting thrown out but he was not selected. He knew some of the men that got selected seemed more capable than him but he had hoped that he would be chosen. He was very disappointed and as he was packing his gear to go back to his unit in Fort Hood, Texas, one of the Special Forces' officers approached him and said that the Psychological Operations (PsyOps) people wanted to talk to him about becoming a member of a PhyOps team.

Being a PsyOps member would have all the benefits of being a Special Forces person, only he would not be allowed to wear the Green Beret. PhyOps recruited many people who almost became Green Berets, but for some reason they were not selected, especially if they were smart and had language skills. He asked to think about it for a couple of days, and then accepted. Now, all the training and learned skills had put him on this airplane for Hanoi.

For the last three weeks he had been trained in Vietnamese culture for the Hanoi area as it is today, not when his parents were in Vietnam. They brushed him up on language skills that would make him sound like he was from North Vietnam and not from the south.

His mission was to fly into Hanoi as a tourist, which would be no trouble, since many Americans visited Vietnam now; even cruise ships visited there. He was to rent a motorcycle and pretend to tour the back country of North Vietnam. His real mission was to go to Quyet Tien, hide in the woods, and find the small clearing where the American POW's were being held. He was to observe only, and he was not to be detected. From a distance he was to take pictures and learn all he could about the prisoners. How many? How healthy did they seem to be? How many guards were there? Who else was there besides the prisoners and guards? He was to observe for five days and then return to the Hanoi airport and come home.

He was told that a CIA agent would make contact with him and provide him with a PRC-137 radio; a Special Forces favorite. The 137 was a high frequency radio on which he could send and receive secure text messages and pictures from anywhere in the world. A NSA listening post in Hawaii would pick up the information and relay it to Washington.

Washington would use the information to help the Army's Delta Force team which was preparing for a POW rescue operation if the President gave the operation a green light. Delta Force is the best of the Army's Green Berets and specializes in hostage rescue as compared to the Navy's Seal Team Six, which is the best of the Navy Seals and specializes in counter-terrorism.

About half way through the flight a young Vietnamese woman

got up from her seat and sat down beside Sgt. Trang and started a conversation. She was attractive and he enjoyed talking to her, actually he was flattered. He had been in training for so long that he rarely had time to develop a relationship or even talk to a "nice" girl.

They had been talking for about forty-five minutes when she said, "Has it ever snowed in Hanoi?"

He was stunned. It was the first part of a three-part coded phrase that his CIA contact would use to identify himself or herself as the case seemed to be. He paused for about five seconds and responded with, "Only when Ho Chi Minh died."

She responded with the third part, "Yes, that was a cold day in hell."

Trang could only look at her for a few seconds.

"Close your mouth", she said. "You'll catch a bug or something."

Embarrassed, he closed his mouth and finally said in a whisper, "I never imagined my CIA contact would be someone like you."

"Good. Hopefully, neither does anyone else."

"What happens when we reach Hanoi?"

"You take a taxi to your hotel and check in. I will come to your room around 8:00 pm. I will have a present for you."

"Is there anything else you might be giving me?, Trang asked with a mischievous smile.

"Absolutely not. I'm not that type of girl". She did not say it angrily because she did not want to hurt his feeling. She was actually attracted to him.

"If you came earlier we could have dinner", Trang persevered.

"Nope. Might attract unwanted attention. I'm going back to my seat now."

"OK— I'm sorry that I made you feel uncomfortable and scared you back to your seat."

"You didn't scare me. See you later." *Ouu*, she thought, *he likes me*. But with her personality and looks she knew most men did.

I didn't even get her name! Trang thought. *Oh well, be cool. I'll get it tonight.*

The men were sweaty and tired. They were sitting on the edge of a clearing in the panhandle of Florida near Hurlburt AFB, drinking water and watching the sunrise. They are an A-Team from the Army's elite and secretive Delta Force. They were resting after a nightlong exercise simulating a hostage rescue on a small clearing in a simulated jungle setting. Every night they practiced their specialty, hostage rescue, on a dozen Army specialists who pretended to be hostages. They had done this same exercise, with small variations, for two weeks, and they would continue doing it every night, except for Sundays, until they were actually sent on the mission.

They had no idea where or when the real mission will take place but scuttlebutt was that it would probably be in South America. These exercises did not seem too different from other exercises that they had performed in the past but the men had noticed one obvious factor that was different. This time, instead of using helicopters, they were using a Air Force V-22 Osprey, an airplane that can take-off and land like a helicopter. The advantage was greater speed, range, and capacity and it was about seventy-five per cent quieter than a helicopter. They were comforted by the fact that they could mount an M-134 minigun, a type of Gatling gun, on the back ramp of the airplane. It gave them tremendous firepower. It could literally obliterate a small village or an opposing force in seconds, if need be.

Kim-Ly's taxi ride from her apartment to Sgt. Trang's hotel took about ten minutes. She clutched her oversized purse near to her body. It contained the secretive radio that Trang would use to send and receive messages while he was on assignment. She did not know what his assignment was exactly, but as his handler, for the five to seven days while he was in North Vietnam, it was her responsibility to see that he got the assets he needed to complete his mission. She knew the radio, as secretive as it was, had been somewhat compromised in Afghanistan. One of them had been captured by the

Taliban in an ambushed convoy, but, they nor anyone else, had ever been able to break the encryption device on it.

Her thoughts turned to Sgt. Trang. She could not suppress or figure out why she was attracted to him. He was about her age and underneath he was Vietnamese just like her, although his upbringing in American society had given him a completely different personality and attitude from what she was used to. She had spent some time in America herself, mostly her college years, but her psyche was Vietnamese, not American, but that did not mean she was a loyal Vietnamese. Her eyes had been opened in America, where she could see what real democracy was. She wanted that for her country. She loved her country but she was not loyal to the present political regime.

The taxi stopped at Trang's new and modern hotel where many foreign tourists stayed. Kim-Ly paid the driver, walked inside, and rode the elevator to his floor. *Here goes*, she thought. *My first real assignment.*

Sgt. Trang jumped when he heard the knock on the door.

He opened the door a few inches, saw Kim-Ly, smiled and said, "Hi."

"Let me in", she said smiling back.

"Oh, sorry, come on in."

She walked in and sat on the bed. He sat down beside her, eyeing the large purse.

"Is my radio in there?"

"Yes, it is, but tell me first. What did you do this afternoon after you checked in?"

"Nothing in particular. I walked around this area of Hanoi, visited a couple of shops, ate in the hotel's restaurant for dinner, and came back to my room to watch some Vietnamese TV. Now that's a hoot; watching Clint Eastwood being dubbed in Vietnamese."

She smiled. She knew the movie he was talking about. It had been playing all week on the local TV. Satisfied with his answer she pulled a package out of her purse. It was wrapped in black plastic. She unwrapped the package and handed the PRC-137 radio to him.

He smiled when he touched it. "It's like what I'm use to working with. Where's the antenna wire?"

She pulled a wire out of the plastic wrapping and handed it to him. He checked it out for a few minutes and then wrapped it back in its plastic wrapping.

She watched him put it in his back pack and said, "Tomorrow you will check out of the hotel and rent a motorcycle from this rental agency." She handed him a map and an address. "We have an agent there who will give you a very good and reliable bike. You should be able to make it to your assigned area by tomorrow night. Get yourself and the bike off the road and hide the bike. Take your backpack with your radio, GPS, and supplies as you navigate to your assigned position."

"Do you know what my assignment is?" Trang asked.

"No, I don't know the nature of the assignment but I know the general area you're to go to. I can't imagine what you would be doing there. Although, I know what used to be there, but that's long gone, I'm sure."

"Maybe, maybe not", he said softly.

She wondered what he meant and said, "It will take you a day to get there. Three to five days for observation. The third and fourth days depend on you. It's your call. It'll take another day to get back here. When you check back in here, someone will notify me. I'll be looking for you in five to seven days. If you're not back in eight days, then a search will commence. Understood?"

"Yes, understood."

The attraction was becoming stronger. She wanted to grab his arm and pull him to her and tell him to be careful but she was his handler not his girlfriend. She knew from her conversation with him on the airplane and some CIA background material that he had never had a serious relationship with a woman. Maybe a broken heart or two in high school but the Army had occupied too much of his time for him to have had a serious girlfriend since then. *Hmmm*, she thought. *He's never been really damaged by another woman.*

She stood up and he remained sitting on the bed, looking up at her. She said, "Get a good night's sleep and start out early tomorrow. I'll see you in a few days." He did not say anything, he nodded as she left.

The more Kim-Ly thought about it the more she worried. She knew he was a highly trained army specialist with many skills and he could surely handle himself on this assignment. In his tee shirt and jeans he looked like a little boy and she was becoming scared for him, although she did not really know why. The two countries were not at war anymore. There were foreign tourists all over the country. He should be ok unless he was to spy on some secret army base that she did not know about.

She thought about that for a moment. *If the Americans think that there is something there, then they must have a good reason,* she thought. Trang's words of, *"maybe, maybe not"*, flashed through her mind again. Then she had a moment of realization. *Oh my God! It can't be that—that's impossible, there's none of them left.*

The motorcycle was a good one. The man at the rental place, a CIA front, went over the details of the bike with him, including a hidden compartment. The man had gone over the map with Trang and showed him pictures of intersections where he had to turn when the roads became confusing. He also showed him a photo of a place, near his target, where he could get off the road and quickly disappear into the trees. He would be able to hide his bike and trek in about five miles to his target area. It would take him all day and into the early evening to reach his destination.

The traffic was light on most of the roads once he got outside of Hanoi. There seemed to be no real rules of the road, just common sense. People passed slower traffic and you had to dodge children and animals in the road. Later in the afternoon he stopped to get something to eat. He found a roadside stand that had soft drinks and some American-looking granola bars. He bought two granola bars and a soft drink. From here on out it would be Army, ready to eat meals in a pouch. They would be generic with no indication of being military or American. He topped off his bike with gasoline since they had a pump. He wanted to be ready to go once his mission was complete.

He drove late into the evening and as the time approached 10:30 pm he knew he was getting close to his target area. The GPS told him that he was almost on top of his arrival point. He slowed down and started looking for the landscape that matched the picture he had been shown that morning. He was beginning to think he had missed it when he suddenly recognized the landscape. *Thank God for a clear night and a half moon*, he thought, or it would have been hard to recognize.

There was no one else on the road and no houses nearby, so no one noticed him when he cut off the bike and pushed it into the woods. It was a tough push for about a hundred yards. It was uphill with underbrush, but that would make it easier to hide. He built a small blind around the bike, camouflaged it, marked it in his GPS, and started walking toward his target following a path his GPS had laid out for him. The GPS was a special piece of technology. It looked normal but there was a panic feature on it that would allow him to push a three-button sequence and all instructions, directions, and past history would be erased and be unrecoverable.

It took him about two hours to get close to his target. He could have done it quicker but he tried to be as stealthy as possible. Soon, as he pushed some brush out of his way, he could see that a clearing was coming into view. It was about fifteen yards ahead. He stopped right there and unloaded his backpack and other equipment. He got his binoculars out of the backpack and crawled near the edge of the clearing and scanned the camp. It was like the satellite pictures they had shown him. There was the men's dormitory, the guard's building, what they thought was a medical dispensary, an open hut where they cooked and ate, and the graveyard.

Man, I would love to go tell them that we know that they are here and that help will soon be on the way, he thought, but he knew he could not do that. They might start acting different; someone could become suspicious, and they could be moved again.

175

He crawled back to his equipment and spent the next two to three hours setting up his camp. He had a small one-man pup tent to protect him from tropical rains that happened almost every afternoon. He had to dig a latrine and a refuse hole to dispose MRE packages and whatever else he needed to get rid of. They were small holes but it took time. He took branches and built a blind around his tent for camouflage and help with the elements. He changed into his camouflaged outfit. It was not an army camo uniform, but camo jeans and a camo long-sleeve tee-shirt. He darkened his face with some camo face paint. Finally, when he felt he had everything like he wanted it, he took out his radio and checked it for operation and reception. Everything checked out to his satisfaction and he sent a message indicting that he was on site. He set his watch to vibrate at 5:00 am. He had learned to sleep with his wrists under his head so he would have no problem feeling the vibration when it was time to get up. It was a trick that the LRS units had taught him.

At 5:15 am Trang crawled to the edge of the clearing and chose a place where he had good visual position, while at the same time not exposing himself. He set his binoculars on a small six-inch tripod, not so much for steady visual observation but to steady the lens for taking pictures. The binoculars could take digital pictures. The binoculars also had a port where he could download images straight to the PRC-137 radio. They would not be close-up pictures like a telescope could give you but it was good enough for the analysts back in Washington to work with. The lens of the binoculars was also coated with a finish that greatly reduced any light reflection that might come off of them, lessening the chances of anyone noticing him.

The light was getting better and Trang was getting a good visual layout of the camp in his mind when four women walked out of the woods on the far side of the camp and went to work in the mess hut. That worried him that they could quickly appear out of the woods and not the small dirt road that lead into the camp. Someone could walk through his little campsite.

Eleven men came out of the men's dormitory around 8:00

o'clock and sat down at a couple of the tables in the mess hut. Four guards also joined them in the hut but sat at a different table. There did not seem to be any animosity between them. They actually waved and acknowledged each other's presence. A few minutes later four more men emerged from the woods where the women had come from and joined them.

As they were finishing their meal, two more people emerged from what he thought was the medical dispensary and were served their breakfast. It was a man and a woman. The man was taller than normal, wore glasses, and had a stethoscope around his neck. The round listening end was pitched back over his shoulder. The female could be his nurse but they seemed closer than that, almost affectionate. She could be his wife.

As the morning progressed and the sun fully illuminated the clearing, Trang turned his binoculars on the area where the four women and men had emerged from. He could see it now. About ten yards back in the woods were four huts. This must be a case where four of the prisoners had taken local women for wives and were allowed to have separate living quarters on the camp premises. Occasionally he could see children through the doorways. A dog walked into the clearing near where the children were playing, sniffed in his direction, gave a couple of obligatory barks, and returned to play with the children.

After breakfast the guards took positions near the buildings and the men tended their gardens while it was still cool. Occasionally a prisoner would go to the medical dispensary and come out a few minutes later. Later in the morning some of the children from the huts in the woods came out to the clearing and played games. At lunch when they were all gathering at the mess hut, a soldier in a much better looking uniform joined the crowd. *This must be the commandant*, Trang thought.

It was a tranquil lifestyle as far as Trang could see. In the afternoon some of the prisoners took some tools to the graveyard and worked on some of the graves. There was one fresh grave. One prisoner put some more soil on the grave where it had settled and

177

raked it out. He finished by adjusting and straightening the grave marker. He could not get a picture of the names on the grave markers because they were pointed away from him.

It was the same routine at supper time. Everyone came, ate, and then returned to their respective buildings. The cooks cleaned up the mess hut and took leftover food home for the children. Later that evening, at dusk, one prisoner sat on a bench outside of the dormitory and played a crude looking guitar. Trang could hear it from where he was. The guitar may have been crude but he had managed to get some good sound out of it. He was pretty good. It was a gospel song. He wondered where he got the strings.

Back in his tent, he draped a poncho over himself and the radio. The poncho would not allow any light to escape from the radio or his small flashlight as he typed his report on the small keyboard of the radio. He prepared the report for upload to the Hawaiian NSA listening post. It was a lengthy written report and in addition there were twenty-five digital pictures to be sent. He needed to get this off tonight. Remote as it might be, he could be discovered and there might not be a chance to get the information transmitted later.

Before dawn, as he started to go to sleep, he took one more look toward the peaceful clearing and thought, *I wonder what'll happen to all these people when an A-Team hits them.*

The next four days were almost exactly like the first day. The routine was the same every day. On the third day some of the children ran around the clearing and came within ten yards of him as they ran by. They never suspected anything but their dog did. He stopped and sniffed the air and looked in Trang's direction. One of the children ran back to the dog and took one step into the brush to see what the dog was looking at, but then shrugged his shoulders and made the dog follow him as they ran to catch up with the other children.

He ate his MRE's but had to ration his water intake. On the fourth day it rained and he was able to make a catch basin out of his poncho and funnel it into his canteen. He knew he was losing about three or four pounds a day but that always happened when he was out in the woods, whether it was training or on actual assignment.

On the fifth day he disassembled his camp, filled in the latrine and refuse hole, packed his backpack, changed clothes and washed the camo off his face. When he reached his motorbike he put the radio in the hidden compartment. He pushed his bike to the edge of the woods and made sure no one was in sight. It was 5:00 am and it was easy to get on the road unnoticed. After a couple of hours he stopped at one of the numerous roadside stores and drank two soft drinks and ate a large candy bar. It gave him such a high that he felt like he was floating.

Getting back to Hanoi seemed to take a shorter amount of time since he knew the way now. He got to the motorcycle rental shop right before they closed. His contact greeted him and helped him get a taxi. He left the radio in the hidden compartment as Kim-Ly had instructed him to do.

Trang barely had time to take a shower and get dressed when Kim-Ly knocked on his door.

"Come in! It's open", Trang shouted.

Kim-Ly opened the door and saw Trang sitting in a chair with his feet propped up on a footstool drinking fruit juice. He was in a tee shirt and short pants. She was shocked at how much weight he had lost. His neck, arms, and face were covered with insect bites.

"My God, Trang, you look awful. Are you all right?"

"Yeah, I'll be OK. I'm just a little weak. I'll be stronger tomorrow. It usually takes me about twenty-four to thirty-six hours to get back to normal."

"Well, you can't gain back that weight in that amount of time."

"No, that takes a couple of weeks. It comes back quick. Most of it is water anyway."

"Are you sure? I was going to see if your offer to take me out to dinner was still good, but now I'm not so sure you're up to it."

"Yes, I am!", he said, jumping up out of his chair but he had moved too quickly. The room swirled for a second. He grabbed the edge of the chair and his senses returned to normal.

"Don't worry", he said to her. "I just moved too quickly. Let me change my clothes and we'll be on our way. You can pick us out a nice place to eat."

"I know a good place, but take your time. I don't want you passing out on me."

Kim-Ly took him to a restaurant in downtown Hanoi that she knew other Americans enjoyed. She ordered for him and picked out some dishes that had plenty of meat and proteins.

"Would you like a drink?" Trang asked.

"Yes, I'll have some Lychee wine. What about you?"

"I would like to. I really would, but I'm afraid that if I had even one measly beer, I would be passed out on the floor. It would look awful for you to have to drag me out of here by my feet."

She laughed. She should have thought of that. He was charming when he wanted to be. He had a cute smile too. They talked over a lengthy dinner and in a disguised sort of conversation let her know that the mission was a success and there were no unexpected surprises.

Trang was glad that his assignment had gone so well. When things go badly on assignments, no matter how good the soldier, it did not reflect well on them. It might not go on the soldier's record but the brass knew who had trouble and who did not. It was a reflection of who was thinking their assignment completely through and who was not.

When their dessert arrived at the table, Trang reconsidered and ordered them both a small glass of brandy. It went well with the ice cream and chocolate wafers, but even so, after he paid the bill and stood up from the table he could feel it. Kim-Ly watched him sway and steady himself but said nothing.

Kim-Ly made sure that he got back to his hotel room safely. She sat down beside him as he lay on the bed.

"I'm drained and charged up all at the same time. I don't think I'll be able to sleep for a while", Trang said.

"I think I can fix that", she said. She leaned over and gave him a passionate kiss. In a few minutes they were in the throes of lovemaking.

180

Fifteen minutes later she rolled off of him. He turned his head to look at her. They locked eyes and she said, "You should be able to sleep now."

The next morning they had room service bring breakfast to their room. As they ate she got back into handler mode and said, "I shouldn't be seen taking you to the airport. So we'll say our goodbyes here."

"When can we see each other again?" Trang asked.

"In a month I'm scheduled to go to the United States for training with our parent export company in Seattle. I will spend some time there and I'm also eligible for two weeks' vacation. Would you like to spend some time with me?"

"Of course. You know I do. I have plenty of leave coming to me. Let me know the dates and I'll get the time off. Here, let me give you my address and cell number."

"Don't bother. I know how to get in touch with you. You forget who I really work for."

"Oh yeah. I guess I did."

"I'm going to leave now. Kiss me bye and I'll be in contact."

They kissed a long good-bye and she said, "Oh, I almost forgot. Behave on the airplane. There will be someone observing you."

"Why would you guys need to spy on me?"

"Don't think of them as a spy. Think of them as more of an observer and guardian, if need be."

Sgt. Trang boarded the airplane and as he walked down the aisle he tried to pick out who the observer might be, but they all looked like normal passengers to him. He got a window seat and after take-off started reflecting on the last few days. This has been the most exciting event of his life. All his training resulting in a successful mission, not that difficult to be sure, but still the mission was accomplished in a foreign country, and best of all, a budding romance with a beautiful and exotic woman. Wow!

The Naval Base at Pearl Harbor was bustling today but the

Harbor Master had taken time to train his binoculars on two Arleigh Burke Class Destroyers as they were leaving port. Their destination had been hand-written in as "undisclosed". What was so interesting to him was that there was an Air Force, V-22 Osprey, aircraft on the helicopter platform of each ship. That was strange to him. *Why aren't there Marine Ospreys on those ships, instead of Air Force Ospreys*, he thought. What he did not know was that there was also a Delta Force A-Team on each ship. It was to be an Army/Air Force operation. The Navy would be their transportation.

In Washington, at the very highest levels, the debate raged on whether to commit to a POW rescue mission or not. The military desperately wanted to do it but the State Department and other high-level politicians were afraid of it. Assets were being put in position. The President would have to make a decision soon.

> *When going through hell, keep going.*
> -*Winston Churchill*

Chapter Sixteen

Sudie awoke with the same headache. It never really went away. At least the sea was fairly calm with only a two foot chop. Much more than that and she would get seasick on top of her other problems. She felt like throwing up most of the time but she had learned to live with it. It had been fourteen days since they had escaped from Bandar Abbas and at least she was not in the hands of Iranian Intelligence. *I wonder how Shaheen and the others are doing. Did they escape too*, she wondered.

Adel was like a father who was protective of his child. He watched over her, made her drink her fruit drinks, encouraged her to eat, mostly bread, because that was all she could get down, and did anything else he could think of to make her comfortable. When she tried to talk about their situation, he would shush her and tell her not to worry; that was his job. It was something in their culture that made them feel protective and responsible for someone to whom they had offered asylum. They were serious about that. She promised herself that if she ever made it out of this situation and survived, she would do all that she could do to see that the CIA protected and compensated Adel, Shaheen, and the others.

Adel came down the ladder to where Sudie was lying in a hammock. He took a fruit drink out of the small refrigerator and handed it to Sudie.

"Do I have to?" Sudie asked, knowing that he would make her drink it.

"Yes, Miss Sudie, you have to drink it and you have to eat some sweet bread, too."

Sudie looked at him and sighed, took the juice from his hand and managed a small swallow. He had started calling her "Miss Sudie" a few days ago. She felt like she was a little girl back in East Tennessee again. Back then, out of respect, one would address a member of the opposite sex, or an elder, with a combination of a title and first name. It showed respect and friendliness, all at the same time. Mr. Barry, Miss Martha, and Miss Sudie was all she could remember her family being called as a little girl. She was almost in first grade before she realized that she had a last name of Sexton.

"Do not be trying to fool me with that drink. I am not going to leave until you drink it all and eat this bread", he said, handing her a slice of raisin bread.

"How much further?" she asked every morning.

Adel did not answer right away this morning. Finally, he said, "We may not be able to go to India."

"Why? What's wrong?"

"Last night, while you were sleeping, some of your people called on the satellite phone."

"And?"

"The whole Iranian Navy has deployed in an effort to find us."

"Oh, great!"

"The American Navy in the Persian Gulf is afraid to release a boat to come after us. They want every boat they have to protect their fleet. Half of the Iranian fleet is playing games with the Americans, the other half of the fleet is scouring the Indian coastline looking for us."

"So, where do we go now?"

"Maybe the Maldives."

"How much further is that?"

"Another two or three weeks."

"Adel, I don't know if I can make it that long. Did they say anything about my antidote?"

"No, but you can and will make it", he said sternly.

During this conversation Sudie had noticed that Adel had kept looking out the window at something. Finally, she asked, "What are you looking at? What's out there?"

"I am not sure. The same fishing boat has been following us for the last two days. I thought at first they were going in our same general direction but they have stayed on our exact course and now they seem to be getting closer."

"This worries you?"

"Normally no, but this fishing boat looks Indonesian. They come here occasionally to fish but mostly as pirates to kill our fisherman and steal their fishing boats."

"Why haven't they closed in already? What are they waiting for?"

"They are being careful and are observing us. They have probably already noticed that there is only you and me on board. It looks like they have finally decided to close in on us."

"We've got guns, don't we?"

"Yes, but so will they."

"Can we outrun them?"

"No, but I do have a surprise for them if they get too close."

"What's that?"

"You will see. Eat your bread. I have to go back up on deck."

Over the next four hours the pirates closed in. During that time, to Sudie's amazement, Adel pulled out an American-made fifty caliber machine gun on a tripod. The bullets were about six inches long and an inch in diameter. He set an ammo box next to the gun and inserted the belt of bullets into the gun. He threw a tarp over it and went back to the steering wheel.

"Miss Sudie, come up here please", Adel shouted.

Sudie climbed up the stairs, slowly, and looked at the nearby pirates and said, "What do you need for me to do?"

"I hate to ask this but when they get about forty yards away, I want you to hang on to the rigging and wave at them. Act sexy. I need for you to attract their attention while I walk over to the machine gun and open fire on them."

Sudie smiled. "I can handle that."

She went down below and folded up her shorts in cuffs as high as they would go. She tied her shirt into a short halter top, put on lipstick, and went back on deck.

Adel blushed and said, Miss Sudie, I am embarrassed for you."

"It's ok, Adel. It's for a good cause. Us."

Adel shook his head and smiled and said, "Ok, go ahead and do your act. They are close enough now."

When the pirates got within fifty yards they used a loudspeaker and told them to stop or they would shoot. Adel did nothing but Sudie started her show.

She grabbed a rope rigging with one hand and struck a sexy pose. With the other hand she grabbed her shirt and pulled it off and waved at the pirates. She still had her bra on but the pirates were going wild.

No one noticed Adel until he flipped the cover off the machine gun and started firing. A fifty caliber bullet can do tremendous damage. He raked the area where most of the sailors were standing, killing several. He concentrated on the wheelhouse and then where he thought the motors would be. Lastly, he put several rows of bullet holes at the waterline of their boat.

Someone must have survived the wheelhouse assault because the pirate boat veered away from them as fast as it could.

Adel smiled at the fifty caliber's handiwork and then looked at Sudie. She was putting her shirt back on and pushing the cuffs back down on her shorts. "Sorry", she said, "I believe that did the trick."

"Yes, it did. I do not think we have to worry about them anymore."

Sudie went below and collapsed into her hammock. For the last ten minutes her adrenaline had kicked in and she had not felt sick but now it was returning. *At least I had a few minutes of relief,* she thought.

The pirates battled the loss of men and a boat that was trying to sink. They plugged every hole they could and limped back toward India where they would try to make repairs. As they got about thirty miles off the coast of India an Iranian Naval Frigate stopped and searched them. The crew related to the Iranian Captain how some unscrupulous fishing boat had opened fire on them, killing several men, and almost sinking them with a fifty caliber machine gun.

The Captain came back to the bridge and said, "Mr. Wu, that was a strange story those fisherman told. They said a fishing boat with only two people on it opened fire on them with a fifty caliber machine gun and almost sunk them."

The Captain and Wu looked at each other for a few seconds and Wu said, "Are you thinking what I am thinking?"

"Yes, that sounds very strange. I think we need to find that boat and search it."

"Did they give you the general area of where it was, and what direction it was headed?"

"Yes, I got the general coordinates, their heading, and approximate speed. We should be able to plot an interception."

"Good. We should catch them now," Wu said.

Sudie strained to climb the stairs to where Adel was. "I know I'm not much of a sailor but haven't we changed course?"

"Very observant, Miss Sudie. Yes, we are heading for the Maldives."

"You still think the Maldives is a safe place to go?"

"Marginally safe. If word gets back to the Iranian Navy about the fishing boat we shot up then they will have a good idea of where we are and are heading. We may have to think about other alternatives."

"Other alternatives! My God, Adel, we're in the middle of the Indian Ocean, what other alternative are there?"

"Africa maybe, although I do not like that one. Too many Somalia pirates around the north half of Africa. We might be able to make Kenya."

"Adel, I can't last that long."

"I know, Miss Sudie, I know. Maybe your American Navy will find us."

Wu handed the Captain a printout from the ship's communication room. The Chinese government had acquired satellite pictures of possible targets in the area of the Indian Ocean that they

187

were searching. The paper listed the coordinates of six fishing boats that were in that area. They studied it and plotted an interception course for the nearest one. It would take them several days to find and search all six boats, but their target had to be on one of them.

That evening Sudie's satellite phone rang again. The message was short and brutal. They could not get a C-130 to them and perform a parachute drop with the antidote because of the weather. The weather was forecast to be miserable for the next few days. No airplane would be able to spot them. Also, they said under no circumstances should they try to go to India or the Maldives. The Iranian Navy had both places covered. They suggested that they try for Diego Garcia, a coral atoll with a large American/British military presence, seven days south of the Maldives.

Sudie and Adel could only look at each other. They were still ten days north of the Maldives and then to add another seven days to get to Diego Garcia would be excruciating.

Seventeen days, thought Sudie, *maybe I can make, but just barely*. She knew that she did not have the strength to fight it after that.

That night the weather front that they had been warned about blew through. Not only were there high seas and rain, there was constant lightning. Adel locked the wheel down and lowered the sails to where there was only one sail at one-quarter rigging. That would keep them from wallowing around in the ocean and give them a little forward motion.

Adel had barely made it into the cabin and closed the hatch when lightning hit the boat. Sudie saw small fingers of lightning dance though out the cabin. It seemed to illuminate everything, especially the electronic equipment. Everything went dark. Adel found a flashlight and they looked around the cabin. Wisps of smoke were coming out of anything electronic. He rested the beam on the satellite phone and it was not only smoking, but sizzling. He ran to it and tried to turn it on. It was dead.

Next he ran to the radio system. The one they used to talk from ship-to-ship or ship-to-shore. It was fried also.

During the next two hours he was able to restore lights and some electrical by replacing two large fuses in the engine room. The engines were not affected. By dawn everything electrical was restored but anything electronic was beyond hope. No satellite phone, no radios, and no ship-driven GPS. The hand-held GPS that had been delivered by the supply bomb in the desert had survived but the battery indicator showed that it was only at three-quarter strength. Usually the indicator would stay at full strength for a long period of time and then fall rapidly. They would have to use it sparingly because the charger had been plugged in during the lightning strike and was also fried.

The storm lasted for three days. They could not control the direction of the boat. They would correct their course once they could work with the sails. The waves tossed them badly and they took refuge in their hammocks which would swing with the waves. Occasionally Adel would change the orientation of the hammocks by ninety degrees by switching the hooks that the hammocks hung on. Sudie was so light that he could change hers with her in it.

During the storm Adel had trouble feeding Sudie. Every time he opened the refrigerator or a cabinet door supplies scattered all over the floor. When he did manage to get something for her to drink or eat she would refuse or hide it. If she drank what Adel wanted her to have, she would have to go to the toilet. She was so weak that he would have to hold her up and walk her to the toilet door. He would open the door, sit her on the toilet, turn his head, and pull down her pants and then do it in reverse to get her back into her hammock. During the storm, she barely drank anything to keep from having to go to the toilet. But now, with calmer seas, she could walk by herself without getting tossed about, so now Adel insisted that she eat and drink more. She knew he was right, but she was getting to the point where she did not care anymore.

At the end of the third day the storm broke. They still had a low cloud cover but the wind and waves had died down enough for Adel to work with the sails and reset his course. He had programmed the coordinates of Diego Garcia into the hand-held GPS unit and turned it on only three times a day to check his track and make adjustments.

While Adel was on deck, Sudie found enough energy to rummage through some drawers and found a piece of blank paper, an ink pen, and a sealable plastic bag. She sat down at the desk used for navigation, composed her thoughts, and wrote:

Dear Eric,

If you are reading this then it means I didn't make it. I'm so sorry. Believe me I tried, but I didn't have the strength to hold on. I have been so sick and so close to giving up every day, but I have not, thinking that there might be a chance of getting back to you. I had every intention of taking you off that shelf in the cupboard and marrying you as soon as I got back to Washington. I think we would have had beautiful children. You would have been and will make a good father and husband.

Grieve for me, but not too long. Live your life. If possible I will watch over you.

Someone once wrote, "If ever a man was loved by a woman, tis thee."

Goodbye Sweetheart, I love thee.

Your Sudie

She folded it, put Eric's name on the outside, sealed it in the plastic bag, and tucked it in her pants pocket.

In Washington, two NRO analysts had been given full access to a satellite that is positioned over the Indian Ocean. They were searching for Sudie and Adel's boat. It is not as easy as one might think. The ocean is a vast area and even finding relative large ships are not that easy unless you know their coordinates. Finding a small ship takes time, especially in bad weather, but infra-red technology helps. They knew the last coordinates given by Adel but they have not heard from him for days now. They had their eye on a "best estimate" area and had been checking out six fishing boats in that area. They had eliminated three boats because there have been a half a dozen people on the decks. They were trying to find a boat with only two people and if the weather would clear up and they could identify one as a woman then they would, with a high degree of certainty, have found their target boat.

The *USS Farragut* had rounded the tip of Africa several days ago and had been given a vector and coordinates for the general area of the three remaining suspect boats. The Captain of the *Farragut* was pressing the boat with a speed of twenty-five knots and he would be in the general area of the two boats in a couple of days. When he was more certain of his target's location he would go to thirty-two knots; flank speed. It was hard on the engines and they gulped fuel but the Pentagon had ordered it. He could refuel at Diego Garcia.

The two analysts had also identified an Iranian Naval Frigate very near the area where the three boats in question were sailing. They gave hourly reports of the area's situation to a team of people from the Pentagon, CIA, and the President's staff. This team was directing the search and hopefully the rescue.

Adel was beginning to worry. They were getting low on food and water and they were still six or seven days from Diego Garcia. They would run out of food tomorrow and water the next day. *Maybe it will rain and I can catch some fresh water*, he thought. He did not want to tell Sudie the situation until he had too. She might give up. He doubted that she could make it to Diego Garcia if the food and water gave out. The fruit drink was the only thing he could get her to consume. They had energy and calories in them but he had given her the last one that morning.

Wu had another message from the frigates communications center. Chinese intelligence had gambled and guessed from satellite imagery that the boat that they were looking for was probably boat number six. It was the one that was the farthest south and it was on a direct line for Diego Garcia. The Iranian Captain set an intercept course but it would take two days.

Chapter Seventeen

Buddy Miller and the *Oriental Flyer* were in the Indian Ocean, headed for India. Once he reached Mumbai he would contact the Chinese Embassy and make his way to Beijing by air. He would have to sell the *Flyer* while in Mumbai. He hated to let her go. She was almost like a family member to him but she was a liability now. Most of the free world was probably looking for him and his boat, including Interpol.

Last week he had beached the *Oriental Flyer* on a deserted beach in South Africa and re-arranged the letters on the boat. With pencil and paper in hand he had run some anagrams through his mind and put them to paper. After deciding on a new name he used the letters from the *ORIENTAL FLYER* to rename the boat. He had peeled the letters off, stuck them to wax paper, and then re-applied them to the back of the boat spelling out *RELIANT*. He removed the home port of Oriental, NC entirely.

He had been a long time at sea. It was lonely and boring and it was a big deal if he even saw another boat. It was hard not to think of Maria but all he wanted to do now was get to India and find safety in China. He was half-way across the Indian Ocean and hopefully he would reach India in about a week.

What's that?, he thought. There was a boat on the horizon heading south. They would intersect close enough to wave at each other. It looked like a fishing boat out of one of the Persian Gulf nations. Hopefully they would be friendly. His catamaran was fast enough if they were not.

Adel saw the catamaran heading his way. *Praise Allah*, he thought. *Maybe they will let us have or purchase some supplies or even use their radio.*

"Miss Sudie! Miss Sudie! Wake up! There's a boat coming our way." No answer.

193

Sudie heard him but was too weak to respond. She would let Adel handle it.

Adel put his sails down and waved frantically. "Miss Sudie, get up here!"

Sudie struggled out of her hammock and managed a couple of steps to a bench where she could sit and look out of a cabin window. *Huh,* she thought, *that could be an exact copy of the Oriental Flyer. Must be made by the same company.*

"I see it!" she called out to Adel.

Buddy could see that they wanted assistance from him, but was it a safe thing to do? He decided to get within about twenty yards from them and see what they wanted.

"Help! Help! Please help", shouted Adel.

"What's the problem?" Buddy asked.

Adel could tell by his voice and accent that he was American. "I have an American lady aboard who is very sick. Do you have some drinks and food to spare? We can pay for it."

Buddy could see a ladies face peering through a port window. She did look sick and very pale. He decided to help. "I'll see if I can get close enough to let you aboard."

Adel threw him a line and after ten minutes they were bound securely together.

"What kind of supplies do you need?", Buddy asked.

"The lady could really use something to drink; hopefully you might have some fruit drinks. We also need food."

"OK, stay here on deck and I'll go below and get you a case of fruit drinks. I'll also fill a box of canned goods. Will that be enough?"

"Yes, if we can have enough to last another week we should be fine."

Buddy came back with two boxes of supplies and Sudie thought, *He looks familiar.*

Adel took the boxes from Buddy and walked them over to his boat. He put them down on the deck and said, "You would do us a great favor if you would let us use your radio."

"Sure, I have a top-dollar high frequency radio that should let you talk to anyone on this side of the world. Just don't say anything about me."

"Certainly. Let me go below and get the frequency I need."

Adel ran below and grabbed a pouch that carried important papers in. It had frequencies that the CIA had provided them with in case of emergencies.

As he ran by Sudie she said, "Who is that?

"I do not know but he has saved us."

Buddy showed Adel down to his radio, turned it on, and waved his hand toward the seat in front of the radio, indicating that he could take a seat and use the radio.

Adel nodded and started turning the dial to the frequency he wanted.

"Diego Garcia radio, come in." He repeated it three times before someone answered him.

"Listen buddy, this is a restricted military channel, please don't use this frequency."

Adel thought for a second. He knew he was broadcasting in the open and anyone could hear him. He had no choice; he had to get help. He took a deep breath and said, "Get this message to your station's intelligence officer. I have Oleander on board from Operation Bamboo Splinter and we need immediate assistance." There was a long pause.

The radio operator had never heard anyone say anything quite like that and he looked across the room to a Navy Commander, an intelligence officer, who had jumped out of his chair and was practically sprinting toward him. The Commander grabbed the microphone and said, "Where are you?"

Buddy was a little freaked out at this point. He realized that Adel was talking to American Military Intelligence, but there was nothing he could do about it now. He would assist and then get out of the area as fast as possible. Adel looked at Buddy's onboard GPS unit and found the LCD readout of their coordinates.

"We are at the following coordinates, heading south at six

knots." Adel carefully called out the coordinates into the microphone.

"What is the medical condition of Oleander?" the Commander asked.

"Very serious, she needs immediate medical attention."

"Very well. Head south and keep in contact."

"I cannot do that. I am on a Good Samaritan's boat and using his radio. I can only be in radio contact for this conversation only. All our electronic equipment was destroyed by lightning."

"The Good Samaritan will not bring you to Diego Garcia?."

Buddy shook his head no. "No, he cannot do that", Adel said.

"Ok, head south, we'll find you. Do you have anything colorful you could put on your rigging?"

"Sir, the only thing I can think of is an orange towel."

"That'll have to do. Secure it to the rigging. We'll have boats and airplanes looking for you."

"Thank you", Adel said. "I will be signing off now."

"Roger, Diego Garcia signing off."

Buddy accompanied Adel back up on deck and watched as Adel stepped over to his boat and untied the ropes that bound them together.

"Sir, I cannot thank you enough. You have saved our lives. Will you allow me to pay you?"

"No, no. I'm glad I could help. You can do the same for someone else someday, but do me a favor and don't tell anyone anything about me. Even the direction I head off in."

Adel was a little puzzled but shook his head in agreement.

Sudie was watching Adel talk with the other person through the port window when it suddenly dawned on her that it was Buddy Miller that Adel was talking to. He had a mustache and goatee now. She was too amazed and weak to do anything. She continued to watch as the boats separated. She looked at the back of the catamaran and saw that it said *RELIANT*, but she also noticed the sticky residue left behind from some lettering that had been removed. She could just make out that it had previously read, *Oriental Flyer, Oriental, NC.*

Should I report him, she thought. *I should, but he probably just saved my life. It's a moot point anyway, by the time I get to someplace with a radio he'll be long gone. I'll tell Langley about it then.* She lay down on the cushioned bench under the window and passed out.

In Washington, Sudie's rescue team had received the news and was in high gear, issuing orders. A C-130 cargo transport plane would be dispatched from Djibouti to locate Sudie's boat. In Ramstien, Germany, the Air Force ordered a KC-135 Medavac hospital plane to Diego Garcia. The Captain of the *USS Farragut* received orders to go to flank speed and intercept Sudie's boat. He was also advised that intelligence indicated that he was probably in a race with an Iranian Naval Frigate to see who could get to Oleander first.

It was late afternoon and Eric was playing soccer with the children at the boy's orphanage. It was a pitiful field; unlevel, rocky, and on each end of the field were two piles of rocks about ten yards apart to indicate where the goal should be and where they were to try to kick a ball between. Somehow it was fun anyway. The children knew no better and thought it was a grand field.

A score had been made and Eric was bent over, hands on his knees, catching his breath when he noticed an army Humvee vehicle heading his way. It seemed to be in a hurry. It pulled to the edge of the field and NCIS Agent Daniels waved him over.

"Eric, get in. Intelligence has some important information for you."

"What is it?" Eric said, jumping in the Humvee.

"Not sure, but I think they have some information on Operation Bamboo Splinter and your Sudie."

It took about ten minutes to get to the CIA office. Eric jumped out and ran in.

"What have you found out?" he shouted as he entered the office.

"We have heard from Sudie's boat. We know their last coordinates, direction, and speed. They're heading toward Diego Garcia." The intelligence officer paused and said in a calmer but serious voice, "We also know that Oleander, your Sudie, has been reported as being in serious medical condition."

"How are we going to get to her?" Eric asked.

"Pack your bags. They've got coordinates on Sudie. We won't be able to locate her tonight but a C-130 will take off at 0600 tomorrow morning and try to spot her boat. You will be accompanied by two Navy Seals. They will parachute to Oleander's boat with supplies and the antidote."

"Do they know how to administer it?"

"Yes, in addition to being Navy Seals, their specialties are in the medical field. At this very moment they're being briefed by a doctor on proper procedure for injection and administration of IV's. You have the antidote. So, give them two of the six vials as soon as you get on the airplane."

"What about me? Do I get to parachute too?"

"Are you kidding? No, of course not. You'd only be a liability to the Seals. The C-130 will fly you on to Diego Garcia with the other vials of antidote and you'll await their arrival there."

"How will Sudie get to Diego Garcia? Surely not on that slow fishing boat?"

"No. A Navy Destroyer is heading toward them at top speed. They should be there about six hours after the Seals parachute down to them."

"Why just two Seals? Why not a whole team."

"Eric, our Navy Destroyer is in a race with an Iranian Frigate to see who can get to them first. I'd rather lose only two Seals than a whole team."

"Can't we send in some aircraft to take out the Iranian Frigate?"

"No Eric. We don't have those types of assets here. Also, if we completely destroy the Frigate, then it'll be an international incident and there'll be retaliation against Americans. We're hoping that our

Destroyer can get there first or even close. If we are close enough then the Destroyer's Seahawk helicopter can fire a Hellfire missile against them that would do less damage than something stronger, say a Harpoon missile.

Eric gave him a doubtful look.

"Eric, the *Farragut* is a powerful ship and the Captain is a smart man. He knows the situation. He should be able to take care of it."

There was not much else Eric could say. He thought about it for a few minutes and then left to go to his quarters, pack his gear, and check on the antidote.

The next morning, a 0545, an Air Force loadmaster, escorted Eric out on the tarmac and up the back ramp of the C-130 cargo plane. The two Navy Seals were already seated and strapped in. They watched him as he sat down. He nodded at them and they nodded back.

Eric opened up a small cooler and took out two vials of antidote and handed them to one of the Seals.

"Here's the antidote."

One of the Seals took the vials and handed the second vial to the other Seal.

"Why do you split them up?" Eric asked.

"Insurance. In case one of us gets tangled up in our chutes while in the water and drowns."

He said it so casually. Eric did not know what else to say. They seemed so cocky and sure of themselves but at the same time, had an air of forced tolerance of outsiders.

Thirty minutes after takeoff the co-pilot walked back to Eric and sat down beside him. He introduced himself, and said, "Listen, it's going to take about five or six hours to locate our target, if we *can* locate it. There's a front moving in that will obscure the area and make visible sighting of it impossible in about eight hours. So we'll need some luck."

Eric nodded his head indicating that he understood.

The co-pilot looked across the aisle at the Seals and then looked back at Eric and shook his head in disbelief. They were asleep.

After five hours they reached the search area and began a search pattern. They started at the last broadcast coordinates and headed in a straight line for Diego Garcia. After thirty minutes and no sighting they turned back on the same line but zigzagged back and forth across that line. They also lowered their altitude to two thousand feet and opened the back ramp where the loadmaster could observe from the rear of the airplane. That woke the seals up and they started checking each other out for their jump. They also had a large bag that one of them had strapped to himself.

"What's that?" Eric asked.

One of the Seals said, "It's an inflatable life raft. Just in case we miss our target and that fishing boat doesn't pick us up. It has communications and a locater device in it, in case someone has to come find us."

Oh, Eric thought, *I hadn't thought about that.*

"I see them!" the loadmaster shouted as he looked out the back of the airplane.

The pilot took the plane down to three hundred feet and flew over the boat rocking his wings. The boat had an orange towel tied to the rigging.

Adel waved at the pilot as he flew by. He could actually see the pilot's face.

"Miss Sudie, an airplane is here. They have found us."

Sudie heard Adel, smiled to herself, and continued to lie in the hammock.

The pilot took the plane up to five thousand feet. This would give the Seals enough altitude to make adjustments as they glided to their target.

Eric watched as they jumped out the back of the airplane. *Brave men*, he thought.

Adel watched the airplane as it crossed over again at a much higher altitude. He could see two men jump out the back. They fell for about two thousand feet and were somehow guiding themselves toward him, and then their chutes popped open. The parachutes were the performance type and they guided them to about a hundred yards in front of his boat where they landed safely. He lowered all sails and started the motor. He slowly guided the boat to the two men and stopped. He threw a rope ladder over the side of the boat and helped the men aboard. They handed up their gear first and then the men climbed up the rope with guns at their chest.

"Thank you for coming", Adel said.

"No problem", one of them said. "Where's the lady?"

"She is below in the hammock."

Sudie heard a commotion and opened her eyes slightly to see two wiry men beside her setting up equipment. One was erecting a portable IV stand and the other was getting an IV bag and tubes ready.

Adel watched from the hatch for a while but then set about resetting the sails and rigging. He looked to the east and noticed a wall of clouds moving toward him. *Another front*, he thought, *They got here just in time.*

Sudie watched as one of the Seals inserted the IV in her arm while the other prepared the first of a series of antidote shots. They were very gentle with her. They had been told that this agent had performed a valuable and dangerous service for the country and had suffered poisoning as a result of it. They knew that the intelligence and the military community were moving "hell and high water" to rescue her.

After they had administered the first shot of the antidote and were satisfied that the IV drip was working properly, one of the Seals opened his pack and pulled out a satellite phone and a commercial GPS system for the boat. They had both units up and running in ten minutes. Soon one of the Seals was talking with a doctor on the satellite phone and was giving him Sudie's vital signs. After that they reported their position, speed, and heading. A few thousand feet above them Eric's C-130 turned south toward the military base on the island atoll of Diego Garcia.

In Washington, Sudie's rescue team was analyzing all of the new information and data. It did not take them long to realize that there was going to be a showdown in about three hours. The Iranian

Frigate and the *Farragut* would both intercept Sudie's boat at about the same time.

An urgent message was sent to the Captain of the *Farragut* to apprise him of the situation. The Captain was sitting in his chair on the bridge when a crewman brought him an urgent message from the communications center. He read it, thought for a moment, and called a junior officer over to him.

"Lieutenant," the Captain said holding out the message to him. "Here's our target's latest coordinates, direction, and speed. Make any adjustments necessary. Continue at flank speed."

He turned to another sailor and said, "Have the helicopter pilots and their maintenance crew in my conference room in fifteen minutes. Have someone from meteorology there also."

The Captain walked into the conference and gave a quick ten minute briefing on the fact that they were racing an Iranian Frigate to a boat that had Americans on board. He wanted the helicopter to be armed with hellfire missiles, in case they were needed. If they could get there before the Iranians, then they were to rescue the four people on board and then destroy the fishing boat.

The meteorologist spoke up and said, "Captain, I don't think that the weather is going to let us do that. There's a nasty weather front that has just socked in that area. They'll be flying on instruments and could be a sitting duck for surface-to-air missiles from the frigate if it is anywhere nearby."

The Captain had already thought about that possibility but continued to weigh the pros and cons for a moment longer and then said, "Get the helo ready for the mission but don't launch unless I say so." When the helo crew had left the room the Captain turned to his aide and said, "Get me Washington on the secure phone."

In Washington, after talking to the *Farragut*, a call was made to the Seal's satellite phone and they were advised of the latest info and that in about two and a half hours, they could be in a hot situation, depending on who got there first. They were instructed to turn toward the southwest in the direction of the *Farragut*.

Two hours and twenty minutes later Sudie was feeling the good effects of the IV and the nutrients that it contained. It made her feel warm and sleepy. She opened one eye and a man she did not know said, "Close your eyes and sleep." She did.

On deck Adel and the other Seal were watching for any signs of a ship breaking out of the low-lying clouds that were hugging the wave tops. They were in a clearing about a mile in diameter.

Both the Iranian Frigate and the *Farragut* were about five miles from the target and they could see each other on their surface radar.

Captain Edwards, of the *Farragut*, grabbed the radio and started broadcasting in the clear, "Iranian Naval vessel, this is the American ship, *USS Farragut*, you are closing in on a vessel that has Americans on board. You are to turn away now."

Fifteen seconds later a reply came over the air. "American vessel, *Farragut*. We are pursuing spies and criminal elements. You are not to interfere with us. We are prepared to use ship-to-ship missiles against you."

Captain Edwards responded immediately. "I hope you do fire your missile. I have adequate protection against it. I would love to have a reason to return fire with a couple of Harpoon missiles."

There was no reply. The Iranian captain knew he was outgunned and he had no intentions of getting into a shootout with a powerful American destroyer.

Wu turned to the captain and said, "If we cannot capture them then we must try to destroy the fishing vessel. Launch you missile against the fishing vessel."

"I do not think that would be wise. The American destroyer might think that the missile is for them. The best thing we can do is try to find them first and sink them with artillery gunfire.

The Iranian's frigate ran hard for about three minutes and then broke into the opening where they could see the fishing boat.

"Prepare the cannon!", the Iranian captain shouted.

"Cannon ready", came the reply.

"Fire three rounds."

Adel and the other Seal were on the deck and saw the Iranian Frigate break out of the cloud bank. "Get below!" the Seal shouted to

Adel. The Seal took a last look at the frigate as he was closing the hatch and saw the flash of the guns. "They're firing! Get down! Things are going to get hot now."

The Seal attending Sudie threw a flak jacket over her and dove for the floor. The first shell went over them and the second one fell short but the third one hit the back half of the upper deck and did considerable damage.

One Seal looked at the other and knew what the other was thinking. *A couple more hits like that and we'll be dead and sinking.*

On the bridge of the *Farragut* they could hear the gunfire. Captain Edwards shouted, "Battle stations, and get the Mark 45 ready!" As they broke into the clearing, they could see the frigate firing again. They had barely enough time to see the shell fall short of its target when Captain Edwards yelled, "Fire!"

The Seals had jumped up off the floor and were looking out the window at the Iranian frigate when they heard firing from a different direction. They jerked their heads around in time to see the *Farragut* breaking out of a bank of clouds that was resting on the water.

The *Farragut's* Mark 45 had fired a three-round burst. The first shell hit the gun that was firing on the fishing boat and put it out of commission. The second shot hit it again. The third shot went a little higher due to the fact that the *Farragut* rose on a sea swell as they fired. As a result the third shell blasted through the window of the frigate's bridge and exploded into hundreds of fragments. Everyone on the bridge was hit but not all were dead. One of the junior officers grabbed command of the wheel and turned the ship away. One of the other wounded junior officers crawled toward the captain's chair and could see that the captain and Wu were dead. Wu had caught a large piece of shrapnel in the neck which had cut his carotid artery.

Sudie was only semi-conscious; but she could tell there was a lot of activity around her. She had the sensation of being moved. The *Farragut* had lowered a boat and she and the others were being moved off the fishing boat and on to the destroyer. The ship's doctor and two corpsmen accompanied her as they took her to sick bay. The Seals briefed the doctor on what they had given her so far and gave him the written instructions that they had received on how to administer the sequence of antidote shots. Sudie soon felt the comfort of a real bed, a comfortable room temperature, and a slight reduction in how much her stomach ached.

On the bridge Captain Edwards gave orders to sink the fishing boat. The gun crew did so with great enthusiasm since they rarely got a real target to engage. He walked down to his conference room, where he held a briefing with Adel and the two Seals. His Executive Officer was in the communications room briefing Washington on the events of the last forty-five minutes.

Washington would have to prepare for the fall-out of an exchange of gunfire with an Iranian Frigate. Even worse, they had no idea that a high-level Communist party member from the *State Council of the Chinese Government*, roughly equivalent to the United State's State Department, had been killed in the exchange.

Four days later Buddy Miller sailed the *Reliant* into the harbor in Mumbai, India. He found an upscale marina and rented a space for his boat. It felt so good to be on solid ground. He wanted to check into an expensive hotel and have a meal at a five-star restaurant, but he decided it would be prudent to go to the Chinese Embassy first.

He walked into the lobby and gave his American passport to the person at the desk and asked to speak to an embassy official. The person smiled, said that their people were very busy, but he would take his request to the proper person. He sat down and waited in the lobby for about fifteen minutes, when suddenly an important looking person rushed into the lobby and asked him to follow him to another room.

When they got to the other room several other people joined them and began asking all sorts of questions. After they figured out that he knew nothing after Beking left him in Grenada, they filled him in on some of the events of the recent weeks, including the assassination of Beking and a Venezuelan Air Marshall and the death of an important Chinese official that was close to the case. They seemed embarrassed and mad at the same time. It was political embarrassment and loss of face. They wanted to get him to China as fast as possible.

Buddy asked, "Can I sell my boat first?"

"No", came the reply. "We will sell it for you and deposit the money in your account in China."

How do they know where and what my account number is?, he wondered, but apparently they did know.

One official continued, "You are not to take a public airline to China. Harm could befall you in flight. We will fly you on a private government jet." They were not going to make that mistake again.

That night he stayed in a room at the embassy, where embassy officials occasionally spent the night, because of business or international situations. The next morning they took him to the airport where a private jet was waiting for him. He was off the ground in a few minutes and on his way to Beijing.

Back in the Indian Ocean the *Farragut* was still at flank speed, straining to get within five hundred miles of Diego Garcia. Once they got within that range they turned the Seahawk helicopter into a flying gas can, loaded up Sudie, the two Seals, one Navy Corpsman, and took off for Diego Garcia. They would be at the tiny ocean atoll in a little over three hours. Back on the *Farragut,* the Captain gave the order to reduce speed to a normal cruising speed. They could almost feel the ship sigh with relief. The strain on the ship and men had worn everyone out. They would push on to Diego Garcia, refuel, pick up their helicopter, and then proceed to their original destination. Another destroyer, already on station in the Persian Gulf, was waiting for the *Farragut* to relieve them. That crew was eagerly awaiting them, so they could go home.

Eric had no idea that Sudie was in the base's medical clinic until a sailor found him at the Officer's Club with a message asking him to report to the medical clinic. The airfield at Diego Garcia was a busy place and the sound of her helicopter arrival never registered with him.

When he arrived, a nurse at the front desk asked him to wait while she made a phone call. Soon, a doctor and a civilian, probably CIA, met him at the front desk to escort him back to the intensive care room. The medical center had one room setup with two beds for intensive care; the rest of the building was for other minor medical problems.

A nurse leaned over to Sudie and said, "Miss, Miss, your boyfriend is here. They've gone to the front desk to get him."

A look of alarm came over Sudie's face. She knew she looked haggard and pale. The nurse seemed to read her mind and said, "Don't worry. I'll have them wait outside for a minute while we fix you up."

The nurse ran out of the room and came back in with a small makeup kit. She and another nurse combed her hair, put on a bit of rouge, and some pale colored lipstick. "That's as good as we can do for right now", the nurse said, and walked to the door to let Eric in.

Eric walked in and could hardly believe that it was his Sudie lying there on the hospital bed. She was so thin, she could have been a skinny twelve-year old girl. She was so pale. She opened her eyes and looked at him as he walked toward her and kissed her.

"Hey baby. I hear you've had a rough time", Eric said.

"Hi sweetheart. I didn't think I was going to make it back to you."

"Well, you did and we're going to get you back on your feet very soon."

"I hope so. I'm so weak and my stomach hurts so bad."

"The doctors are going to fix that, so don't worry."

They made small talk for about ten minutes and then she asked, "Eric, can you find the clothes I had on when they brought me in here, especially the pants?"

"Sure, baby. I'll see if I can find them." He walked over to a closet in the room and found nothing, then he went to a dresser in the room and found her clothes in a plastic bag. He pulled out the pants and took them to her. She took them and laid them beside her.

Eric looked at her, wondering what the deal was with the pants.

She smiled at him and said, "Something in them that I will have to check out later."

Eric could only shake his head and he thought, *Must be some secret CIA thing.*

"Eric, one more thing," Sudie said.

"Sure baby, what is it?"

"I want you to find and meet Adel. He was with me on the boat. He saved my life more than once. Do what you can to see that he gets treated right."

"I'll do it; whatever it takes. You get some rest now."

The doctor came in, said that they needed to give Sudie an injection, and put something in her IV that would relax her stomach and make her sleep. Eric could visit her the next morning.

Eric waited for the doctor in the hall. When he came out Eric said, "Doctor, what's the prognosis? Is she going to be OK?"

"We don't know yet and we won't know for a couple of weeks. Her exposure to the poison was slight but it slowly worked on her internal organs anyway. If we could have gotten to her in the first week after her exposure, then she would have no damage. If we are too late then the poison will have damaged her organs to a point where she cannot recover. If I had to guess, I would say that we are right on the borderline. If we've caught it in time and have counteracted the poison, then her organs will slowly recover, but it could take six months to a year for her body to recover and even then she may never be at a hundred per cent."

"You mean she will always be weak or an invalid?"

"No, if she recovers, she can lead a normal life, but she'll never run a marathon and she might not be able to have a baby."

"That doesn't matter; I'll take care of her."

"Will you be accompanying her tomorrow?"

"What do you mean? Where's she going?"

"She's scheduled to fly out to Washington tomorrow on an Air

Force KC-135 Medavac. That's a hospital airplane."

"I'm sure I'll be with her but I need to go check and make sure."

"Do you have a small purse or clutch that I can have?" Sudie asked the nurse.

"Oh, I'm sure there's one around here that I can round up", the nurse said as she left the room to see what she could find.

When she left the room Sudie reached into the pocket of the pants and was relieved to find the plastic bag with the note in it. She did not want to show it to Eric yet, but she would someday. When the nurse returned with a small clutch, she put the note in it, asked the nurse to put the pants back in the drawer, turned on her side, and went to sleep clutching the bag close to her.

Chapter Eighteen

In Washington, two NRO analysts were watching a live feed from a satellite positioned over Southeast Asia, North Vietnam in particular. The large high definition television showed a clearing in the jungles of North Vietnam. They had been assigned to watch the POW camp, recording anything of significance. Someone was at the post twenty-four hours a day.

"Do you think they're going to go after these guys?" one analyst said.

"Yeah, I think so. It's a lot of time and money to tie up a satellite this long, so they're probably going to do something."

"It's crazy how Beking's photos stirred up such a hornet's nest. I bet he's living in luxury in China somewhere."

"I don't think so. I've seen indications that he may not be among the living anymore."

"So again, what's going to happen to these guys? Rescue?"

"Maybe, I don't really know, but something's up. I can feel it."

"Hey, look. There's the same two guys that sit on the bench every afternoon.

"The one with the guitar and his friend?"

"Yep, that's them."

"Jay, that guitar sounds funny with that string missing", Howie said.

"Yeah, it does leave something to be desired. Dr. Duc said he would bring me some strings next week after he and Han visit their families in Hanoi."

"Has he finished his paper yet? You know, the one about our dreams."

"I think he's doing the final editing now on that television-typing machine", Jay said.

"I bet it's dry reading; very academic."

"Hey, if you were to tell him about your angel dream, then he would really have something to write about", Jay teased.

"Hey, it's not funny. You know it still has some lasting effects on me."

Howie was right. Not only could he sleep now but ever since that night, when the angel touched his head he had become psychic to a certain extent.

"You still think someone is out there in the jungle watching us?" Jay asked.

"No, not anymore. He's gone."

"Who do you think they were?"

"It was a he, singular, not they."

"Ok, who do you think he was?"

"I don't know, but he wasn't from around here."

"How do you know that?"

"I just know, dammit."

"Probably just some curious local peasant. He was Vietnamese, wasn't he?" Jay said, slightly exasperated.

"Yes… and then again, he wasn't."

Jay shook his head in bewilderment and let it rest, but Howie had changed in one respect. He knew things before they happened. He knew when one of the children across the clearing would soon get sick or hurt; he knew when they were going to have a special meal or that the commandant would be showing a new movie, days before it happened. Strangest of all, he knew that Han was pregnant.

"Anything else gonna' happen soon?, Jay asked.

"You're not going to get your guitar strings."

"Why not?"

"Something's going to happen before that. Something bad."

"Lord, what could be worse than being a prisoner in a jungle camp for forty years?" Jay asked.

"Go ahead. Make fun of me but something's going to happen."

"You sure it's something bad?"

"Yeah, I think so. It use to waiver between good and bad but now it's a bad feeling all the time."

"Probably means that one of us here in the camp will die, that's all."

"It's bigger than that," Howie said quietly. They let the conversation drop as Jay started picking a song on the guitar.

The commandant's radio phone rang in the camp's small office that was attached to the medical dispensary. He answered and, as he listened, his face became red and frightened. He ran outside and rang a buzzer. He gave it three long buzzes, which meant for the guards to come to him immediately.

He ran into the medical dispensary where Dr. Duc and Han were working with a microscope and slides.

"Get in the truck! Do not wait! Get in right now! Troops are coming. They will kill everyone in this camp, including us, if we are still here."

He grabbed the doctor and Han by the arms and pushed them out the door and toward the truck. Dr. Duc broke loose and ran back inside and grabbed a flash drive that had his academic paper on it, ran back out, and jumped in the truck. By this time the guards had arrived and the commandant was ordering them into the truck.

One of the guards started the truck and headed it down a narrow dirt road that led out of the camp. At the commandant's urging, he was going fast and it was shaking up everyone on the benches in the back of the truck. Han was scared and tears were streaming down her face.

Jay and Howie watched all the commotion from the bench where they were sitting.

"What the hell is going on with them?" Jay asked.

"I dunno, but I don't think it's good", Howie said, as the truck went around a curve and out of sight. By this time the other prisoners had come outside the dormitory and were wondering what was going on.

"What's that noise?" Jay asked.

"Sounds like helicopters", one of the men said.

Some of the men were getting excited. One of them said, "We're going to be rescued!"

"I don't think so", Howie said quietly and started slowly walking backwards toward the woods. Once into the foliage he ran deep into the jungle.

Four helicopters had crossed the Chinese-Vietnam border, a half a mile north and were now coming over the tree line and landing in the clearing. Chinese Special Forces poured out of them.

China had been embarrassed by the assassination of their spy and angered by the death of a high-ranking Communist member. Retribution had to be dealt out against the Americans before the POWs could be rescued; which would be another embarrassment for both the Chinese and the Vietnamese. The Golden Dragons, an elite Special Forces unit of the Chinese Army, had been sent to deal with the camp.

As the soldiers ran toward them, the POWs understood what was coming. They formed a loose military line and stood stoically waiting for the inevitable. Jay's mind went back to when he was a little boy, sitting in the dentist's chair and thinking, *This won't hurt long.* He stepped forward from the line and watched as the soldiers formed a line and raised their weapons to a firing position. He held out his arms as if he was to be crucified, looked upward, and said softly, "Swing low, sweet chariot."

The soldiers took aim and an officer shouted the order to fire. In less than ten seconds all the men lay dead.

When the helicopters had landed four of the soldiers had run to the huts, in the woods, where the four American POWs that had started lives with local Vietnamese women were living. They dragged the men out of the huts and shot them in front of their families. Other soldiers searched the camp to make sure that no one was in hiding.

A half-mile down the road the truck had stopped. The commandant, the doctor, and Han had gotten out of the truck and listened in horror to the gunfire. Han had her head buried into Duc's back and was crying. They waited about twenty minutes and when they heard the helicopters leave they drove slowly back to the camp. Fifty yards from the camp they stopped the truck and a soldier was sent to make sure that it was safe to come back into the camp.

They watched the soldier as he got to the edge of the clearing. He stood there for a moment. They watched as his shoulders slumped down. His rifle slid off his shoulder and fell to the ground. A few moments later he leaned down and picked the rifle up by the shoulder strap. He walked back to the truck and reported to the commandant that the Chinese had left. There was a single tear running down his face.

They drove back into the camp and saw the bodies lying on the ground where they fell.

Han kept screaming, "Why! Why!"

The families of the four dead men were also screaming at the commandant.

The commandant went into his office and reported to his superiors what had happened. He requested a bulldozer to be sent in the next morning to dig a mass grave.

The two analysts at the NRO were stunned. One of them had pushed the record button as soon as the commandant had come running out and started pushing people into the truck, but now they were too shocked to move or say anything.

Finally one of them shook himself out of it and said, "Get that video onto a disk. I've got to report this…. Man, there's going to be hell to pay."

In Atlanta, Amy Broussard Ferris, was pouring her husband a cup of coffee.

"Morning, baby. You sleep ok last night?" David asked.

She said nothing for a moment and finally said, "Yes, but I had the strangest dream. It was so real."

"Were you having a nightmare?"

"No, nothing like that....it was about Jay."

"Really. What did my old Navy buddy have to say?"

"He said he was glad that I was happy and married to you. He said he was especially proud of Jayce. I asked him if he was ok and he said that he was in a good place now. He took me to a beautiful field where his parents and relatives were waiting for him, and then, poof. I woke up."

"Are you ok? Did it upset you?"

"No, I feel very calm about it, but he said the strangest thing?"

"What?"

"He said to tell David, 'thank you, for being a man of his word.' What do you think he meant by that?"

David was silent.

"Honey, are you all right?"

"Yes. I think I know what he meant." David fell silent again and seemed to be in a trance, thinking back to his time on the carrier and his promise to Jay.

"Honey, please tell me."

"One night, on the carrier, we were talking to each other in our stateroom. We had both flown two, four-hour missions, and we were beat. Two aircrews, four men, had been lost that day from our ship and we were wondering if we were going to make it back alive, ourselves." David paused and got lost in his memories again.

"And?"

"Jay asked me to look after you if anything happened to him and I promised him I would."

"You never told me about this before. Is that why you married me, to keep a promise?"

"No, you know not. When I came back to NAS Meridian, as an instructor, my intentions were to visit you and make sure that the Navy was treating you right, just like I had promised. I was going to make sure that you and Jayce were getting all the help you were entitled to. I had no idea that I was going to fall under your charms and marry you. I had girlfriends in Pensacola but I couldn't help it, before I knew it, I was in love with you."

"I know honey. You were all business at first. It took me a while to ensnare you with my womanly charms and get you away from those Pensacola hussies."

David smiled at her humor and said, "Anyway, if Jay really did appear to you in that dream and asked you to thank me, then I think that's what he meant."

Amy walked over to David and put her arm around him and said, "I'm glad I had both you and Jay in my life. After Jay was declared dead I didn't think my life would be much, but you have given me and the children a wonderful life. Thank you, sweetheart. You know I love you."

> *.....Come home, come home,*
> *Ye who are weary, come home.*
>
> *Softly and Tenderly*
> *By Will L. Thompson, 1880*

Chapter Nineteen

Three days after the Chinese raid, Dr. Duc and Han had returned from Hanoi to the now deserted camp with a borrowed pickup truck to pack their personal belongings. Dr. Duc packed his computer with care for the bumpy trip back, and Han gathered their personal items. She was in the process of wrapping the items with newspaper and packing them in a box, when she felt a presence at the door.

She turned her head slowly and gasped when she saw Howie standing in the door way. He was gaunt and ragged looking.

"Howie!", she cried out and ran over to him, grabbed his arm, and pulled him to a chair and table. He looked exhausted. "How did you escape?"

"I ran when I heard the helicopters coming. I knew something bad was going to happen."

Dr. Duc knelt down beside him and looked closely at his face, examined his eyes, and checked his heart with his stethoscope. "Have you eaten?"

"No. I sneaked back into the camp and drank water from the well, but there is no food here. I ate a few berries I found in the brush."

"Han, give him some of our food", Duc said.

Han opened their backpack and pulled out a sandwich and some fruit and placed them on the table in front of Howie. She poured him a glass of water, stared at him for a while as he ate and finally said, "Oh, Howie, what are we going to do with you?"

Howie could not wrap his mind around the situation in his present condition. All he could do was focus on the moment and eat his sandwich.

217

"Han, we will have to take him back to Hanoi," Duc said.

"Do you think we can keep it a secret", Han responded.

"We have to try. It would be wrong not to help him."

Dr. Duc thought about it for a few minutes as they watched Howie eat. Finally he said, "Han, we will have to hide him at our place for a while. I know a man who can get an American Passport, probably stolen, and forge his picture and put a new name on it. Then we will have to try to get him passage on a merchant ship out of the port of Hai Phong to the United States. From there he will have to use his own wits to get home. That is all we can do."

They made a place for him in the back of the pickup and disguised him as best they could so that he would blend in with the local populace. The conical straw hat helped, but it kept trying to blow off while he was riding in the back of the pickup.

They reached Duc and Han's house in Hanoi after sunset and had no problem sneaking Howie into their house. It took Howie a couple of days to get use to the sounds of the city and sleeping on a real bed. He watched Duc set up his computer and listened to the explanation of all the things that it could do. Howie was proud that it was mostly an American invention. He could make sense out of word processing and he thought a spreadsheet was a marvelous thing, but he had trouble fathoming the internet.

Dr. Duc made contact with a person who assured him that he could make a passport that would get anyone though any American entry point. The man came, set up a camera, and took several pictures of Howie. He said he would have the passport ready in a week.

After the man left Howie asked Duc, "How much is this going to cost you?"

"A tidy little sum, but do not worry about it. I'm glad to do it for you."

"When and if I make it to the states, I promise I will repay you," Howie said solemnly.

"That would be nice but it is not necessary."

"No. I'll do it. Can you receive mail without it being opened or censored?"

"Yes, of course."

"I've memorized your address and one day you'll receive a money order from me and you'll know that I'm doing well."

Ten days later Dr. Duc and Howie drove to one of the docks in the port of Hai Phong. The altered passport looked genuine and he had been given the name of William "Bill" Hart. After a half-day of searching, Dr. Duc made arrangements for Howie to travel on a merchant ship headed for Seattle, Washington, later that day. They had chosen a ship going to Seattle because that was Howie's hometown.

The irony of the situation was not lost on Howie. Forty years ago he had helped bomb Hai Phong Harbor in an effort to stop all shipping, but today he was counting on one of its ships to take him out of the country. *Sorry about that,* he thought.

He carried a gym bag packed with a couple of pants, shirts, underwear, toiletries, some socks, and a lightweight jacket that Han said he would need in Seattle. The socks and shoes were something that he was having to get used to. He had worn sandals for the last forty years and the shoes felt hot and confining. Han had also included three English paperback books for his voyage. He had not realized that his vision had changed so much and that he could not make out the words of a book, so Han had gotten him a cheap pair of reading glasses.

The ship was owned by a European company but was manned mostly by Philippine nationals, although the ship's officers were Dutch. The trip to Seattle would take ten days, weather permitting. Howie watched the dock workers finish loading the ship. As soon as everything was secure, the Captain ordered the ship to depart the harbor.

That evening Howie watched the night lights of Hai Phong disappear over the horizon and he suddenly felt a great sense of relief and freedom. He was sixty-four years old and had spent almost two-thirds of his life on Vietnamese soil. He was finally beginning to feel like he was really free. He was actually starting to believe that he might make it back home. It felt good to lean on the ship's railing and watch the marine life in the ship's wake. There was luminous plankton in the waves, flying fish, and the warm ocean breeze felt like freedom. He stayed up late, leaning on to the ship's railing, feeling the wind on his face. He could hardly sleep that night.

He had a simple cabin with a bathroom. No radio or television. He read one of the paperback books the first day but soon learned that there was an entertainment room where crew members could relax by watching movies. The fact, that they could put in a shiny round disk in a machine and a full-length motion picture would play on a wide-screen TV, amazed him. They also watched television. He did not quite understand it, but they said they received a signal by satellite. Occasionally he would catch an American television broadcast from Los Angeles. He was amazed by the fashions and all of the events that were happening on the West Coast of the United States.

He took his meals in the galley with the rest of the crews. There was a meal served every six hours. That took care of all of the crew's shifts. On the second day, after the noon meal, one of the female Filipino stewards took an interest in Howie and sat down to talk to him. They talked for about thirty minutes. There was something about him that intrigued her. She sensed a wounded soul but he was not damaged enough that it had destroyed his kindness and compassion. He still had an air of gentlemanly class about him.

She was not sure what his story was but she felt an attraction for him. Her name was Josie. She looked like she was in her thirties but Howie knew that Asian women could keep their young looks until they were well into their fifties and then suddenly, overnight, they were old and wrinkled. She laughed when Howie guessed her age at thirty-five and then confessed that she was forty-nine. He was also surprised to find out that she had a college degree from a university in Manila, but even so, this was still the best paying job she could find.

That evening, after the 6:00 pm meal, Howie was again leaning on the ship's railing, enjoying the wind in his face, and the sense of freedom when he heard footsteps behind him.

"Good evening, Mr. Hart", Josie said.

"Oh, hi there, so they finally let you out of the kitchen?"

"Yes, Mr. Hart, my shift is over."

"Please, call me Bill."

"Ok, Bill." She stood beside him for a moment and then asked, "Can I ask you a question?"

"Sure, go ahead."

"When we were talking earlier today you mention that you had been gone from your home a long time. How long have you been away from your family or wife?"

Howie thought for a moment. "It's been over forty years. I don't have a family, a wife, or children. My parents are probably dead. I do have a younger sister, though."

"You do not know if your parents are alive or dead?"

Howie could not speak; he could only shake his head no.

"You are coming from North Vietnam. Forty years is a long time. Were you in a place where you were not allowed to leave?"

Howie looked at her for a moment, wondering if she knew or suspected the truth. Finally he said, "You're very perceptive. Yes, I was, but I can't talk about that."

They did not speak for about five minutes and then Josie asked softly, "How long has it been since you have been with a woman?"

Her sensitivity and understanding, combined with the realizations of the things he had missed in life, made him tear up, but he managed to say, "Not since I was a young man."

Josie put her arm though his, pulled close to him, and said, "Let's go to your room. I have something for you."

Howie looked at her eyes; their faces were only inches apart. He put his hand behind her head and pulled her toward him until their lips met.

They made love every day for the rest of the voyage. It helped him come out of a shell. Instead of avoiding people, he was beginning to feel more outgoing and willing to talk to strangers. Parts of his old personality were re-emerging.

Every evening after lovemaking, they would go to the railing of the ship and watch the flying fish as they rode the ship's wake. The voyage started a healing process in his mind and Josie had an instinctive awareness and ability to sense his troubles and help him talk through them. They both knew that once they arrived in Seattle, their relationship would be over. But still, Howie asked for an address where he could write her. She gave him an address that would reach her shipping company and then would be forwarded to her. She also gave him an email address and said that he might learn to use it one day soon. Unfortunately, he could not tell her where he could be reached. He did not know what was going to happen to him. He wondered if the Navy would even be interested in knowing that he was alive.

The ship arrived at the South Port of Seattle early on a Saturday evening. Howie's psychic instincts told him to wait until after midnight to exit the ship and go through customs. Before he left the ship Josie came to his room and they made love one last time. He had been a little rusty at sex at first but after a couple of days she had him up to speed and he could now perform and do what it took to please a woman.

At midnight he walked down the gangplank and turned toward customs. He stopped and looked back at the ship. Josie was watching him from the railing. He waved and she blew him a kiss. He turned back, took a few steps, saw an American flag waving nearby, and realized that he was finally back on American soil. He closed his eyes, took a deep breath, and smiled. *Home*, he thought.

It was a half-mile walk to customs and it was 12:45 am when he arrived. He was the only transient in the custom office. He walked up to a sleepy looking customs officer, put his gym bag on the table, and held out his passport.

The customs officer looked at the passport and ran it under a scanner. A look of puzzlement appeared on his face.

"Oh crap", he said. "The whole friggin' system is down two hours for a software update."

"Does that mean I have to wait?"

"Maybe not. You're traveling awful light. What kind of traveling are you doing?"

"Just seeing the world on tramp steamers. Going as cheap as I can."

The officer looked at the passport, the meager gym bag, and a man dressed in modest clothes. He had seen these guys who travel on the merchant ships before, seeing the world on a dime.

"Listen, Mr. Hart. The system is down. Your passport looks ok, so I'm going to let you go through. Just put your index finger in the machine and let it scan your fingerprint. I'll scan your passport too and upload your information later." Howie watched in fascination as the light in the machine moved back and forth, scanning his fingerprint.

"Now, just in case a problem comes up with your passport, let me know where you'll be for the next couple of days."

"Is there a cheap motel nearby?" Howie asked.

"Yes, there are two or three about a mile down the road."

"I'll be in one of those."

The officer looked through his gym bag and said, "Ok, go ahead."

Howie started walking. He was not going to stay in one of those hotels. He was going to walk all night, find his childhood home on the outskirts of Seattle and see if anyone he knew was still around.

Seattle had changed a lot in the last forty years, but he managed to navigate his way toward his old neighborhood. Many buildings were gone and new ones were in their place, but, at least, the main street names were the same. Every now and then he would stop and sit on a bus stop bench.

At two o'clock in the morning he was sitting on a bus stop bench when a police cruiser came by and slowed down to a crawl. The two officers looked at him closely but did not stop. They went on down the road, but came back in about five minutes. Again, they slowed down to look at him.

Finally they stopped and one of the officers said, "Sir, do you have any ID?"

"Yes, I do." Howie reached inside of his coat pocket and pulled out his passport, walked over to the cruiser, and handed it to the officer.

"Most people give us their driver's license, not a passport."

"I don't have a driver's license. I only arrived in Seattle today on a merchant ship."

"Where are you going?"

"I'm walking to my parent's home on the southeast side of town."

"That's a long walk."

"Yes, but I don't have a car and the buses don't start running again until tomorrow morning. Wanna' give me a ride?"

"Sorry, not going in that direction."

"You could, if you wanted to."

"Have a good evening Mr. Hart", the officer said and they drove off.

He walked the rest of the night and the next morning. Around six o'clock, he stopped at a breakfast restaurant near his old neighborhood. He had to pay the staggering amount of five dollars for breakfast. They wanted almost two dollars more for coffee so he just had water and had to pay twenty-five cents for that. Miffed at the price, he left no tip and continued his walk. The hundred American dollars that Dr. Duc had given him would not go far at those prices.

At eight-thirty he was standing in front of the house that belonged to his parents, or at least, it used to belong to them. The trim was painted a different color and someone had added a garage. He had no idea who lived there now. Maybe his sister, if he was lucky. It was relatively early and he did not have the nerve to ring the doorbell yet, so he sat down on the steps near the sidewalk and rested. Maybe someone would come by that he would recognize. *Fat chance*, he thought.

He fell asleep for a few minutes, while sitting on the steps and was awakened when the lady across the street came out to get her Sunday morning newspaper. She gave him a quick look. A minute later he heard the phone ring in his parent's old house. A couple of minutes later a middle-age man came out of his parent's house. He could see the man's wife peering through the door as her husband approached Howie.

"Can I help you?" the man said.

"I hope so. This was my childhood home. I grew up here. I've been gone a long time and I'm looking for some relatives."

"What were your parent's names?" He seemed suspicious.

"Neal and Dorothy Stanley. Do you know them?"

The man seemed to melt a bit. "Well, yes, in a sense I do. We bought this house from their estate. Their daughter Virginia sold it to us."

Howie paused and swallowed hard. His parents were dead. He had prepared himself for the fact that they would be gone, but now it was confirmed and real for him.

"Do you know where Virginia lives now?" Howie managed to get out.

"Yes, I think we have her address written down inside. Let me go inside and see if I can find it."

A couple of minutes later he came out with a slip of paper and handed it to him. "Listen, my wife is a little leery of your story and she wants me to drive you to your sister's house and make sure you're who you say you are. I see you're walking. It's about twenty minutes by car. I'd be glad to take you."

"Thank you. I would appreciate a ride."

It was a beautiful Sunday morning and Virginia was working in her flower garden. In the past her husband had done most of the gardening. Since he had died of cancer two years ago she had taken on the yard, riding lawn mower and all. Once she was in the garden, digging up weeds and planting flowers, she did not like to be disturbed. She heard the telephone ringing inside the house but decided to let the answering machine take care of it.

As Howie and his driver neared his sister's house, he thought, *This is a very expensive neighborhood, Sis must have done well.*

The man pulled into the driveway and said, "There's Virginia, over there in the flower garden."

"Thank you. I really do appreciate the ride." Howie took a big breath and thought, *All right, let's see how this goes.*

Virginia or Gina, as Howie had always called her, heard the car pull up in the driveway. She turned and saw a man get out of the car and walk to where she was working in the flower garden. He stood there for a moment and did not say anything. "Can I help you?, she said.

"Virginia, I'm Howie, your brother."

Gina stood up and looked at him. "Look, I don't know what you're trying to prove but my brother is dead."

Howie shook his head, smiled at her, and said, "No Gina, I'm not dead."

Then it hit her; his pet name for her, the smile, a close look at his face, and then recognition.

"Oh my God!", she screamed and wrapped her arms around him.

Later that day, at a security center for Customs and Immigrations in Washington, DC, a security analyst was going over passport entries that had been flagged as a problem. The analyst sat there, not knowing what to do. He was stunned at the implications.

Last night a person had come into Seattle's South Port under a questionable passport. Its last port of departure was stamped as the port of Hai Phong in Vietnam. The passport neither passed nor failed. It kept coming up questionable so he ran the fingerprint scan through the database and it turned up nothing. He expanded the search to account for an older range of people and the military. The computer searched for over an hour until it finally found a match. The system had brought up a picture of a Navy Pilot that was listed as "*Missing in Action and Presumed Dead*". It was from the Vietnam era conflict. He looked at the photo of the young Navy Lieutenant and then the passport picture; back and forth, several times. It was the same man, only forty years older.

He picked up the phone and dialed his supervisor. "Sir, can you come down here a moment? I have a situation that I've never seen before. I'm not sure who to contact about this."

Chapter Twenty

Five Years Later

Centennial Gardens, Napier, New Zealand
Hawkes Bay Region of New Zealand (Northern Island)

"Eric, why don't you take the baby and go across the bridge and play in the grass with him. I'm going to sit on this bench and rest awhile", Sudie said.

"OK, let's go little fellow", Eric said as he grabbed the boy's hand and started out for the bridge. The toddler had been walking for a few months now and he was eager to walk with his daddy and not be carried.

Sudie watched them walk across the picturesque bridge in the small park. She could also see the waterfall from the bench. The bridge, the waterfall, and all the beautiful flowers would be pleasant to take in and enjoy while she rested and waited until Eric and the baby returned. The park was near the ocean and she could hear the waves crashing faintly in the background. She was glad that they had made the effort to take the trip. They had taken almost all of their vacation, six weeks' worth, and had decided to see New Zealand and Australia. It was a bit of a struggle with a two year old, but he was a good child and the trip had been wonderful so far.

New Zealand was so beautiful. Yesterday they had driven around Te Mata Peak and enjoyed the beautiful views. She would have liked to have made that trip on a bicycle, but she knew she lacked the endurance.

Five years ago she could not have even imagined such a trip as this. After she had been flown to Washington, she had spent the first six months in an upscale recovery center and the next six month at home. The doctors said that she was not permanently damaged, but would never be one hundred per cent again. She could lead a normal life but she would tire easily. She had a desk job as an analyst with the agency now, and she could handle it with only occasional periods of fatigue.

Eric was moving up fast at the FBI and it was a struggle for him to make sure he took enough time to be with his family. Since Sudie's father had died, they had moved her mother into the mother-in-law wing of their house. She was a big help to Sudie and the baby. Her mother had made a special effort to befriend Eric and as a result, they had become good buddies, sometimes to the exclusion of Sudie.

She could catch occasional glimpses of Eric and the baby through the trees on the other side of the bridge. She turned her attention back to the flowers near her and then noticed a couple carrying a small girl. *That's them, she thought.*

The little girl was about one year old and they were walking down the pathway in her direction. The bench where she was sitting was beside a walkway that led to the waterfalls and they seemed to be heading in her general direction.

The CIA had inserted a mini-assignment into their vacation. A week before they were to leave for New Zealand, Sudie's boss had come to her office and asked her to perform a small assignment.

He sat down in her office, cleared his throat and said, "Sudie, we need you to take care of a small matter for us while you are in New Zealand."

"You're not going to make me do company business on my vacation are you?" Sudie said.

"It's just a minor matter. I think it's something that will interest you."

"How so?" she said suspiciously.

"It has to do with Buddy Miller."

That did perk Sudie's interest and her eyebrows shot up. "Continue.", she said.

"British Intelligence located Buddy Miller a couple of months ago in New Zealand."

"How did they manage that?"

"Facial recognition, I think," he said.

"I know that the British are big on facial recognition in England, especially London, but I'm surprised that it extends to their commonwealth nations," she said.

"I don't think it was a British camera, it was probably done by New Zealand security at a big event of some sort. I don't really know. Anyway, footage was shared with the British and their facial recognition technology recognized him."

"So what do you want me to do?"

"Nothing much. Like you, he is protected from retribution by our agreement with China, but we want him to know that we know where he is. It's just enough to make him feel uncomfortable. We can't do anything to him but he committed a treasonable crime and we want him to be a little bit uncomfortable. I don't want him to think he got away with it, scot free. We want him to know that we know where he is.

British Intelligence has set up a scenario where his wife and small child have won a free photography session. The location for the photo shoot is at a small park in Napier, New Zealand. The photographer will lead the family past a park bench where you will be sitting. She will take some pictures of Buddy and the little girl on the park bench and then take the mother and child toward the waterfalls for some more pictures, hopefully the photographer can work it where Buddy will remain on the bench while she and the mother and child go to another location."

"Won't I be in the way on the park bench?"

"No, there is plenty of room for the photographer to work with Buddy and child if you sit on the far end of the bench. You shouldn't have to move."

"What do you want me to tell him?"

"Just have a general conversation with him and let him know a little of his history with the CIA which will be more than enough to let him know that we have an eye on him."

Sudie thought about that conversation as she watched Buddy's family, and the photographer walk toward her.

The photographer approached Sudie and asked if she minded if they took some pictures on the bench. "You won't be in the way. You'll be fine where you are on that end of the bench."

For the next five minutes she took pictures of Buddy and the little girl. Then the photographer said, "Buddy, you look tired. Why don't you sit here and I'll take your wife and baby down to the other end of the park, near the waterfalls, and finish taking the pictures."

Buddy's wife looked at him and said, "You're feeling ok, aren't you? You do look tired."

"Yes, yes, I'm fine. You two have worn me out today. Too much sightseeing. I'll be ok, just let me rest a few minutes. You have to expect it when a forty year old man is married to a twenty-six year old young woman."

She laughed, cradled the child against her hip, and walked toward the waterfall with the photographer.

He turned his head toward Sudie and smiled. They nodded to each other.

"I hope you don't mind my sitting on the bench with you. Those two have worn me out today", he said.

"Please, don't worry about it. I'm here for the same reason", Sudie replied. She gave him a good hard look and thought to herself, *Yes, it's definitely Buddy Miller.* He still wore a mustache and goatee. It was greyer now, but there was no doubt, it was him.

"That's a pretty little girl?" Sudie said, trying to continue the conversation.

"Yes, she is. Fortunately, she gets her good looks from her mother." He paused for a moment and then continued, "I would have never thought that I would feel this way but she has really added something to my life that I didn't realize I was missing."

"Yes, children will certainly do that. My little boy and husband are on the far end of the bridge. That's him holding on to our little boy and looking over the bridge rail, looking at the fish. What Buddy did not know was that Eric was also keeping a watchful eye on Sudie. Buddy looked and said, "Yes, I see them now. Looks like a very active little boy."

"Oh yes, he certainly is. Tell me, are you from around here? We're visiting and looking for suggestions of places to see."

"Yes, we live about forty miles from here. It's inland a ways. We have an orchard where we raise fruit and berries. I had thought about a vineyard but that's too much work."

"Well, I bet a fruit orchard is not that easy either."

"It has its moments but I have some good help. You should come visit our orchard. We show tourists around all the time. We own and run Nance Orchards and have a gift shop. I should introduce myself. My name is Buddy Nance"

Sudie paused for a moment, sighed, and said, "No—it's not— It's Buddy Miller, past captain of the *Oriental Flyer* and the *Reliant*."

Buddy jerked his head toward her and his face drained of color.

"My name is Sudie Dawkins. I'm a CIA analyst." She watched him struggle with his emotions. "Now don't panic. There's no need to run or be scared, no one is after you."

"How did you find…. How did you recognize me?"

"Buddy, I would know you anywhere. I was the agent in charge of finding you when you and Beking were making your escape through the Caribbean. I followed you all the way to Grenada where you and Beking separated. By the way, I actually found you at Pagau Bay in Dominica.

"Do you remember when you got a message that the CIA knew where you were; in that little hotel on the bluff overlooking the ocean? Do you remember when you were pushing the catamaran out of the river and a woman was sitting on the bank of the river under a poncho watching you? That was me. We had a team on the way that would have been there in about twenty or thirty minutes, but you got out of there before they arrived."

"That was you sitting on the river bank with the dogs? I remember it."

There was a pause in the conversation and then Sudie said, "You know, Maria is still waiting for you."

Buddy hung his head and said, "I'm sorry, but there's nothing I can do about that."

231

"I know… you're right. If you had contacted her, we would have known."

"I have a new life now with a wonderful woman and a child…. so what happens now?"

"Probably nothing and I should explain why."

Buddy swallowed hard and said, "Yes, please." His life, as he knew it, depended on what she had to say.

"Five years ago when I stopped tracking you and continued on after Beking, I was given a mission to assassinate Beking. I posed as a stewardess on a Venezuelan Airline and managed to poison him and an air marshal." Sudie watched his face as he realized that he was talking with a CIA assassin. She let it sink in and continued, "The flight landed in Iran and I had a narrow escape out of the country. We made our escape on a fishing boat to the middle of the Indian Ocean. By that time I was very sick because I had been exposed to the poison. We were out of food and water and our communication equipment had been destroyed by lightning. I was close to death when, by chance, an extraordinary chance, another boat showed up and gave us food, water, and let us use their radio. It was a catamaran called the *Reliant* and it saved me.

"During the next two years I slowly recovered from the poisoning, got married, and had a baby. They said I could never have one, but I did. I almost lost him, but, somehow I managed to bring him into this world."

"You were the sick lady on that boat?"

"Yes, it was me and you saved my life. I owe you."

"It seems we keep running into each other. What happens to me now?"

"Buddy, there were serious consequences to what Beking did and *you* helped him escape. More than a dozen people, very special people, died later on because of it. I paid, and will always pay a price for killing two people and I'll never have full health again. I wanted you to know that before I tell you this. You have been given a gift; sort of a *"Get Out Of Jail Free Card."* You are free to travel and not fear arrest or being pursued by the CIA."

"Why is that?"

"Three years ago there was a spy swap between the United States and China. In addition to the swap, part of the agreement was that there would be no reprisals against me for my part in the assassination of their spy. In return, they requested that there would be no reprisals against you either. Both sides agreed to the bargain. That's why we are both free to travel. Now, that being said, I don't think it would be wise for you to visit the USA or any of its territories. You might get through with a new name and passport but with the new face recognition technology that's being implemented now…well, they would eventually recognize you. Some rogue agent might, because of the special people that were killed, decide to take revenge on you. That's a remote possibility, but still, take my advice and stay away from the USA or any of its territories."

"I had wondered why the Chinese said it was safe to leave after only two years there. They said it was safe to go to New Zealand and that was about three years ago."

"Yes, that would be about the right time frame."

"So, I'm free to get up from here and walk away. No one is coming after me. You're not going to report this meeting?"

"Yes, you're free to continue your life. I will report this meeting and where you're living, but it won't make any difference because of the agreement with China. You're protected."

They were silent for a moment and then Buddy spoke, "Could I ask a favor of you?"

"Maybe. What is it?"

"If I were to write you a check for $10,000, would you see that Maria gets it and have someone let her know that I can't come back into her life?"

"Yes, I'll do that for you…and for Maria… I can see that the Chinese rewarded you well", Sudie said, watching him dash off such a large check on what seemed only a moment of thought.

Buddy smiled, silently acknowledging her statement as he wrote out the check, handed it to Sudie, and said, "Thank you." His wife and daughter were walking toward the bench. The photographer had remained at the waterfall to take more pictures. He stood up and joined them.

As they walked off his wife asked him, "That certainly was a pretty lady that you were talking to. Who was she?"

"Just another American tourist. She had a lovely southern accent."

"Are all American girls that pretty?"

"No, she's exceptional. By the way, honey, you know that trip abroad that you've wanted to take?"

"Yes", she said with a puzzled look.

"Let's do Europe. Now's the time."

"With a one-year old? We'd need a nanny, besides I thought there were some reasons why you shouldn't leave the country."

"I think that's over with." He stepped close to her, put his arm around her, and pulled her close to him, and said, "This is hard to explain and there are things about my past that I can never tell you, but I've been given a gift; a gift of life and fortune. I would like for you and little Becky to enjoy that good fortune with me. Let's travel, see the world, and enjoy a gift that was dearly bought."

The End